Second Saga, Book Three: Deis' Purpose

Jill Marie Denton

BookLocker

Published by BookLocker.com, Inc., St. Petersburg, Florida.

Printed on acid-free paper.

The characters and events in this book are fictitious. Any similarity to real persons, living or dead, is coincidental and not intended by the author.

BookLocker.com, Inc.
2020

First Edition

Library of Congress Cataloging in Publication Data
Denton, Jill Marie
Second Saga, Book Three: Deis' Purpose by Jill Marie Denton
Library of Congress Control Number: 2020905035

In patience, there is wisdom.

In faith, there is hope.

In love, there is peace.

In purpose, there is resolution.

*****

Chapter 1

DeAnna Sarafian awoke with a start, the violent vibration in her pocket interrupting fleeting dreams of more peaceful places. Instead, she awoke in a place of panic, pain and death for the patients she fought to save.

The cot in the pediatric hospital's doctor's lounge was far from ideal sleeping conditions. A quick check of her petite Rolex showed only twenty-six minutes had passed.

"Good enough," she muttered aloud to no one, sitting up with a scowl.

She'd survived on far less before.

Volunteering for that swing shift in the emergency department had been a terrible choice for her internal clock, but it had been a terrifyingly rewarding evening. She'd managed to paddle a teenager back after a fentanyl overdose, to talk a young mother through necessary but painful injections for her toddler, and to suture a boy back together after he fell on a kitchen knife, all in a few hours' time. She'd saved all but one of the department's intakes.

But the emergency department wasn't her place. The previous sixteen-hour shift proved it in spades.

After that quick nap, she had another shift before her. Fortunately, this one was in her home department of pediatric diagnostics. Figuring out what ailed the hospital's most precarious patients, the ones that mundane medicine just couldn't cure, was more her speed.

And when she wasn't diagnosing extremely rare pediatric cases, she was playing bass in Second, the band she and her friends formed two decades ago.

Lifting the still buzzing phone from her pocket, she turned off the alarm and checked incoming messages. She'd been conversing with Emmi, her oldest friend and Second's lead singer, about their mutual friend and Second's guitarist Rai. Her recent engagement to the suave British comedy writer Stephen Cooper was front-page news. Emmi, despite her best efforts and insane workload as the band's manager and lawyer, had also fallen head over heels for another Brit, superhero actor Simon Piers, the month before.

Moving Second's home operation to the UK had resulted in more than just better music for the quintet of friends. It had resulted in love for two of them, too.

At this moment, though, Second's bassist DeAnna, nicknamed Deis many years before, was a disaster. Her blinks were sluggish and her pockets were filled with used gloves and spent syringes.

When better rested and better dressed, she loved being on stage with her friends and helping to keep Second a family unit. She also wrote many of the hit songs the band chose as radio singles and was commonly used in their marketing efforts as a sultry and exotic Armenian-American front woman in their all-female ensemble.

DeAnna became Deis when Emmi first realized her potential. When anyone asked who'd be willing to head up a group or to coordinate just about anything, "De is" was Emmi's casual reply. Her maternal instinct and ambition were to blame there, two traits her friends continued to exploit in the subsequent years. The new name became her calling card, though, something that defined her as much as a pediatric physician as a musician and producer.

Emmi, Rai, Deis and their cohorts Destiny and Marilyn had spent years on the road furthering Second's success while working through their college educations all the while, much to the detriment of their social and family lives. But, as Emmi always drilled into their heads, fame is fleeting but family is forever.

"It's forever until you drop dead of exhaustion," Deis scowled to the empty room.

She rose, stretching long arms and legs before slipping back into her tattered clogs. Refastening her long chestnut locks into a tight bun, she exhaled a heavy breath.

"Come on, girl. One more. You've got one more in you."

She was blissfully close to being done with her rotation. Months of work were coming to an end. Her final twelve hours here at the hospital would no doubt center on problem solving, mystery unravelling and never-ending parental consent forms.

Eleven hours later, she was called back to the lounge. With no reason given, she headed to the vanilla room with caution and suspicion.

She was prepared for the worst. The birthday texts had been flooding in since dawn broke.

Sure enough, the third-floor doctor's lounge was an explosion of yellow crepe paper, golden balloons and confetti-topped tables when she stepped in, her caramel eyes narrowed.

"Surprise!"

Deis released a rehearsed scream on cue, her hands swept dramatically to her mouth. The other doctors, in starched lab coats and khakis, leaped out from behind doors and chairs, goofy pointed hats on their heads and noisemakers whirring to life in their fingers. With a good spirited laugh, she swatted at the closest conspirator.

"We couldn't send you off without cake!" Doctor Carolyne Peters declared, sweeping forward to capture Deis' forearm before the birthday girl could escape. "Come on, it's marble."

"Ooh, my favorite, though I'd swear it's actually yours," the besieged pediatrician pointed out with a smirk.

Dr. Peters, the chipper brunette in horn rims, escorted the birthday girl into the maelstrom. Helplessly cornered, she eased into the awkward attention. It was her last day here in the monogrammed coat, after all. She wouldn't miss the workload, but Carolyne was another story. She was a valuable peer in a male-filled specialty and she'd been a source of kindness and empathy on the toughest days.

Even now, the jubilant doctor was encouraging the others to enjoy the cake they felt obligated to decline. The hospital's contest for weight loss was still in full swing and Carolyne was angling to win by temptation. Deis was a few days behind on workouts and said no as politely as she could. Yoga only did so much.

After the cake was cut and the guests had dispersed to their units throughout the building, Deis helped plate leftovers for the young patients who were healthy enough to enjoy.

"So, you're off to London tomorrow, you lucky dog. You're not going to fall in love while you're there, too, are you?" Carolyne jibed with a wink.

"Not on my agenda, no, but I don't think it was on Emmi's or Rai's, either."

One of Dr. Peters' crutches, as Deis well knew, was checkout-aisle celebrity gossip. The picture of Rai, smiling like a lunatic and posing with the Hope Diamond-like bauble on her finger caught Carolyne's attention, and Deis had been peppered with inane questions about the engagement ever since.

"And Emmi's leaving Simon's side somehow, headed back here to America to work with some band of upstarts. I read that somewhere online, I can't remember. How she can walk away from him for even a moment, I'll never understand. He's unbelievable, all dark and muscled. She'd better keep an eye on him. I have no idea what Rai sees in that tall, lanky nerd of hers."

Deis hid her disinterested eye roll, turning to dump the dirty cake board in the tall trash bin. Patting crumbs from her long jacket, she turned back to her friend while the prattling continued. She'd miss the normalcy of this place, and of her accomplice, the pediatric surgeon, drama queen and insufferable chatterbox Carolyne.

The hospital had been much more demanding on this rotation, and while she enjoyed caring for these junior patients, she was ready to move on, to take a break of sorts. As normal as it felt to work full-time amongst doctors, this workload plus managing Second's stateside home and studio Spire was taking its toll. Keyboardist and producer Marilyn flitted in and out on endless assignments, leaving the manor house and its housekeeping entirely to the beleaguered bassist.

Every time the Eastern Shore Children's Institute called, though, as they often did, Deis acquiesced. As a top trauma center and the country's highest rated children's' hospital, located a few dozen miles from her childhood home, they recruited the absolute best, and Doctor DeAnna Sarafian was honored to be included among them.

After her early graduation from med school, she applied for a sought-after fellowship at this very hospital and was chosen over thousands of other bloodthirsty candidates. She'd made so many sacrifices, had endured so many sleepless nights to meet the hospital's residency requirements. But now, in her opinion, the debt she owed the hospital was fully satisfied. She'd spent a collective total of four years in the pediatric diagnostics department here, sliding in hours of service when Second's music paused or when emergency cases popped up.

Now finally, after months of hearing about its wonders, she'd see their British home, Haven, for herself. The freshly built manor and shiny new studio spaces were calling her name. Rejoining the music efforts and having a break from the often heart-wrenching field of pediatric diagnostics was just what the doctor ordered.

"Did you remember to say bye to Carlos?" Carolyne asked, interrupting her thoughts.

"No, I figure I'll stop in as I'm leaving. He'll be disappointed. I don't want him to have a lot of time to stew."

"He'll definitely miss you," she agreed, standing alongside the freshly wiped table with her arms crossed. "We all will, but he's your biggest fan."

"I'm fortunate that he recognized me at all. I had an in. Otherwise, he'd have deteriorated until he couldn't say no to treatment any longer. His parents were getting desperate."

"Imagine his delight when his attending turned out to be in his favorite band, and the hottest one in the band, if you ask him."

"He's just fixated."

"Which guy around here isn't? With you gone, I actually stand a chance of getting a date again."

"Oh, shut up, Carolyne."

She laughed, stepping over and taking Deis' arm companionably. "Let's go say bye and get my social life back up and running, shall we?"

She waited until she'd clocked out to visit Carlos. Outside his door in her tan suede overcoat, she looked to the floor with dampened palms. This was the part she dreaded most.

His television pumped out the telltale sounds of high-velocity cartoon violence, simulated gunfire and dramatic music. His favorite show was well underway as was his treatment. She felt sorry for interrupting it, debated internally, talked herself out of cowardice and stuck out her chin.

Tapping on the doorframe, she peeked around at her pre-teen patient.

His beaming face greeted her as he reached for the remote. "Doctor Deis!"

"Hey, buddy." She stepped inside, her smile automatic and genuine as she settled into the black chair alongside the bed.

A plain blue kerchief wrapped around his bald head. He was wearing his favorite Captain America shirt, emblazoned with the round shield the hero carried. On the nightstand was a foam Hulk fist, a plastic tumbler in the shape of Iron Man's helmet and assorted action figures ready for action or lying on their sides, previously vanquished in battle.

If not for Emmi's interest in such nerdy things and her coaching sessions about them, Deis would've been clueless about his source of inspiration. Instead, she'd been able to entertain and enthrall him in conversations about their superpowers and personalities with a little help from her blonde manager and friend.

The monitors perched over his head beeped monotonously with an IV bag of cloudy liquid hanging alongside in a sling. It was nearly empty, maybe ten minutes of chemo left to go.

"How are you feeling?" The doctor asked with the broad smile. "You're almost done already. Not as tired today, huh?"

"Nah, I sleep better now. They give me the juice later in the day like you asked them to."

"Glad you let them give it to you at all. You're turning into a softie."

"I want to go home," he confided, muting his television before turning to her fully. "How much longer do I gotta be here?"

Deis sighed. "I don't know, dude. You're doing well, but you've got a tough disease. It could be a few weeks or a few months. It's too soon to tell."

His eyes slipped to his lap, his lips turning down. "I hate cancer."

Deis reached for his little hand, gripped it. "You and me both, kid."

"You going home?" He asked, his tawny eyes inquisitive on hers.

There was such hope in them, a kind of dependency she hadn't felt since she was a kid herself. He still saw a future and envied the strength of his idols, even though she knew it likely wouldn't be

11

enough. His prognosis was dismal, but he still believed. And she held onto hope because he did.

She squeezed his palm in hers once fiercely. "I'm leaving for London tonight."

She watched the news confound him, worry him as his eyes clouded. "Like, in England? On vacation?"

She shook her head. "Not exactly. I'll be staying there a while."

It took a few seconds, but he pulled his hand back and hid it under his blanket. "You're leaving me. You're leaving me for good."

"I have to, Carlos. Work's waiting for me there."

"But you work here, too," he argued, his eyes narrowed. "You have work *here*. *I'm* here."

"I worked here, yes, but my rotation's over. It's time for me to do music for a while."

He huffed, pouted and crossed his arms, jerking the IV cord. The nearly empty bag of cloudy liquid swung dangerously.

She rose instinctively to check the flow. After flipping his forearm over and reassessing the injection site, she eyed him patiently, sitting back in the chair.

A knowing smirk teased at his lips at her reaction. "You're still acting like my doctor. Why can't you just be my doctor?"

"It's been a pleasure being your doctor and your friend. You watch the best TV shows. You get the best snacks. But you know how I really make a living. I know you do."

His lip tucked in tight. "You guys are awesome. I watch the YouTube videos."

"That means a lot to me. And Emmi needs me in London. Besides, I could use a few weeks away from all you sick jerks."

She reached under his arm, tickled where she knew it would work and watched him squirm. He tenuously held the chuckles back with staunch, boyish pride.

"I'll miss you," Deis admitted with a somber look. "I'm not supposed to have a favorite patient but you're it."

He nodded slowly. The defeat in his eyes dropped a twenty-ton anvil on her heart.

When she rose, walking to the door, she checked over her shoulder to see him staring at his own lap, limp and dejected. With a deep breath and heavy heart, she turned to leave.

"Doctor Deis?"

She turned back, tipped her head as he continued.

"Emmi's a doctor, too, right?"

"Uh huh, why?"

"I'm okay with you leaving, and I'll keep taking my medicine like I'm supposed to, but only if she comes and visits me. And I want a selfie with her. My friends all think she's hot, but none of them will believe that she came here just for me. Pics or it didn't happen."

The doctor's eyes narrowed. "Carlos, are you blackmailing me?"

"I did the same thing to get you as my doctor. And it worked, didn't it? Besides, my friends are stupid. You're way hotter." He grinned, lifting his replica Captain America shield between them.

"You conniving little pipsqueak."

She slid back to his bedside, reaching out to tickle around the barrier while he cackled.

Back at her suite on Spire's second floor a few hours later, with bags packed and travel documents ready, she did her best to relax pre-flight. Red-eye travel over oceans shattered her internal clock, which was already upside-down from her endless shifts at the Institute. She imagined arriving to find Haven in havoc and having to set it back to rights without pause.

Emmi was spending a week between Haven's door and Spire's in Bora Bora with Simon. With feckless Rai left alone in that manor house, she feared there would be artwork lying in the halls and instruments leaning against every piece of furniture.

Releasing a deep breath, she assumed the downward dog position on the pristine white yoga mat. With eyes closed and peaceful music full of bells and gongs floating around her, she wrestled back the hells of her day, the panicked looks on children's sick faces, the overbearing parents in the emergency department. Alone in her meticulously organized space, and with another full breath, her heart lightened like a helium balloon.

Before finding yoga, the only anti-stress activity in Deis' life was more work. She and Emmi shared the same work ethic, nauseatingly intense and unwavering no matter the outside distractions. Take on more, achieve more. But when music commitments overlapped with caring for terminally and chronically ill patients, anxiety crept up slowly, building up like bricks until it boxed her in. With yoga, she could finally ease out from under it, coax the angst away and find respite in the few minutes of time she found for herself.

She completed her routine in the lotus position, the music shifting into quiet piano. With eyes still closed, her mind flashed back to her teen years, the endless hours in her room studying, memorizing the endocrine system and learning the implications of drug interactions. Her mind was so logical, so analytical, even back then. Strumming a borrowed bass guitar became an escape from the studies and exemplary expectations. The hollow, soulful tones made the instrument seem lonely, like it needed her somehow. In time, the instrument and the player needed each other.

Her parents, strict and dutiful Armenian emigrants, mandated flawless grades, but they deigned to let her play music after she wept desperately for a bass of her own. Despite the musical interest drawing away some of her attention, she knew four languages by her thirteenth birthday, took her MCATs at sixteen, a year before Emmi, and graduated the top-rated pediatrics program at twenty-one, all while performing for audiences three or four nights a week for cash. Confused for a patient at the children's hospital, she'd faced criticism, ridicule and dismissal in the medical community in the dozen years that followed.

But music had always been there. As a balm, it soothed the rough edges of her life and raised her self-esteem. On stage under hot lights, she was a goddess. She commanded the audience's undivided attention. There was no self-pity, no unachievable expectations and no condescending self-judgment. Her parents had encouraged her musical skill as another form of superiority, demanding that, if she intended to dedicate herself to song as well as medicine, she needed to be the best at that, too.

Instead of railing against it, she accepted it and dealt with it, practicing until her fingernails chipped and her lower back ached for days on end.

Keeping her parents proud wasn't as important as it once was. As they aged and as she progressed, as her photos graced magazine covers and as medical texts published her dissertations, their pushing eased back to lackluster nagging.

Their latest kick was the toughest yet. When would they be grandparents?

She could fetch any man she wanted. She'd make such beautiful, smart and eloquent children.

But only if she married before menopause.

Her eyes snapped open with a huff. So much for relaxation.

In the mirror over her antique walnut dresser, she peered at her reflection. The oval glass displayed glittering amber eyes, flecked with gold like her father's, below a cascade of slightly wavy, mink brown hair. Smooth skin, naturally tan like her father's, was uninhibited by the heavy stage makeup she often wore. From her mother came the slight chin, high cheekbones and narrow build, accented with petite breasts and subtle hip. Yoga kept it all toned and missing the occasional meal kept her weight low enough to please the media.

Unlike Emmi, who was frequently vilified for her curvy, zaftig shape, Deis' photos were rarely critiqued. The fashion industry had come knocking a few times over the years, had approached her about the possibilities, but her sensibilities, workload and dignity had her laughing off the requests as politely as she could manage.

Hot shower, flat iron, almond-scented lotion, huge cup of black coffee. With the post-yoga routine complete, she waited by the door for her ride. Her bags were labeled and ready. The airport was waiting.

Not long after, seated in the first row of first class, she watched Spire, the hospital, her hometown and recent history fall away as the plane ascended.

Chapter 2

Sunday, November 30

"We're fine. Stop palpitating, woman," Rai barked into her cell phone.

"Oh, I couldn't palpitate if I tried. Too much rum in me for that."

In fact, Emmi had spent the last fifteen minutes gloating in the guitarist's ear about the wonders of the island paradise. Glass panes in the tropical hut's floor revealed fish swimming beneath her bed, their adjoining pagoda had a fireplace in it, and the sea was bathwater tepid versus the winter chill in England.

In the background, Simon called out saucy demands and Emmi was gone with a giggle and a click.

Eyes rolling, Rai replaced her cell phone on the kitchen table while Anna-Lena, the stout chef de cuisine of Haven, eyed her inquisitively from the stove. She covered a huge pot, billowing with the scent of beef and vegetables, with a metal lid the size of a manhole cover.

"Had to go, did she, little bird?" Her heavy voice, tinged with an enduring Eastern European accent, carried across the immaculate kitchen.

"Sounded like Simon had something to show her." Rai lifted a brow and had the chef wagging her finger.

"Obscene. Those two, gallivanting off to the Pacific like lusty teenagers. It does my heart good."

"I guess she deserves some time off. I just wish she hadn't left all her work to me."

"Do what you must and only that, little bird. No more."

"Oh, and she left me here with the Armenian Diagnostic Machine," Rai glowered. "Thank God she's been laid up since she got in."

Anna refilled Rai's teacup. "Sleeping like the dead. Henry's itching to launder her sheets. He's already snuck in to unpack and hang her things. Brought an embroidered lab coat along with her, he tells me."

"Oh, I'm not surprised. You never know when they'll need a doctor at the pediatric hospital here. God forbid she just does music for a while."

"Sometimes one task makes a person better at another. You are a swimmer. Imagine working with that demon Robbie without your outlet."

"If medicine is her idea of an outlet..."

"I'd be, what, a glutton for punishment?"

Deis stood in the doorway, hands on her hips and her brows lifted at her cohort. Anna chuckled, caught red-handed, and retreated to her stewpot without another word.

"Well, yeah," Rai shrugged, lifting her mug. "If you soothe work stress with work stress, that's pretty pathetic."

"I've been called worse things," Deis tossed over her shoulder, stepping to the chef. "Anna-Lena? I'm Deis."

Anna bowed slightly in greeting. "Lovely miss, welcome to Haven. Your breakfast is ready, and lunch is nearly done, whichever you prefer. I've taken the liberty of brewing your coffee and preparing your infused water exactly as Emmi instructed. Henry, Haven's butler, will deliver your meals unless you choose to eat here in the kitchen."

With a palm on the chef's shoulder, she smiled pleasantly. "No need to deliver anything. I have no intention of missing your meals. I've lived on Marilyn's terrible leftovers, cafeteria food and vending machines for months now. That was when I remembered to eat at all.

Today, I'm eating whatever you made. Tomorrow forward, just try to keep the calories in check. I'm on a high-protein, low-sugar plan when I can be."

She sat at the table and watched Anna serve her a flawless stack of blueberry pancakes, two sausages the size of chubby fingers and a mug of Colombian coffee, just as she preferred, black as night and just as deep.

"It might just kill my waistline but I'm going to love this place." Deis lifted a fork and inhaled deeply.

"Anna, there should be a candle on those," Rai added. "Her birthday was Friday."

Shock mixed with shame on the chef's face as Deis held out a palm. "No, that's not necessary. I've had thirty-three sets of candles already. I'm good. Really."

"I'll bake a little something."

"This is more than enough sugar, Chef," Deis argued with a head shake, digging unceremoniously into breakfast.

As Rai explained White Light's progress, Myopic's upcoming recording sessions and her work with yet another up-and-coming band, Deis continued to plow through her meal. It was an odd relief to be away from the hospital, away from Carlos, though her mind often flashed back to him, his IV, his replica shield. She was still thinking of how to coerce Emmi into visiting. She'd have to offer up some sort of boon.

Rai's phone rang mid-conversation and she leapt up to answer it outside earshot. As Deis watched her flee with a brow raised, Anna stepped over to fill her mug.

"That must be Steve. He calls twice a day, late morning and just after dinner, like clockwork."

"Frankly, I'm shocked. She wouldn't commit to a movie show time a year ago. Now she's in magazines with this older, dignified and cultured Englishman. He must've cast a spell on her or something. I didn't remember him being so insistent."

The dutiful chef nodded, cradling the carafe in both hands. "Magic is in the air here. This Haven, it's a beautiful place. Two overwhelmed and lonely women found love inside these walls. It does an old woman's heart good."

"I know you're not referring to yourself," Deis replied dryly.

Anna smiled warmly. "I'm not thirty-three. Go on and finish your breakfast, miss. When Rai's done, she'll have you down in that studio working it off."

Deis shot her a conspirator's wink. "You think she can boss me around? Oh, Anna, you don't know me at all."

Downstairs, Deis ogled over the futuristic equipment in the generous studio space. Haven's studio trumped Spire's and that was an achievement. Spotlessly clean, meticulously organized, it was a combination of Henry's tireless efforts and Emmi's careful design. With state-of-the-art brands, handmade instruments, custom acoustics and warm mahogany details, it was posh in the truest sense of the word.

Rai stood back with her arms crossed as Deis examined every microphone, every key on the piano and keyboard, every string on the guitars. The room was perfectly scrubbed. There were no faults to find, but Deis was a former tenant of her immigrant mother's life-sized dollhouse, immaculate down to the last detail, and that air of perfectionism had emanated off the bassist ever since.

"Have we passed muster, Lieutenant?" Rai quipped.

Deis grinned, stepping over to lay an arm over Rai's shoulders. "Indeed, cadet. That butler is a gem and that boss of ours, I've known her twenty-plus years and she still amazes me."

"She's a one-of-a-kind pain in the ass, but she sure can design a space."

"No arguments."

"But this peace is short-lived, isn't it?" Rai lifted a brow. "You're going to argue with me, aren't you?"

Deis turned to her. "Why are we arguing already? I just got in."

"I'm sure Emmi gave you instructions. She gave me a bunch, too. Should we compare notes?"

"My instructions were clear." Deis' thumbs hooked in her skinny jeans' pockets, a smirk curling her rose lips. "I don't think there's anything to compare."

"I knew it. Damn it," Rai moped, flopping down into the leather chair alongside the soundboard. "I'm stuck with that devil drummer Robbie."

Deis planted a condescending kiss on her head. "Sorry, dearest. I'm with Myopic when they record next week, and I'm supposed to lay bass tracks on our new songs until then. I'm only here three weeks, so I'm not taking on White Light's resident asshole. He's yours. We'll call it 'continuation of care.'"

Rai huffed in a little tantrum. "Of course, because I've been so stellar at it up until now."

"Oh, shush," Deis scoffed. "It's my first night back in London. Why don't we live a little? Forget about Robbie. Show me around. We should catch up with everyone. And I should see Steve again. He was eyeing Emmi last time I saw him. He changed his tune pretty quick."

Rai spun the seat, her eyes narrowed bitingly. "Oh, I'm not taking *any* chances with you, hot stuff. You're not getting anywhere near him alone. I don't trust hot Middle Eastern bassists near guys I plan to marry."

"He's on set with beautiful actresses all day," Deis contended, turning away from Rai's accusation without care and heading to the ascending stairs with Rai glowering at her back. "Aren't you worried about them, the ones you haven't known your whole life?"

21

"He works with that goof Bernie, not hotties."

Bernie Overland, Steve's mentor and comedic foil, was certainly not as attractive as a leading female would be, but his shock of red hair and boisterous cackle certainly garnered attention. Steve and Bernie made fast friends with Emmi the prior summer, negotiating a backstage visit at Second's September Wembley show as a gift for Bernie's better half, Jane. That was the last time Deis saw the two lads.

"I'm sure they have their share of female devotees." Deis replied amicably.

Rai chased Deis to the top of the studio's stairs and into the atrium. "Seriously? You're going to give me a complex."

"He gave you this," Deis grabbed and lifted Rai's left hand. The cobalt diamond the size of a dime glittered from its place on her third finger. "I heard all about the sabotage and surprise, too. You guys are golden. Nothing's coming between you two, least of all me."

They retreated upstairs to their suites without another word, ready to celebrate away from Emmi's watchful eye.

Both musicians settled into the plush seating area above the crowded downtown nightclub at a little past nine. The square room on the mezzanine was private, roped off with red velvet and flanked by bouncers in all black. Rhythmic, thumping music erupted from speakers. Sweeping lights illuminated dancing patrons, their faces dim and mysterious in the voluminous crowd. The club smelled of beer, men's cologne and old wood. It was the kind of place Rai enjoyed but the kind that made Deis awkward and suspicious.

Between their shared leather sofa and an identical, unoccupied one across the way was a squat table, topped with trays of cheese squares, berries, grapes and thin crackers. Their hosts had yet to arrive but had seen to the pleasantries.

"How did we beat them here? I thought they left an hour ago," Deis asked Rai, her tone raised over the din of pulsing music below.

"They're heading in from Brighton. Some meeting there. I expected Jane to beat us, though."

"Hey, I'm here, I'm here!"

The joyous female voice rung out as the late-thirties female headed up the stairs with a pint glass in her thin fingers. Deis recognized the trim brunette in a pink V-neck sweater, jeans and boots instantly as Bernie's better half. Jane was a serious Second fan and a delight to be around. She embraced Rai with easy comfort. When she turned to Deis, blissful hazel eyes twinkled genuinely.

"Deis, it's so nice to have you back in town."

The bassist smiled back in kind, taking Jane's free hand to bypass a hug primly. "Thanks for entertaining us."

"Oh, it's an honor. You've entertained me much more, I assure you."

Jane set her beer down on the table as the back-entrance door slid open, two gents in full laughter sauntering in. The room exploded into life as Jane ran to and hugged Bernie sweetly. Steve sidled to Rai, lifted her several inches off the floor to even their statures and kissed her fiercely, possessively, in a way that made Deis' heart ache.

She'd forgotten how Steve Cooper towered over them all, how his dirty blond mop and blueish eyes captured the light and how welcoming it was to be around him and his cheerful friends.

"Deis!" Bernie shouted, stepping over to wrap her up despite her body going to stone in his arms. "A vision, as always."

"Hi Bernie. It's... nice to see you and Steve again." She gasped motionless in his tight embrace.

Once he peeled himself away, Deis turned to Steve as he dropped Rai onto the couch like a heavy sack. "I'm not allowed to be within five feet of you, apparently, but hello."

"Welcome back," Steve greeted, already stepping up for a hug, but resorting to a handshake as Rai cleared her throat a little too loudly behind him. Deis backed up with palms out like a suspect.

He dipped his head down to murmur to Deis alone. "Progress on the whole trust thing is a bit stymied."

"Good luck with that," Deis remarked sarcastically, stepping over to drag a worn armchair alongside the two couches, now occupied by two nauseatingly adorable couples.

"How long are you sticking around?" Steve asked, his arm tossed around Rai.

"Three weeks or so, unless Emmi has such a good time with Simon that she doesn't come back."

"Oh, the honeymooners," Bernie jested, laughing with Jane.

"Honeymoon?" Deis' face grayed. "What are you talking about?"

"Oh, no worries," Steve interjected with an outstretched hand. "Them being married is only British tabloid fodder. And there's a baby on the way, too, apparently, if you believe their atrocities."

"Oh, that," Deis sighed with relief. "Good Lord, I know I work too much, but there's no way I could've missed all that."

"It's ludicrous," Jane remarked around a swig of beer. "The media's been gamblin' on when your nuptials'll be." She gestured to Rai with her half-empty glass.

"No hurry. He's mine and that's fine for now. Besides, I doubt the boss will give me time off any time soon."

"Emmi's the workhorse, so stop complaining. Simon had to steal her away from here," Deis quipped, referring to the Bora Bora vacation scheme. "There's no way you're working harder than she is. During her last vacation, she built Haven. If he didn't drag her off to someplace without Wi-Fi and fax machines, she'd be sneaking in work there, too."

"Of course, you'd take her side over mine," Rai grumbled. "She's been running me ragged for weeks."

"She also balanced recording a top-selling rock album at home while managing your sister's health down to the tiniest detail at the downtown hospital. Or am I wrong?"

"Don't remind me."

Earlier in the month, Rai's sister Kara ran away from home, straight to Haven with a serious opioid addiction problem and a stolen credit card. Emmi's medical expertise and penchant for security kept the entire fiasco from turning into a giant PR nightmare. Only after detoxing and promising Steve she'd keep on the straight and narrow for Rai's sake was she given clearance to fly home without her sister's overbearing scrutiny. As a former addict herself, Rai was dead set on keeping Kara on the sober path herself, but thanks to Steve's handiwork in negotiating, Rai was free to stay in London with him while Kara completed her treatment stateside under his strict guidelines.

Steve turned to Deis. "Kara emailed. She kept her appointment with your colleague last week."

Deis nodded. "Her therapist audited my psych course in college, and I have no problem asking questions and evaluating the doctor's approach. I feel confident she's receiving the best care."

"She'd better be," Steve added, finishing off his lager. "That was the only way to keep my fiancée here where she belongs."

"I heard," Deis commented, the glass of white wine resting in her fingers. "It seems to me that she's taking sobriety seriously. I think seeing Rai happy is the bulk of the reason, but it works all the same."

Bernie burst into laughter suddenly, causing Deis to bobble her drink. While he recounted some dizzying tale of onset drama, Deis' mind drifted off, back to the emergency department at the Institute.

The four-year old patient's heart had stopped. Sirens, shouting, code blue. Nurses scrambling and parents wailing in the slow motion of her memory.

Clear, paddles, shock. Silence.

Clear, paddles, shock. Silence.

Nothing but the hollow, high-pitched squeal of the flat line on the monitor.

Little girl, curly red hair. Type 1 Diabetes.

Thirty seconds. No pulse. Too long.

Turn it up. Clear, paddles, shock again.

Flat line.

"Deis!"

"Huh?" Deis snapped back to see Rai glaring at her.

"Welcome back," her friend jibed. "I asked you a question."

"Sorry, I... I was somewhere else."

She refused to let herself be embarrassed. With an exhale, she reset her attention, wondering if she'd ever get used to failing her patients and living on without them.

Chapter 3

Monday, December 1

Hangover symptom number one, the nauseous pull in her belly, faded once Deis dragged herself to the shower, but the excruciating headache lingered like a virus as she dressed.

She'd had three glasses of wine, more than she'd had in months. Rai had her two beers, as per her contract with her sister after her own addiction issues, and had no doubt escaped unscathed. Deis, on the other hand, was pitifully out of practice.

Downstairs, enjoying a dish of Irish oats and fruit at a snail's pace, the suffering bassist perused the music Rai emailed her. Lyric, guitar and percussion were in place, waiting for her parts to be written in. She'd already dreamed up most of it and had envisioned the pace and rhythm. It was just a matter of putting pen to paper, music to the page and completing the sound. Bass was music's building block, the fundamental element in rock, and her parts would round out the overall feel of the album.

Anna refilled her coffee with the pity of a woman who knew a hangover when she saw one. Deis downed it quickly and desperately as it scalded her tongue.

Rai fluttered into the kitchen like a bee, her hair still wet from her post-swim shower. Laps in Haven's Olympic pool was Rai's morning exercise routine. All hums and energy, she snagged a mountainous cinnamon roll from the glass-domed tray and accepted the plate and coffee Anna offered with a perky smirk.

Barely functioning, scalded from the inside out by the Colombian magma, Deis watched Rai exhaustedly, hiding her disdain behind a thin veil. She imagined that having a man in her bed last night would've done wonders for her energy level, too.

Unwilling to start the day so peevishly, she rose and carried her empty mug to Anna. Rai and the chef exchanged knowing glances as the bassist retreated silently to the studio to start her day of recording.

Fortunately for the ailing bassist, the tracks came together effortlessly. Relieved that she'd make quick progress, she tossed off the rest of the hangover and focused on the music.

Rai's sarcastic and cruel lyrics on track four were inspired, and with her piece added in, the tune took on a crassly energetic tone. She'd have to record background vocals on three tracks once Emmi approved the bass lines.

Her voice mimicked Emmi's the closest. In the rare case that Emmi fell ill or couldn't pull off the right sound, Deis was her primary backup. It was yet another aspect of Second she appreciated, that they could each switch roles seamlessly and still maintain their signature sound. A twisted ankle, sprained wrist or sore throat never caused Second to miss a show.

A few hours later, the bulk of the writing work was done. After tuning the beautifully polished onyx bass guitar she found, she stepped into the booth, donned headphones and put her mind to task. She rarely had the opportunity to work without an audience or the frequent stops caused by her band mates. Her foot tapped out the rhythm as her fingers rapidly found their place, her head bowed down toward the sound.

Her eyes closed naturally. The soulful, humming strum of complex riffs took her mind off medicine, back to the primal pleasure of making music. Suddenly she felt at home, in the heart of sound, and insecurity and heartache ebbed as she ripped into the solo opening of the album's second track.

From outside the booth, a silent observer watched her pour herself into the instrument. The passion, the fire he felt through the glass was so tangible that he nearly reached out for it. Here was this exotically beautiful woman, ethereal with her golden-streaked hair, unpainted almond-shaped nails and long eyes that he knew glittered under stage lights though they were closed firmly now. She hunched over the bass, the pale green tank holding on tight and showing off toned arms and shapely physique over narrow, indigo jeans and bare feet. Reverence tangled with unabashed lust in his mind as she played through an intricate bass part with fluid grace and swift fingers.

When she ended the tune and eyed the sheet music on the stand beside her, a sharp explosion of applause had her grasping her heart and bobbling the bass. Her banshee scream echoed inside the glass cage.

He laughed, shame coloring his cheeks as she jumped to her feet. She gradually and markedly regained her composure with deep breaths and wringing hands.

Her breath was harder to catch, though. Imagine her surprise at being eavesdropped on by such a handsome stranger.

When she stepped from the booth, the bass hanging by its strap over her shoulder and her brows raised in demand, his apology tumbled out like an avalanche.

"I'm so sorry. I meant no offense. I didn't know how to interrupt properly. It was so brilliant, it would've been rude to disturb you. Apologies."

Sweet British accent, she thought. Thicker than Steve's, a bit slower and with a touch more twang. Raven hair in soft strands brushed over his forehead as they made their way south of his ears in a long, easy sweep that her fingers craved to touch. Piercing blue eyes, like sapphires nestled in pale sand, focused on her alone. That bright, conspirator's smile, sharp cheekbones, firm chin and chest under a white Henley and dark, loose jeans over heavy black boots made a very nice first impression.

She peeled her gaze away. It had been so long, too long, since she'd had such a visceral reaction to a man. It was demeaning and thrilling all at once.

"It's okay. I just wasn't expecting an audience. Clearly. I'm Deis."

Her hand outstretched and he took it in his rough palm. "Charlie."

Deis filled in the blanks instantly. "Lead singer of White Light. I've heard the recordings. You have real talent. Congrats on earning Emmi's support. You must have impressed her. That's an achievement right there."

"Thanks. Means a lot coming from you. We're all fans, and we owe Second in every way, though not well reflected by the behaviors of certain band mates of mine."

His voice was like rolling thunder, bold and deep. She giggled a little too lightly and coyly before she could rein it in. "Robbie and Liam. Yes, I've heard. Apparently, you're the tie that binds now that your manager's moved on to greener pastures."

He shrugged, wide shoulders lifting easily as his thumbs tucked into his back pockets. "He was too young to manage us fools. I'm the oldest and I stand in front, so it just happened that way. When did you get in from the States?"

"Saturday, early." She lifted the guitar from her shoulders and placed it back on the custom lacquered stand. It was so beautiful that she took a moment to appreciate it. "I'm still not through being impressed by this place yet."

"Light's certainly not," he admitted. "Doubt I'll ever be. It's more than we could've asked for."

Deis turned to him, lifted a brazen brow. "You'll work for it. Don't think Emmi's the type to ease up. She'll never lower her expectations. It's a never-ending race to perfection."

His grin lifted his lip, showed off the sexy, sharpened incisor underneath. "Oh, I bet. I've heard bits and bobs of your new album, her vocals, Rai's guitar, and now your bass line. We'll need a miracle to keep up but we're here for the long haul."

The taunting smirk, the gleam in his eye, lit a match in her soul. She stepped closer, her eyes fixed on his, replying with a challenging tone. "You want to keep up? Good luck with that. You'll need it."

As she breezed by and up to the first floor, he inhaled the perfume and promise she left behind, all honeyed and captivating. Her molten voice lingered in his mind as he followed up the steps a few calming, solitary moments later.

Emerging from the studio and up into the atrium of the manor house, he witnessed Deis and Rai in conversation. Outside earshot, he watched the two women nod in agreement to each other's' points after adding in their bit of dialogue. Rai's fingers tucked into her jeans pockets, her posture relaxed, while Deis' arms crossed over her chest, stiff and professional.

He was stunned to silence by them both. Rai was fascinating in a casual, approachable and unassuming way, with her diminutive Asian features, affinity for beer and well-worn attire. But Deis was something else. She was exquisite; an ideal, golden damsel. It was no challenge to watch them talk and flush his mind of every other thought.

And when she laughed at whatever Rai said, her cheeks rose into lovely little apples and showed off a dazzling smile he'd do anything to keep around.

How brilliant to discover that she was even more beautiful in person than in print.

Rai turned to him as Deis stepped away and began climbing the grand staircase. "Hey, Charlie. You looking for me?"

He nodded, intelligible words still outside his ability to find in the bassist's wake.

Rai took his forearm and led him back to the studio. "The pieces today are a little gruffer. You ready to dig down deep?"

31

"Just watch."

With the Armenian vixen's challenge issued, inspiration would be easy to find for his afternoon session.

Upstairs, Deis used Emmi's well-appointed office to send off the tracks she'd finished. Waiting for file transfer, she meandered and eyed every antique her boss had collected. It felt royal, dignified, unlike her relaxing spa-like rooms back at Spire. There was a quiet formality here, and as she passed by the crystal vase of perfectly dried dahlias, forever a bright violet, she found her lips curling in a knowing smile. Simon and his heart were just as much a part of this space as Emmi now. He'd gifted the blonde singer those blooms months before and now she was off on an island adventure with her superhero and male counterpart. He was just as headstrong, just as conniving as she, no doubt her equal in so many ways.

The thought made her chuckle. She'd never imagined such a splendid guy for her overbearing friend. Emmi loved work, whether it came as a fixer-upper band or hopeless man, but flawless actor Simon seemed to bring out Emmi's best without adding to her workload.

As she rounded the end of the hall to begin the descent down to the atrium, reverberating voices below stopped her dead. She watched Rai escort Charlie to the front door as they shared a laugh. He took her palm, kissed the back of it with a wink and laughed off her good-natured slap to his bicep.

Deis faded back into the shadows of the hall. A burning under her heart made her feel awkward, silly, like some covetous child.

Rai's ascent was interrupted by Deis stepping out and into her path. "All done with Charlie?"

The guitarist and Light's chief producer nodded, stopping at the top to eye her band mate curiously. "Yep, today was just some background stuff. You waiting for me?"

"No, I just... I was just headed downstairs, but I didn't want to interrupt."

The twitching gestures, the averted, insecure eyes and the stammering made Rai's gaze narrow. She could read her old friend's tells like a poker pro.

"Come with me." Rai smirked, dragging the shamed bassist by her wrist. Inside Deis' west wing suite, Rai closed the door and leaned back against it. "What's going on? You're uncomfortable. You're never uncomfortable."

"Nothing," Deis waved her off and turned her back. "It's nothing. And I'm not uncomfortable."

"Hmm, let's see." Rai dashed over and hopped up on the made queen bed, her chin in her fingers like a police inspector. "You asked if I was done with Charlie. You didn't want to interrupt us. You were practically hiding up there while he... Ah hah, while he kissed me!" Rai's eyes brightened. "You think he's hot. Well, duh. He is. And his voice is like suede. You should hear it unmodified. It's a little gruff but, wow. Color me surprised, Deis' not completely dead inside."

"Shut up," the doctor snapped, flopping onto the red velvet stool by the vanity, her cheeks ablaze. "I've been attracted to men before. It's no big deal."

Rai shook her head with a wide grin. "I got it in one. *Damn* I'm good. And you haven't looked at a man with anything close to lust since you finished college. I haven't seen you flirt with any guy in years. Admit it, you're in a slump."

"A work-filled sabbatical," Deis corrected. "You try being social while doing twenty-hour shifts at a children's hospital. The only guys showing up there are dads with sick kids and pharmaceutical reps. And the doctors? Forget it. Most of them sleep with their pocket protectors in or with their assistants, or both."

Rai chuckled, lying back on the crisply seamed blanket. "Oh, Deis, you poor thing. It's so much fun to chase, to flirt, to watch a man's libido fight with his logic. I'm done with the whole sordid thing. It'll be nice to watch someone else play the game for a while. Enjoy it."

"There's no game-playing in my plans. I'm here for work. Next week, I start producing Myopic. I'm headed back right after I'm done. Holidays with the fam. Besides, I know his name and that's about it."

"That's a good start." Rai sat back up, watching Deis pace the plush carpet. "Your bed's too hard. Steve would like it. I bet Charlie would, too, especially if he got to break it in."

"Oh, *shut up*. Seriously, or I will hurt you."

"You couldn't if you tried. And besides, what you don't know is he may, or may not, mind you, have asked about you already."

"He did not," Deis contested half-heartedly.

Rai nodded slowly. "Nothing major, but he opened communication about you at least. Now he can ask again. A stealthy, careful tactic but an effective one."

"And what did you tell him?"

Rai climbed to her feet, stretched. "I just answered his questions. He only asked two. Like I said, basic openers. Nothing a newspaper hasn't covered."

"Then why bother?" Deis lifted her cell phone off the nightstand as it chimed.

"Am I talking to a houseplant?" Rai asked no one in particular, spinning left and right with her arms out at her sides. "So he can ask more questions later. All I did was confirm his suspicions that you're a pediatrician and that you're not seeing anyone."

Deis whipped around, dropping her phone in the process. "He asked *that*?"

"No, but I told him anyway." The schemer grinned evilly.

Dodging Deis' fists, Rai danced her way out of the room with rolling laughs.

Left alone, she sat on the foot of the bed with a sulk. She knew Rai was trustworthy when it came to secrets. While the guitarist always dodged the uncomfortable, passed the buck, she was able to hold her tongue in the face of brutal questioning. And loyalty amongst Second's sisterhood was steadfast, especially against the media.

But Rai would tell the rest of the band, that gossipy hen. That would cause some troublesome ribbing, but she'd been devoid of female stirrings for too long. It seemed healthy to explore the lust she'd shelved.

And he was handsome. Emmi had been right about accents, too. Rai herself had fallen for some English gent. She was certainly allowed to admire.

And she was already being defensive.

With a sigh, she flopped down, closed her eyes and quickly passed into sleep again, still worn from months of hospital rotations and producing obligations at Spire.

"I sent her a message. She didn't answer and that's not like her. Is she still sleeping?"

Emmi's voice was edgier, more challenging than it had been on her last check-in call. Rai rolled her eyes at the kitchen table, waiting for Anna's lasagna to be served. Simon, even with his dark charms and sexual proficiencies, couldn't keep the manager at bay forever. The tiger was looming again, too far to supervise Haven directly but still ruling from afar.

"I checked on her. She's out like a light but she sent you the bass tracks. She's done the whole album already. She slept for a day and half, worked a few hours like a madwoman then crashed again."

"Those shifts at that hospital are too much," Emmi conceded with a sigh. "I feel bad sending her more work."

"More work? Myopic's not here yet and she's done with our tracks. What's left to do?"

"It's not music. I received a message from the director of that London hospital that sponsors me, asking for a consult. Apparently, this patient's related in some way to one of the board members and they're pushing the case up the chain to diagnostics. She's seventeen, so it's a borderline pediatrics case. That's her specialty."

"So you're telling me that you want that exhausted doctor upstairs to go back to work at a hospital here? That's cruel. And her license is still stateside anyway."

"They'll sponsor her, too. I already checked. And this kid's been in and out of clinics all over town. They need a diagnostician with some outward thinking and creative tactics. The doctors at the hospital are scared to misdiagnose with their jobs and reputations on the line."

"So you'll let Deis' reputation take the hit? Either that or you're overly confident that she'll find something that no one here has. It had better be the latter."

"Sure, but you know who's always down for a challenge and isn't scared to face a tough crowd?"

"De is." Rai replied in a sigh. "I'll have her call you as soon as she shows her face again."

"Much appreciated. I guess I'll owe her big for this one. Oh, and if this whole mess at the hospital takes longer than a few days..."

"Yeah, I know, I know. I'll be doing Myopic, too."

"You're the best."

Rai knew Emmi was grinning on some zero-gravity chair, on a pristine white beach half a world away and hated her even more for it.

"I know. And you'll owe me, too, if that happens."

"Deis' a brilliant diagnostician. I have every faith that she'll have it figured out in no time."

"Unless she's too busy with a certain dark-haired musician we're both acquainted with."

36

"What?" Emmi's voice cracked. "Who? She's only been there a few hours. Dear God, tell me he's a decent human. She's been out of the game so long, she'd fall for the first conniving bastard she finds."

"He's no bastard. He is out of her league, though. No worries."

"No one's out of her league. You're gonna tell me, right?"

"Not a chance. This is way too much fun."

It was Rai's turn to grin as Anna laid a plate in front of her. The chef's brow rose curiously, intrigued by the gossip just as much as any eavesdropper, but Rai shook her head. Defeated, the chef turned back to the stove.

"I'll trust your judgment for now and beat it out of her later."

"I'm looking forward to it. Bye-bye, boss lady."

Rai hung up and lifted her fork, ready to dig in just as Deis stepped in with a yawn. "Welcome back to the land of the living. Chef made lasagna and biscotti."

Deis wordlessly sank into the chair across from Rai and yawned again, rolling her head over her shoulders.

"Still recovering?" Rai asked, digging into the layered pasta as Anna served Deis a meager portion. Alongside was a petite filet and a pile of bright green broccoli florets, plain as far as Rai could see. "And that's what you're having?"

"Apparently, and apparently," Deis replied to both inquiries drably. "I can't do enough yoga to burn off so many carbs. Was that Emmi on the phone?"

"Unfortunately. Simon is losing the war against her workaholism. She'll be back to Spire by the end of the week."

"Did she get to the bass lines yet?"

"Nope but she said she sent you a message."

Deis poked at her veggies. "I got it. I figured I'd better eat first. I'm sure it's just more work she needs done."

"It's a weird telepathy we all have," Rai mused with a chuckle. "Of course, it's more work."

"Is it the kind of work I want to do?"

"It's the kind you'll enjoy but the kind that I'd run from at full tilt."

"You'll have to be more specific."

Rai shot her the middle finger as Anna chuckled from beside the sink, dishtowel in hand, drying the dripping utensils and observing their byplay. The dutiful doctor was home, and it tickled her how they related so easily despite their varied styles and backgrounds. They were sisters in the truest sense.

"I'll let Emmi fill you in, but she owes you big. That's all I'm saying."

Deis' eyes lit up, remembering her favorite patient back at the Institute. "Perfect. I just so happen to have something in mind."

Chapter 4

Tuesday, December 2

In her doctor's coat, black slacks, and with her hair pulled back demurely, Deis strode into the lobby of the downtown hospital with an attaché case tucked under her arm. At reception, she introduced herself, signed an autograph for the sprightly secretary and sat nearby as instructed. The hospital was abuzz with elevator dings, chattering visitors and ringing phones.

She powered back her nerves. This wasn't an interview. It was barely a consultation. Just walk in, diagnose, recommend treatment and go.

In her bag was her preferred manual of disorders, two extra notebooks sized for a breast pocket, her favorite felt pens in black and blue, a few business cards, her cell phone and a chef-prepared lunch.

It felt strangely and comfortingly like a school day.

"Doctor Sarafian?"

Rising instinctively, Deis offered her slender hand to the approaching figure, a stout British man in the basic gray suit, well-worn loafers and half-moon glasses on the tip of his nose. He was securely in his mid-fifties, balding, and staunchly professional.

"Yes, but please call me Deis."

"Deis, a real pleasure. Doctor Abram Gordon. Welcome to my hospital."

She nodded and followed behind as he led her through two sets of glass doors. Beyond was his office, a sharply lit space devoid of charm except for the immense walnut desk with twin picture frames and a ticking clock on its corner. He gestured to the guest chair and she sat obediently, setting her bag alongside.

"Doctor Gordon, I'm curious about your willingness to sponsor my credential transfer. I understand Emmi's affiliation after Kara Donovan's case, but I haven't proven my worthiness yet. It's a considerable investment."

"Doctor Deis, it's a pleasure to affiliate with you both, and I'm convinced you will accomplish great things here. I've investigated your credentials and case history. The pediatric institute had nothing but glowing accolades to share. And not only do your colleagues regard you highly, but your patients do as well. You're certainly aware of websites for physician ratings?"

"Yes, I'm aware. Second contracts with a social media manager and her workload includes those review sites as well as our social media accounts."

"You're fortunate to have help, and I'm fortunate for yours." Doctor Gordon handed over a four-inch thick ochre file. "Here is the patient's file."

"Goodness." Deis gritted her teeth, opening it to scan the documents inside. "A life-long record for a geriatric patient with a few chronic conditions wouldn't be this thick."

"Agreed, but our patient is related to one of our most-esteemed board members, so her maladies have been well and thoroughly documented."

No kidding, Deis thought with a hidden scowl. The standard childhood illnesses had nearly full-page synopses dedicated to them. Every fever was monitored and documented in half-hour increments, every injection and immunization meticulously accounted for.

"Impressive," she managed, shaking her head. "I didn't know an MMR vaccination required three-quarters of a page of sign-offs. Thorough is a bit of an understatement."

Doctor Gordon cracked a small smile. "She's been here three times in the past year, forwarded each time from her primary care physician after being seen in his office. I've personally seen to her care the last two visits, since our attending is, wait a moment," he paused, opening a drawer to read a document tucked inside. "'Incompetent,' per our illustrious board member. The attending discharged her without the full diagnosis, so I've been overseeing her case personally ever since."

"Her second visit, this past June," Deis noted, her finger tracing the page. "Intake noted different symptoms from the first visit. Are you sure these illnesses are correlated?"

"She's a teenager and her behaviors fluctuate just as readily as her symptoms. It's a moving target, but there's got to be a common thread causing the weakness, pain, dizziness, lethargy."

"I have your permission to run these preliminary tests again?"

"You have my permission to run whatever tests you feel necessary, after receiving parental approval of course."

"Tell me about the parents." Deis fished a notebook and pen from her case, in full diagnostician mode.

"Only one to speak of. Single mother, the half-sister of our board member. Close enough to keep him in the loop but not close enough for him to visit the patient, thank the heavens. He's threatened to but has kept distant historically. I do hope that continues."

Deis peeked up, took in the director's panicked glance to the door. "Doctor, I asked about the patient's mother."

"Oh right," he snorted, nudging his glasses up a half-inch. "Diane Victor. She works two jobs, at a bakery in the evening and a shipping warehouse overnight. She's absentee to say the least. Thirty-six this past July, brunette, no serious underlying health conditions of note."

Gordon handed her a thinner, practical file with Diane's name on the label. Inside, Deis found records for psoriasis cream, frequent stress-induced headaches and birth records for her daughter, Miranda.

"This is a little more manageable," Deis breathed, tucking both files into her case. "Any other pertinent facts I need?"

"Just the hospital accordance items are left. I've assigned two fellows to this case. They are familiar with the hospital and its equipment, and they'll perform diagnostic tests per your instructions. The physicians on residence have been alerted to your arrival, and I apologize ahead of time for any undue attention they pay you. Many replies were very excited to welcome another Second member. Please humor them."

Deis nodded with an understanding smile. "Many but not all. I understand. And where are we with transferring my credentials?"

"The process is underway, though the American pediatric institute was gutted. I expect progress by the weekend. In the meantime, the fellows in the Diagnostic department will authorize tests. Any documentation from here on will be forwarded to me as I'm still the attending."

"Understood, Doctor. And my team, are they here today?"

"They are indeed, and I've scheduled a meeting with them at one. The Diagnostic department's office and lounge is on the third floor. In the meantime, feel free to acquaint yourself to the hospital. I've authorized access to all functions and supply areas. This is your second, well, third home now, I suppose."

He passed over a small envelope from his chest pocket, sealed. "Here are the access codes you'll need. Now, if you'll excuse me, I must call in to one of the many, many terribly mundane meetings I have slated for today."

He stood, came around the desk and escorted her to the door.

Deis took his hand. "Good luck, Doctor. You'll have my first report in the morning."

"Same to you, and I look forward to your insight," he replied, opening his door and watching as his newest doctor walked away. With a satisfied nod, he returned to his desk and to work in a brighter mood.

She arrived ten minutes early for her one o'clock meeting and found the Diagnostics department unoccupied. The office consisted of a plain, clean-topped walnut desk, a half-dozen year old laptop, an ergonomic office chair, empty bookshelves and a back wall of tall windows overlooking a courtyard in the hospital's center. Through an interior glass door, the adjacent lounge featured a long table to seat six, a petite microwave and toaster, cabinets she assumed were filled with junk food and a wall-mounted television tuned to the hospital's internal station. A whiteboard covered the far wall, wiped clean of notes. Both spaces were impeccably clean, dusted and stocked with the stationary she expected.

It was much more stylish, and certainly more adult, than her tiny office space at the children's hospital had been. London General was well-funded by its benefactors and she'd been impressed at the abundance of modern medical tech, diverse workforce, in-house staffing levels and genial courtesies she'd been shown so far. It made perfect sense that Emmi felt at ease here, and it was no wonder that she'd decided to accept Doctor Gordon's proposal of sponsorship.

As she sat at the office desk, dutifully unpacking her briefcase, a young female in a lab coat entered the adjoining lounge in brisk, quiet steps. The perky blonde dusted the table with a white towel, set out a box of coffee from a take-out café, three paper mugs and a tray of pastries. Sitting back a little so she was out of view, Deis watched the subject sit, reposition, fix her watch, glance at the clock, coordinate the two, and wait impatiently with tapping fingers.

Nervous, Deis realized. Just like she'd been on day one of her fellowship all those years ago. Imagine being told that some new, American doctor was coming in to supervise, to lead this existing team, and that she was moderately famous.

Okay, very famous, she corrected herself with an eye roll.

A moment later, a male, about the same age as the blonde, sauntered in, much easier in gait and with a relaxed expression. His cropped hair, brooding eyes and rounded brows all spoke of a straitlaced upbringing. They shared a few words outside Deis' earshot as he grabbed a pastry and leaned back against the wall by the table's end. He laughed at something he said, though the blonde looked uncomfortable in the joke's wake.

Just a blasé lad in a doctor's coat and a timid little mouse.

Show time, Deis thought with a smirk.

At one precisely, she rose into view and saw them both gape wide-eyed through the glass door. As she approached and swung it open, both doctors perched by the table, eyeing her apprehensively. While she'd kept her makeup simple and her outfit professional, she knew she made an impression. Whispers and rumors had already begun by the time she made her rounds, before she could even introduce herself to her new patient.

Her time of flying under the radar was officially over.

"Good afternoon, doctors," she greeted with a tiny smile. She stood at the opposite end of the table, eyeing them both. "Item one, thanks for being punctual. Item two, please introduce yourselves to me. I'll go last."

In a tiny voice obscured by an Irish brogue, the female volunteered a reply. "I'm Natalie O'Leary, doctoral grad of the University of Belfast. I've been here nearly a year, in rotation through Emergency, Intensive Care and now Diagnostics. I suppose I like a challenge."

"Very good. I hope you like puzzles, too," Deis added, turning her focus to the male doctor, who had his arms crossed over his chest. "And you are?"

"Doctor Phillip Murphy, Phil. Born in Leeds, graduated from Oxford, top of my class, and then did four years in the military. The goal was to teach, but no one wants an inexperienced instructor, so here I am."

"Thank you for your service," Deis replied, to which Phil waved his hand at her apathetically.

"You Americans. It was a job."

"We Americans do like supporting our military, yes," Deis retorted with a brow lift. "And as a veteran, you deserve that respect. The attitude, however, won't garner rave reviews."

"You're a rock star," the male doctor snarked. "I'm sure Gordon is just hoping the patient's a fan so she'll agree to have all the tests redone, since we botched them the first time 'round. Your face and your fame will invariably stop the lawsuits."

Fishing the notebook from her pocket, she began perusing her notes. "Yes, you two messed up so bad, they're hoping a few autographs and selfies will just wipe the misdiagnoses away. It's unfortunate for me and for us as a team that Miranda favors, let's see, 'EDM jams,' and not our 'shite excuse for music.' So, we're back to square one, Doctor Phil."

Doctor O'Leary snorted. "Doctor Phil. That takes you down a few pegs, eh?"

Defeated and scorned, Phil sat down with a huff. "Whatever. We mucked it all up and now this American's here to show us up."

Deis tucked her notebook back in the pocket and crossed over to the whiteboard. "True enough, you doctors are big losers, and as I see it," she paused mid-sentence, lifted the marker and drew a horizontal line. "We can either be up here." She drew an arrow up above the line. "Or down here, mired in failure and unwilling to actually diagnose and heal patients, which we all committed to do when we accepted our titles." Alongside the down arrow, she drew a coffin with a cross on top. Above the line, she drew a gravestone and some tufts of grass. "Personally, I'd rather give it a shot than resign myself to failure right off the bat. This is a damn good sketch, though.

Art's not my strong suit. Fortunately for Miranda Victor, diagnostics is."

Natalie, hearing all she needed to, opened the patient's file and began reading the past admission paperwork while Phil exhaled.

"Fine, so where do we start?" He tapped his pen on the table.

"You're the doctor. Where would you start?" Deis replied, erasing the whiteboard. "Feel free to pitch in since you've already decided I'm just a rock star and a pretty face."

Deis turned around just in time to see Natalie's eyes rise pensively at Phil, who looked away. When he finally spoke, it was a few decibels quieter.

"Fine, I spoke out of turn. I know you're a doctor, pediatrician by specialty, with exemplary records. Emmi was a brilliant doctor even though she's famous, too, and I figure you are who you hang with."

"Oh, please. You're making me blush," Deis replied flippantly.

Natalie cleared her throat and pushed the file in Phil's direction. "She's been through the battery of tests already, twice this year at this hospital alone. We took her history, again, asked her the basics, again, and detailed them in her file."

"I saw that," Deis sighed, sitting and fishing out her notes. "I also took the liberty to ask some pertinent questions which no one else seemed to. I read the file in its entirety."

"You," Phil ogled. "You read that massive file this morning?"

"Twice," Deis answered absently while her eyes scanned her jottings.

"Twice," Natalie repeated, in awe.

"Yep, and I did my own intake summary. Miranda Victor, seventeen, type A-positive, nothing genetic in the file, from the mother's side, anyway. Father ran off before her eleventh birthday. Mom Diane is overworked, out all night, and so she's on her own a lot. Wears cheap makeup and uses self-tanner. Presented yesterday with intense but sporadic stomach pain, diarrhea for the past three days and lack of appetite. Vegetarian since age fifteen. The over-the-counter anti-diarrheal meds aren't working, and she's getting weaker. It seems the dizziness and weakness are the two symptoms we can count on."

"Weak and dizzy's nothing to go on," Phil retorted. "She said she's missed class the last two days, but her friends and the school nurse report that no one else has similar symptoms. Mum's not sick, either, so we can rule out environmental toxins."

"Only if home and school are her only two environments," Deis countered, closing her notebook and tucking it away. "We've got to assume a seventeen-year old with carte blanche isn't at home much, or at least has a social life, especially with her music preferences. Any friends visit her yet?"

"No," Natalie answered, paging through her own notes. "Just mum and rotating doctors in her room the past two days. She told me she parties a little, drinks occasionally, but hasn't in a few weeks. I guess the guy she was dating broke up with her so she's a bit out of sorts. "

"This isn't consistent with alcohol abuse," Phil argued. "And she swears she doesn't do drugs. We tried for a tox screen but the first blood panel was such a bear, it seemed irresponsible to run another. We ran blood cultures at intake. She said the pain died down afterward when we tried to administer meds, but she also had a panic attack and tunneled during the draw. Severe dehydration and having blood drawn took her dangerously close to going under. It doesn't seem right to risk it again when she's barely lucid."

Deis nodded. "She's on fluids but the diarrhea's too persistent to be irrelevant. The most logical cause is bacterial. Keep fluids on around the clock, push difenoxin IV hourly for the next four hours. Monitor her gut response. The spasms should slow. We have to stop the digestive symptoms before we can go in for a better look."

"No tox screen?" the female fellow asked, looking up.

"I already ordered an oral swab," Deis replied, standing and stepping toward her office. "I guess Doctor Murphy forgot about that option. It should be back within the hour. Have the results of the tox screen and a comprehensive description of her typical diet on my desk by sundown."

Stepping into the office and over to the desk, she lifted the phone and paged the intensive care nurse. Her fellows made their way to the patient room as Deis ordered the medications and sat down to continue her analysis.

Remembering that a favor needed repaying, she lifted her phone to dial Emmi.

Her lifelong friend murmured drowsily after the third ring.

"Hello, manager lady. You back home yet?"

"Got in about three hours ago. It was a sixteen-hour trip back," Emmi replied with a yawn. "I haven't slept in three days. This better be important."

"Oh, I think it is. It's a matter of repayment."

A few minutes later, Emmi hung up with a muted growl of discontent. Deis grinned, reopened Miranda's file and imagined how delighted Carlos would be the following afternoon.

At her desk just after dusk, Deis sorted through prior lab results with leaden eyes. It had been a long day of studying dry documents. At the sound of tapping on the office's door, Deis glanced up and welcomed in her fellows, reporting with the materials she'd requested earlier.

Fresh from Natalie's hand, the tox screen came back clean. Curious but not surprising.

"And where is her diet analysis, Doctor Murphy?"

"Here, boss," he replied, handing over a single sheet of paper. "There wasn't much to write. She's pretty restrictive."

She scanned the sheet, disappointed to only see five items listed. Citrus, spinach, tomato, a fat-free dressing and peanuts.

"Okay, I asked for comprehensive detail." Deis shoved the paper back into his hand. "This is a shopping list. Where's the rest?"

"I asked her what she eats in a typical day. She said orange or grapefruit juice that she juices herself in the morning, spinach salad with tomato and that dressing, or she'll have two tablespoons of peanut butter instead, and she rarely eats dinner. She said she might have three or four pints of water a day. That's it, boss."

"First, it's Doctor or Deis. Second, she's not vegetarian. She's vegan." Deis lifted her brows. "I have a very hard time believing this is what she eats all day, every day."

"She," Natalie began, then faded, her voice barely a murmur. "She used to drink alcohol but... Well, she hasn't recently."

Deis sat back. "All right, we're moving on. Is the difenoxin working?"

"So far," her female fellow supplied. "No occurrences since it was first administered. More blood cultures were taken. The results should be in shortly. She was finally hydrated enough to give us a few vials."

"Hallelujah for small favors. Schedule an endoscopy for Thursday. We need to look in that intestine as soon as possible. No other tests until we get the endoscopy. I don't want any potential side effects. And she fasts until then, IV fluids only."

After handing Natalie orders for their patient, Deis booted up the laptop, astonished to find the archaic machine so responsive. "I have a few hours of documentation to do. In the meantime, get the blood panel results back. Look for mineral levels, thyroid and any other possibilities in there. This diet has me concerned about her glucose and triglycerides. Have the report to me first thing in the morning. Doctor Gordon will be expecting a full update by then."

"Gordon's throat's exposed on this one," Phil added under his breath.

Deis felt her chest tighten, her patience and kindness waning with each snarky remark her fellow tossed back. Anger bunched her hands into fists as she rose, circled the desk and stood two inches from his face. Tired, confounded and stressed, her amber eyes narrowed hotly while his widened.

"It's *Doctor* Gordon. You seem to have trouble with proper nouns and titles. I think you might have missed a lesson on respect among your peers."

She turned to the gawking female fellow and ripped the documents from her hands. Turning back, she thrust them into his chest. "You get to stay tonight. You'll do all this work plus the documentation on the desk. I'll see Doctor Gordon in his office at seven a.m. sharp, and I will go through every line with him personally. If there's one understated detail, one thing missed, you'll be getting your experience by following nursing assistants around, stocking incontinence supplies and scrubbing dentures in the geriatric ward."

She grabbed her briefcase, strode past the two stunned fellows and left the hospital with a slightly elevated heartbeat to accompany the sense of accomplishment. Emmi's cutthroat management style suited Deis just fine.

Chapter 5

At the breakfast table, Deis recounted the standoff with her fellow on Tuesday evening, and of Wednesday's morning meeting with the director. Rai enjoyed every minute of the gossip, digging into a three-inch thick Belgian waffle with a heavy fork. Deis avoided temptation and settled for fruit and yogurt instead.

"So he did it all?" Rai asked. "You made him stay and do everything?"

"Absolutely. Natalie's this timid little mouse, and I'd bet my ass she does all their work. I showed him respect from the jump and he's yet to prove he deserves it. Once I told Doctor Gordon that I assigned the notes away as a sort of growing pain for my fellow, he understood and pardoned the lackluster grammar and dim observations."

"But you fixed them."

"I had to. This girl's file is a tome. I've never seen anything like it. Even cancer patients who've been on chemo for years don't have files like that. I can't let his misspellings make their way into those notes, not with my name at the top of the page."

"Any idea what's wrong with her yet? Only four days until Myopic's back to record their stuff."

"Yeah, I know," Deis glowered. "I can't share a lot of details, but I will say that her endoscopy's today. I expect to see some sort of anomaly there. Tests are coming back normal, which I didn't expect. The symptoms fit with heavy metal toxicity, maybe even an underlying blood process failure."

"You'll figure it out. You and Emmi always do," Rai replied, sitting back and patting her non-existent gut. "I'm so glad I didn't go the

"Where's your mom?" Deis asked, handing over the file and op instructions to her while Doctor Murphy disconnected her IV.

"Sleeping. She's knackered, between work and being here. She left an hour or so ago, said she'd be back later during her break from the bakery. I wish she'd just stay away."

Deis' brows nearly touched. "Why would you want that?"

"I'm just sick of it. She keeps asking me what I did, accusing me of stuff. I've been here with a needle in my bloody arm. It winds me up."

Deis borrowed back the file and added to the notes. Difenoxin had side effects, specific and potentially dangerous ones, so she detailed every emotion she saw. Unease, aggression, anxiety.

Handing the file back, she stepped to Miranda's side. "You ready?"

"As I'll ever be," Miranda exhaled and closed her eyes as the medical team wheeled her gurney to the hall.

In the procedure room, the two fellows worked without hesitation. Outside the suite, watching from behind glass, Deis observed their fluid, practiced movements. She was prepped to help but was still waiting for her credentials. Trusting the pair of doctors to perform at her level pushed her patience to the limit.

Phil said a few words to Miranda, and Deis watched the girl's face twist into panic. He showed her the face mask through which the nitrous would be delivered while she shook her head. Natalie took the patient's forearm to comfort with an impressive air of maternal grace.

But Miranda was unmoved. As she covered her face with her hands and slid even farther into terror, Phil stepped away and out into the hall. Deis prepared for the worst.

"Doctor, she won't take the nitrous. We can't do this with her conscious."

"She's asking for her mother," Natalie called through the glass as her patient's hands slipped to her chest and clutched at her gown.

The monitor hanging alongside whirred to life in frantic beeps. Both Deis and Phil ran into the room as Miranda's heart rate sped up like a Ferrari on a straightaway.

"Damn, she's tachycardic. She's going to crash. Crash cart. Now!"

At Deis' command, Phil dashed into the hall to retrieve it while Natalie pulled the med cart over from the corner.

The sound of a flat line had them all glancing up at the monitor in unison, pausing with mouths agape. From one-eighty to zero, her heart slammed the brakes hard, and every previously clenched muscle of her body went limp as she fell unconscious. A code blue was called on the public announcement system overhead while the team scrambled.

"Damn it, v-fib. Push lorazepam. Paddles!"

Phil prepped her paddles with gel, handed them over. Deis rubbed them together and then to the patient's chest on either side of the still heart.

"Clear!"

The pulse exploded into Miranda's torso. Her chest boosted off the table in a sharp arch.

Still, the flat line's drone echoed around them.

"Go again, charge one-twenty. Clear!"

Her body rose and flopped again. Bystanders alerted to the emergency stood outside the glass with their hands over their open mouths as Deis charged the paddles again.

The red-headed four-year old diabetic, Deis' last v-fib victim, snuck back into her conscience. With a grunt, she forced the image back.

"Go, one-sixty. Clear!"

Another shock blasted into Miranda's chest. Ragged, staggered blips appeared on the monitor as Natalie sighed with relief. Phil took the paddles from Deis as she stooped in with a penlight, lifting her patient's eyelids to examine pupillary response with a few practiced passes. They turned to slits as the ray of white light skipped by.

"She's back in sinus rhythm." The male fellow exhaled, pushing the crash and med carts to the wall.

"Oh, good Jesus," Natalie breathed, watching Deis take a manual pulse at Miranda's wrist. "I thought we lost her."

"No," Deis replied quietly, stepping back with a deep, restrained breath. "She's here, but the endoscopy's off the table."

Back in their lounge, Phil cradled a cup of stale coffee, standing against the wall while Natalie paged through the file again. Deis swept in from the hall, blowing out a sharp exhale.

"I just called Miranda's mother. She's leaving work to come in. Doctor Gordon and I are taking her off difenoxin. The atropine in it can cause v-fib and we're not risking it."

"She'll have GI symptoms again," Phil added with a brow raise.

"Still better than her heart stopping," Natalie argued.

Deis sat at the end of the table with arms folded. "All right, back to differential. What causes diarrhea, heart issues, loss of appetite, weakness?"

"Infection. Something in the blood," Natalie volunteered.

"Blood panel was clean," Phil fired back. "We ruled out toxins, environmental and internal, multiple times. All not guilty."

"The blood panel might not be normal now," Deis mused in a murmur. "Something's different. She had no heart symptoms before, and even if it was just the difenoxin, we should expect to see something different. Run the panel again in a few hours, once fluids are back underway."

"You want to run it again?" Natalie asked incredulously. "That's three in as many days."

"You have a better plan?" Deis asked in a simmering tone. "We have nothing to go on. Her symptoms are sporadic. For what it's worth, I figured we'd see an abnormal endoscopy today and she'd be on her way home with an antibiotic by dinner. Now her heart's an issue. Fortunately, there's no long-term damage, but that can't be risked again. We have a limited window and very little data. Run the blood again, look for viral, pathogens, anything that explains it all."

Deis rose and retreated to her office as her deflated staff deserted the lounge to head back to the patient's room.

Sitting at the desk, she began her notes. She'd taken an incredible risk by defibrillating the patient herself, but instinct had taken over. Doctor Gordon had agreed with her decision in retrospect, but in the moment, she'd charged in completely unlicensed and taken over the care of a patient whose heart had stopped. If she hadn't recovered, it would've been a very large and very costly problem for the hospital.

She couldn't help questioning her role. This case was a patient barely considered pediatric. Two fellows looked to her for guidance and instruction but were more experienced in this hospital space than she. And they were credentialed.

Naïve, green, struggling, but credentialed.

She opened the laptop and booted it on. There was no point in her working the case unless she was legally able to do so. She'd draft an email to Doctor Gordon. She'd explain her hesitation and insist on a pardon.

An email from the Medical Commission waited in her inbox.

Dear Doctor Sarafian,
*   We are pleased to report that your credentials have successfully transferred to the United Kingdom*

Registry of Licensed Physicians. As a private contractor, your medical institution, its director and Board are responsible for administering and maintaining your credential for the life of your affiliation. Your institution's director has also been notified to expect your credential documents within twenty-four hours. Fees and liabilities are to arrive directly from your institution of affiliation. Congratulations once again, and welcome to our esteemed assembly of world-class diagnosticians.

With a defeated sigh, Deis closed the laptop and sat back.

She was ordained now by some Grand High European Doctor League of sorts. With a simple email, she became an international diagnostician. It was supposed to be an accomplishment, an honor. Instead, it felt like a curse.

With no choice now, Deis opened the medical file software program and typed well into the evening, copying Doctor Gordon on every word.

When the moon disappeared and the sun rose over the trees, she finally completed the last note. She'd spent hours poring over her medical texts, researching potential ailments and going over every inch of Miranda's file with a fine-toothed comb. She turned off the laptop with a yawn, standing to stretch as Natalie knocked quietly and entered the office.

"Good morning, Doctor." Laying a paper to-go cup on her desk, she cradled her own with both hands. "I didn't see you add anything to your coffee before, so I kept it black. I hope that's all right?"

"Good eye, and thanks," Deis replied amicably, scalding her tongue with the fresh dose of caffeine. "You normally here so early?"

"I'm an early bird. Doctor Murphy should be in within the hour. I couldn't sleep anyway. I wanted to check in with Miranda."

"And?" Deis asked, setting down the cup.

"Better than I figured. She's stable right now. The pain's died down, her stomach's empty but quiet and she slept thanks to the Ativan I administered before I left. The chart shows no arrhythmia issues in the duration and the lab results should be ready in a bit."

"Great. Let her rest. I'm sure her mother will have her anxious again by lunch. Momma stormed in here last night in a tizzy. I managed to explain v-fib and the changes in her treatment before the wailing began. She'd already called this board member relative of hers, so I couldn't step in front of that, but Doctor Gordon called him to explain the new treatment and ease his concerns."

"I saw the director in the lobby. He filled me in. And your credential came in by courier just then. Congrats, International Physician Deis... Wait, have you got a surname?"

Deis chuckled. "I do, but I work with kids, so first names are better. And since it just sounds like the first letter, it's easier for them. Between you and me, I hope I won't need the credential much after this."

"I imagine you have loads to do. That new studio space is supposed to be unbelievable. I've heard the new Fighters LP that was recorded there. It's extraordinary. And the album you did for Myopic? It's brilliant. Practiced doctor, pro musician and noteworthy producer. It's an honor to work with you."

Deis glowed, the apples of her cheeks tinting pink. "Thanks, I appreciate that. It's a lot of work, all of it, but I love every second of it."

"Another band I really like, White Light, they're working with you, right? I've seen them knocking around town, playing a few locals. Four talented, rough and tumble guys. It's fantastic that they're getting a shot."

"That's Rai's handiwork. I've got Myopic. They're all amazing musicians and pleasures to work with."

"Speaking of White Light, though, I could've sworn I saw their singer in the lobby when I came in. But when I turned the corner, I... Well, it might've just been wishful thinking. Can't help hoping to run into him in my personal life."

Deis' eyes narrowed. "I hope he's not here. They're supposed to be working this week. I'll call over to triage, make sure his name's not on the books."

"I'll go to the lab, check on Miranda's results." She turned back when she reached the door. "Oh, and Doctor? It's a pleasure being on your team."

As the blonde strode off on her red ballet flats, Deis took a deep breath, taking a selfish moment to enjoy the praise.

There was no one by the name of Charlie on the sign in sheet, so she decided to check the emergency department to ease her curiosity. Rai hadn't called to report an illness or accident, nor were there any adult male patients waiting to be seen. Upon checking the intake binder, only one patient had been admitted in the past four hours, a Ruby Taylor. Age eight, nausea, achy and short of breath. Deis shrugged, assumed norovirus and replaced the binder.

On her walk through the bustling department, nurses rushed by to take vitals, hand clipboards to droopy-eyed doctors in their white coats and consult family members sitting in chairs alongside patients' beds. There was a general sense of tension here, one she despised. It felt like weights on her chest whether she was on duty or not. Every doctor that passed by was scrutinized by waiting families, analyzed and chastised silently for not having an instant cure or the proper diagnosis already in mind.

She turned the corner, her mind endlessly toiling over Miranda and her next moves.

"Look who's here. What a splendid surprise."

She gasped in fright at the voice to her left. As her eyes rose to the source of the deep resonant sound, her honeyed eyes met the deep sapphire of his. Dark hair, five o'clock stubble, bright grin and worn leather jacket.

Charlie.

She swallowed back the astonishment, the palm-dampening reaction to his rugged looks, and managed a delighted smile.

"Charlie. Sorry, I didn't see you. I guess I'm in doctor mode."

"Speaking of, the look suits you," he remarked, rubbing the lapel of her doctor's coat in his fingers. "So official. I knew you practiced but not here in Britain."

Her heart pounded against her ribs as she watched him play with her professional attire so casually. "I'm official as of this morning. I'm here on a case for Emmi."

"Impressive. I never expected to see you here. I wonder if your patient is doing better than mine this morning."

"Your... Your patient?"

"Come on, introductions are in order."

He took her hand confidently, unabashedly, and led her down the hall to a private room at the end. As his foot crossed the threshold, he dropped the doctor's hand just as suddenly as he'd taken it.

"Hey, beautiful," he called out with a grin.

Her heart stung with jealously before she could viciously swat the reaction. With a deep breath, she followed him inside and instantly hated herself.

The pretty raven-haired girl, dwarfed by the big bed, had his rosy cheeks, onyx hair and icy eyes. She was no more than eight, cute as a button, but no doubt feverish and unwell. Deis grappled with the sudden urge to jump in and play doctor. This type of patient care was much more her speed.

"Hi, Daddy," the girl replied, holding her arms out as he approached. "I've been waiting for ages. Have you got it?"

"Yep, got one just for you," he replied, sitting in the chair alongside her pillow and fetching a soda can from his pocket. She cheered as he popped the top and handed it over. "Ruby, this is Doctor Deis. She works in music, like me, and here at the hospital, too."

"Hi," the pixie murmured, averting her eyes as she brought the can to her lips.

"Deis, this is my best girl." He smiled proudly to them both in turn.

The doctor's heart sang loud enough to ring in her ears as she stepped closer. The resemblance between father and daughter was astoundingly beautiful.

"It's nice to meet you, Ruby. Why are you here instead of at school this morning?" She grabbed her chart from its rest on the footboard of her bed, shifting into a familiar diagnostic routine as she lifted the top page to read her admission summary.

"My belly hurts and I don't feel good." She brought the blankets up around her shoulders and shivered as Deis glanced up. "Daddy brings me lemon fizz. It makes me feel better."

"Thank goodness for daddies, huh?"

Charlie reached out calmly, patiently, taking the soda from her and tucking the blankets under her tiny frame.

She scanned the attending physician's notes. A few diagnoses were scribbled down, tests were ordered. This was her third visit since school had started in early fall. The diagnostician inside her peeked out, demanded the spotlight.

"You've been here a few times already this year, huh, Ruby? Same symptoms then, too?"

"Uh huh. I was cold all summer and Daddy put me in jumpers. It was bollocks."

The simple observation made Deis chortle. "It was hotter this summer than normal, too. I was here at the very end of it. Do you recognize me?"

"From telly, and the magazines at the market line, yeah. You talk funny. Are you American?"

"Guilty," Deis replied easily, replacing her chart and stepping up alongside, sitting in the chair opposite Charlie. "I'm from a tiny little state on the east coast of America, right on the other side of the Atlantic Ocean. And I play music. That's why I'm on TV and on those magazine covers. Your daddy, he sings, but I play a type of guitar called a bass."

"You sing sometimes, too," she flashed a knowing smile. "You and the yellow-haired lady up front."

Charlie chuckled. "Tattletale."

"The yellow-haired lady, she sings the most, but you helped. Daddy and I watched that hotel show. And your guitar is so shiny and pretty. I want one just like it."

She thought back to the fundraiser they'd performed at the London hotel, to her crimson bass guitar and to the songs they performed. "That's my best one, but I have a dozen of them. You like red?"

"It's my favorite." She lifted the tiny pendant from her neck. A round ruby the size of a pencil eraser hung from a thin gold chain. "Daddy got me this for my birthday. And the princess stuff for my room, but that's purple and pink. They're my second and third favorite."

"It's perfect, a ruby for Ruby. The black-haired guitar player, the one that stands on my left? Her name's Rai and she loves little rubies too. When you meet her, make sure you ask to see her secret one."

"A secret ruby! Like a treasure?"

"Uh huh. Steve, her future husband, hid it so only she can see it. But she'll show you if you ask nicely."

Deis patted Ruby's knee under the stiff linens before turning to Charlie. "Can I see you for just a sec? Ruby, I'll bring him right back, I promise."

"I guess," she murmured. Her eyes followed them as they disappeared into the hall, the door closing behind.

In the hall, Charlie turned to her with concern clear on his face. "What? What's the chart say?"

"Has Doctor Heimer seen her yet?"

"No, just the admission doctor, um, Howards, I think. Why? Who's Doctor Heimer?"

"He's chief of the Oncology department."

Charlie's mouth dropped, his eyes darkened as his voice hushed. "What? They think she's got…"

"It's on the table," she interrupted, dissatisfaction clear in her eyes. "Asthma is, too. There's a pulmonologist on the way to check her for that. It's a waste of both those physician's time, if you ask me."

"You don't think it's asthma or…"

"Cancer? No. That's a bit of a leap. I'm guessing he thinks these symptoms are some sort of paraneoplastic syndrome. That's a cluster of symptoms showing an immune response to cancer, but there's no reason to jump to that. I'm sure Doctor Heimer will run the battery of tests and come up with nothing."

"Interesting. And I see you've got no issues undermining fellow physicians?"

The male voice over her shoulder made her wince. She turned and couldn't hide her cornered look as Ruby's attending physician, Doctor Emmett Howards, approached. They'd met on her tour and he'd been less than impressed at her presence. The squat English bulldog, complete with narrow glasses and paisley tie, eyed her suspiciously.

She inhaled, trying for confidence at being caught. "Doctor Howards. It seems your patient's father and I are acquainted."

"I think a great many are *acquainted* with you, Doctor," Howards grunted, the posh North London accent shadowing his words. "And you seem to know quite a lot of this case."

She turned to Charlie with a glance that told him to retreat quickly or be subject to fallout. He ducked back into Ruby's room and pulled the door shut behind as Deis turned back to the edgy physician.

"She's a patient, not a case, and yes, I read over the file. He asked questions since he knows me, and I felt obliged to answer them. Do you mind sharing your thoughts with a colleague?"

"There's nothing to tell," he snapped, his head tipped as he glared over his narrow frames. "The specialists will, as you say, waste their time testing, but that's the diagnostic process of exclusion. I'm sure you learned that in med school, back home where perhaps you're better suited to practice your intrusive and assumptive medical style."

Deis wanted to recoil but her spine leapt into her throat. She'd earned her place here as his peer, whether he deigned to show respect or not.

"I'm sure I graduated from just as prestigious a school as your alma mater here in Britain. We can both agree that this patient's prognosis is our sole interest. We can deal with each other as contemporaries, or we can condescend to insult each other. I prefer the first option."

"Very well, Doctor. Since you've only spent a few minutes with her and I did the intake and history, tell me, what have I overlooked, then?"

"Not cancer, not asthma. In taking those few minutes and actually speaking with Ruby, I was able to unearth a few more details you might need. This kid is freezing cold in the heat of summer. Her belly calms with carbonation when that would normally irritate it. Those facts are missing from her write-up. But let me guess, after the respiratory analysis comes back normal and her scan shows no sign of cancer, it'll be a Crohn's diagnosis? It's missing in the diagnostic plan, but it fits some symptoms."

"I've ruled out Crohn's. The intense pain is absent, and it's not in the family history. In fact, there's no family history of anything pertinent, which I'm sure you also read."

"I did," Deis nodded, proud of the doubt she saw in his eyes. "Well, I wish you luck with your diagnosis, and I sincerely hope she doesn't end up back here again. I'd take her on as a pediatric patient in Diagnostics, where this sort of work is commonplace, though that probably wouldn't look good to your peers who've also decided to waste time confronting a new colleague rather than spending that time comforting their customers."

Poking her head inside Ruby's room, she bade farewell to the patient, shooting a quick wink to Charlie and brushing past the hoity doctor and his opinions.

Ready to be done for the day, she made her way to the rented SUV and back to Haven, boiling on the inside but determined to prove her skeptics wrong.

Chapter 6

Saturday, December 6

Two days after her confrontation with the pigheaded doctor, Deis returned to the emergency department's triage bay at breakneck speed. She'd navigated through the late afternoon traffic fiercely after calling the police for clearance. The flashing lights in her rearview mirror fought to keep up as she weaved around cars and bicycles.

Tossing her key to the nurse at check-in, she rushed inside and up to the third-floor patient room where Miranda was waiting, covered in an itchy rash and wailing in pain. She threw on her doctor's coat outside the room while her fellows caught her up on her patient's condition.

"Yesterday, the diarrhea came back as expected. Atropine withdraw brought the nausea back but again, we expected that." Natalie explained in a quick tone.

The male fellow sighed, shoved his hands in his jacket pockets. "But the rash, it started on her forearms and spread inward. She said it's itchy like poison ivy but there's no chance of exposure. She hasn't been out of bed in days."

"And the pain, on a scale of one to ten?" Deis asked.

"She says eight, as bad as or worse than at admission, but now it's persistent." Phil added.

"Run high-dose NSAID until I know the atropine and difenoxin is out of her system. Push eight-hundred milligrams IV ibuprofen now, again in three hours, and monitor pain."

"I'm on it," he replied, rushing off.

"I'm coming with you," Natalie added confidently to the charge doctor, ready to follow behind.

Deis nodded and stepped inside the patient's room just as the young patient released an agonizing scream. The doctor's blood turned to ice in her veins.

"Miranda, I'm starting pain meds," Deis shouted over the howling, grabbing her patient's forearm. Her mother Diane had her other arm tight in her grip as her daughter clenched and groaned. "I have Doctor Murphy starting them for you. It won't take the pain away all together, but it'll take the edge off."

With teary eyes and gritted teeth, Miranda begged. "Please. Please help me. I can't. It's torture." Her arms pulled against their holds, wriggling and begging to scratch.

"I'm going to start a non-steroid cream for the itching, but I need you to relax. Tensing up is going to make this worse. Doctor Murphy can't push meds if you're tense. Please, Miranda." Deis lowered her head within inches of her patient's, upturning and softening her gaze. "Control it. It's your body. Take control. I know you can."

She watched Miranda close her eyes, pant fiercely against pain. With deep breaths through her mouth, she opened her palms. Tears spilled out as she eyed her mother.

Diane laid her cheek on her daughter's head and consoled while Deis moved aside. With the medication pushed and Natalie slathering on the cream with blue-gloved hands, Deis added to her file of notes. She glanced over the symptoms, putting them in order and forming a connect-the-dots diagnosis.

Once Miranda's pain was at a manageable level and her hands were outfitted with cotton mitts to prevent abrasive scratching, the doctors retreated to their lounge.

Doctor Murphy paced the floor, wringing his hands. "Now the pain's back, big time. She's uncomfortably itchy with rash, has the GI symptoms and is still weak. We're adding symptoms."

Deis touched her fingertips together, resting her elbows on the table and leaning forward. "She's getting sicker. That in and of itself is a symptom."

"Brilliant docs we are, doing a world of good, pen-pushing while she circles the drain." He moved to the whiteboard and wrote her symptoms, old and new, in spastic penmanship of all capital letters.

Deis wheeled her chair over to consider them all. Diarrhea, nausea, weakness, dizziness, pain, heart arrhythmia/tachycardia, rash.

Common denominator? There were dozens.

"You ran blood panels Thursday. Any oddball findings?" Deis asked aloud.

Natalie spoke up without hesitation. "Nothing that explains it all. These symptoms, are they paraneoplastic?"

That word brought back memories of her clash with Doctor Howards outside Ruby's door. Bile rose in her throat and burned like magma.

"Go on," the senior doctor muttered.

"Well," Natalie sat forward. "It fits most of these symptoms. Paraneoplastic typically includes pain, weakness, ataxia, dizziness, and sometimes rashes. The pain could be related to the growth itself, maybe an intestinal tumor?"

"Doesn't explain the heart," Phil chimed in, passing the marker between his palms.

"Okay, a systemic cancer, one that affects the body as a whole," Natalie amended grumpily.

Deis' eyes closed slowly, the unfortunate truth emerging through the fog and bringing disappointment in a suitcase along with it. It was a terrible prognosis, potentially a terminal one, but it explained the symptoms on the table better than anything else.

"Do a lymph node feel, look over the CBC on that last blood panel."

Phil turned to Deis, his eyes drawn. "Damn it all. You think it's leukemia?"

Deis nodded. "Systemic. You can't get more systemic than blood. Did she bleed excessively after her blood draws? Any bruising?"

"She has a few, but she's a teenager and she said she's been weak and dizzy. And she bled enough to show on the bandage but not profusely."

"Any reported ataxia? Is she unstable on her feet? Uncoordinated?"

"Like I said, weak and dizzy," Natalie scowled with her palms up.

Deis stood and laid her palms on her hips. "Doctor Murphy, do her lymph feel and Doctor O'Leary, see to the CBC levels. If in doubt, get another sample. I'm going to see her mother."

Deis strode out and into the hospital hall. It was already weighing on her heart, the prospect of telling a young mother than her teenager had cancer and convincing her to sign off on a painful and hopefully fruitless biopsy.

Doctor Heimer, prestigious head of the Oncology department, was starstruck and overwhelmed as he showed Deis to the armchair by his desk. The fine-looking late-thirties doctor with auburn hair, hazel eyes and a faint German accent had a much-coveted corner office, complete with a brickwork terrace topped by potted winter camellias exploding in flamingo pink blooms. On shelves on the far wall, miniature models of spaceships and airplanes took up residence alongside photos of young children and golden retrievers.

"Doctor Heimer, thanks for seeing me on such short notice." Deis sat as instructed while the doctor circled his desk.

"Oh, please, call me Garren. I'm a big fan. I heard your team is well underway finding a diagnosis for Miss Victor."

"Actually, that's why I'm here." From her briefcase, she pulled out Miranda's huge file and laid it on his oak desk. "If you'd take a look, I'd appreciate it."

"Oh, a consult? I'll admit, I hoped this was a friendly call, but I'm honored either way."

He laid classy reading glasses over his nose, scanning each line of her scholarly notes with a smirk. "It seems she's been quite the patient. I knew she's was a frequent flyer but not to this extent. She's received better care than the royals."

Deis nodded with a polite smile. "It seems so, but we're still looking for an answer. The recent symptoms seem indicative to me."

He nodded. "I see. Paraneoplastic, but some symptoms are irregular. Your fellow did the lymph feel?"

"Slight swelling."

"I see." He closed her file and opened his day planner. "I can see her in the morning, assuming you've received consent."

"I have, thank you," Deis replied, astonished at his consideration. "Doctor Gordon signed off already. I've explained to Miranda and her mother that a bone marrow biopsy is painful but necessary. She said it can't be worse than the pain she's in."

"She'll be surprised," Doctor Heimer replied dryly, checking his watch before writing in his day planner. "I'll see her at nine precisely. Have her prepped in the operating theatre at a quarter 'til. April, my charge nurse, will attend. You'll need to schedule the anesthesia."

"Thank you for your promptness, Doctor. I expected a weekday appointment after a few days' wait."

"Not a problem, Doctor. I'm on the Board with her uncle. He's a pushy bastard but it's more about concern than strong-arming. He has no children of his own."

Deis nodded, retrieving and stashing the file back in her case. "We'll have the patient ready and will handle the other details prior to your procedure."

"Excellent," he replied. "And how are my other colleagues treating you? I've heard a few nasty things and have corrected the behavior appropriately, but I imagine it hasn't been the friendliest reception in this boys' club of ours."

She paused to find a diplomatic response. "It's been a bit of a challenge, but I'm used to being the new kid in town. A few doctors have been difficult, seemingly due to my gender, bedside manner, primary occupation or citizenship, but most have been very friendly, like yourself. And I appreciate your efforts to stop the rumor mills."

"Certainly." He handed over a CD jewel case. "Now sign this."

"Blackmail, Doctor? For shame."

With a laughing grin, she retrieved her felt pen and did as asked.

There was always a trade-off, she realized, walking away with a biopsy in exchange for a signature on their first album and a selfie to place alongside the photos of his purebreds.

Doctor Gordon was in her office when she returned from the cafeteria, waiting in the guest chair with a folder on his lap. As she approached, he stood and offered a hand in greeting. After taking it cordially, Deis stepped around her desk, set her premixed salad and bottle of water down and turned her chair to face him.

"Pardon the interruption, Doctor Deis, but I wanted to discuss your findings. The Board member we discussed often was contacted by Doctor Heimer a few minutes ago. I read over your notes on the system and agree with your findings but want to be ready to brief him when he calls me, as he no doubt will."

"I'd expected that. Let me send over my notes."

She jumped on her laptop and emailed Doctor Gordon her synopsis and observations, along with the pre-op procedures and care plan she'd created. When his work phone dinged with a new message, a pleased smile crossed his face.

"I knew Miss Victor was in good hands. His schedule is even tighter than mine, yet he somehow had time for her tomorrow. What did you do to gain his favor so quickly?"

"Doctor Gordon," she scolded lightly at his insinuation. "All I did was ask him nicely. And condescend to his blackmail. He wanted my autograph."

"As I figured. You've got quite a few fans here. How have the other doctors been treating you?"

She considered her options. If she snitched on her peers, it would no doubt bounce back to her in some way, but if she lied to her director and he found out, it would affect her trustworthiness. Doctor Heimer had known of her hardships, so the office grapevine was a tighter noose than she'd figured.

"The vast majority nurture working relationships, though one particular physician gave me a hard time. He and the situation were properly handled."

"And this doctor, is he on your team?"

She laughed, sitting back. "No, Doctor Murphy's been agreeable since I assigned him all my duties as punishment. I think he realized that being in charge means a whole lot of paperwork."

"Then who is this troublemaker? I will have words."

"No, please," Deis interjected with an outstretched palm. "I'm an adult and I handled it with my own words. Fortunately, I don't work in his department and we don't cross paths often. In fact, I've only seen him twice. I have no interest in changing his mind or in furthering the issue."

"Very well. Please know my door is open. I hire a diverse staff, foster learning through inclusion and don't appreciate open hostility. Tell me if there are any other issues and I will handle them appropriately."

"Yes, sir," Deis replied with a nod. "Please let me know if any more questions arise about Ms. Victor's care."

Deis escorted her supervisor to the door and showed him out. Turning back, she exhaled and uttered a silent prayer.

Back at her desk, she took a moment for herself and ate her diet-friendly yet already limp salad. Before long, she'd be chowing down on burgers and chips like the other staffers if she remained trapped here. For now, while her willpower remained intact, she ate her meal in silence, jotting down ideas for Myopic's production the following week.

As she finished her water and spun her chair, tossing the bottle in the recycle bin behind her desk, she heard a delicate tap on her door as it slid open. Surely it was Natalie, the mild and considerate fellow, and not her brutish coworker.

"Come on in, Doctor. I'm done." Deis called over her shoulder.

"Oh, I'm no doctor," the thick male voice replied.

Whipping around, she saw Charlie step inside with his hands in his pockets. The leather jacket was on today, too, over a plain black crew neck tee. He looked tired, still unshaven, but his face was an arrow to the heart even so.

"Oh, hey," Deis managed, standing and stepping over. "Sorry, one of my fellows knocks every time she comes in. It's her office, too, but I guess it's her version of courtesy."

"Oh, the blonde one? She seems a touch meek. Maybe she's intimidated by your persona."

"My persona?" Her brows dipped.

"You ladies, all the hats you wear, it can be a bit intimidating. I'm sure people think Stage Deis is a character, and perhaps that Doctor Deis is one, too. I think they're all little bits of you, but others, maybe they think it's all a big act."

"If I'm an actor, than who am I really?" She asked rhetorically. "I wish I was that clever."

His smile lifted the corners of his eyes, the azure gems twinkling. "I think you're very clever. That's why I'm here."

"Oh?" Her breath caught as she fought the urge to step back, scolding her lusty response down deep. "It's late. What do you need at this hour?"

"I need your help." His tone softened as he closed the distance. "My girl, she's still here. That doctor, the one you took the piss out of? He's waffling. I met that Doctor Heimer and he's confident it's not cancer. You don't think it is, either. Please," he sighed, met her gaze with a fire that made her heart throb. "Please come see her again. I know she's his patient but he's a bit dim. I need you."

She released a deep breath. Personal connection. Concerned father. Someone else's patient. It was dangerous ground to tread.

Before her mind could argue, she instinctively reached out and squeezed his forearm. "Let's go."

In Ruby's room, she found the girl sitting up, bundled to her chin and watching a cartoon show she didn't recognize. Charlie called her beautiful and opened a can of soda he fetched from his pocket once again.

"It's a good thing it's not diabetes," Deis jested to Charlie, stepping to Ruby's bedside. "You're going to turn into a can of lemon fizz if this keeps up."

"That's fine. Lemon fizz likes being cold. I don't." Her tone was indifferent, exhausted.

Deis looked over her file once more, noting the changes since her last visit. Doctor Heimer documented normal lymph nodes, was skeptical of cancer diagnosis, and confirmed symptoms unrelated to paraneoplastic syndrome. Flipping back, she looked again at her symptoms at admission plus the ones noted after her confrontation with the attending.

"Hey Ruby, sorry to interrupt your show, but I have to know a few things." She closed the file and tucked it back into its cradle. "How hard is it for you to breathe? Is it all the time?"

Charlie flipped off the TV with the remote, disciplining her silently with a fierce look when she let out a tiny grumble in protest. With a sigh and lowering the soda can, she replied meekly. "No, not really. When I'm in a hot bath, or when we run laps at school. Sometimes when I just wake up from a nap."

"Gotcha," Deis acknowledged, lowering her face to Ruby's. "Do me a favor, Ruby. Tip your head back, look up at the ceiling."

As her head tipped up, Deis shined her penlight on the girl's neck.

"Now, turn left and look out the window. Can you see any stars out there?"

She did as commanded, straining and stretching to see through the frosted glass. The doctor checked the skin above collarbone while she was fixated.

"Now, look at your daddy. Get your face in as close to him as you can. Give him a big nuzzle."

She did as commanded, giggling when he pecked her cheek.

Deis stepped back, laid her hands on her hips. "Okay, one more thing. Can you stretch up and try to pull the ceiling down? Stretch up really high with both arms."

She reached her fingers toward the ceiling. Deis leaned in and saw the truest symptom of all on her underarms, clearly visible in the narrow beam.

"That was great, thank you," Deis praised. "And I have a little secret for you."

"Like Rai's ruby?" The girl asked earnestly.

"It's kind of like that," Deis squinted dramatically while leaning in, playing up the drama for her audience. "But it's *your* secret. Have you ever heard of a fairy named Addison?"

"No, who's that?" She asked, her bright eyes tinged with curiosity.

"Well," Deis sat on the foot of the bed. "She's tiny, and she only picks a few people, the ones she likes best. She hides in them, and she's in you. The coolest thing is that she leaves footprints wherever she walks. Lift your arms up again and I'll show you."

With her cell phone, Deis took a photo of her underarm and showed Ruby. "See? See those little dark spots? Those are her footprints. That's how small she is."

Ruby snatched Deis' cell phone away and showed Charlie, whose brows raised in mock excitement. "Wow. Daddy, look! She's leaving marks all over!"

"What does Addison do?" Charlie inquired, his anxious gaze on the doctor as his daughter ogled the snapshot.

Deis exhaled, gathering her thoughts. She turned away from Charlie's glare, instead focusing on the patient and her excitement.

"Addison does like to cause trouble and she's always hungry. She loves to dig into the little cabinets inside you and eat up all your cortisol, which is an ingredient your brain needs to make happiness. She sneaks in, eats up whatever she finds and leaves you with none. Not having cortisol might make you feel sick in your tummy or might make feel chilly. It also might make you dizzy sometimes or tired on certain days. Right now, you have a lot of those problems plus a few more, but I can help make it better."

"You can?" Ruby asked with furrowed brows. "Will it hurt Addison?"

"No, it won't hurt her or chase her off, but it will help keep that cortisol in your body's pantry where it needs to be. You'll need to take a little pill. If you take one every day, she'll get the cortisol she needs and leave what's in your cabinets alone. But it won't make her leave."

"Will she ever leave? I don't like being knackered and frozen."

"I bet you don't, but she's here to stay. Sometimes, you'll have to bundle up when everyone else is in shorts, and sometimes, especially when you get a cold or the flu, your daddy might have to bring you back here. She causes more trouble when your insides aren't in tip-top shape. Cortisol is important, so I'm going to start those little pills right away and tell Doctor Howards about Addison, too. He'll want to know where she's been, so make sure you show him those footprints, okay?"

"Okay." She smiled a little and brought the blanket back up around her little shoulders. "Maybe Daddy will sleep now that Addison's here."

"Tattletale," Charlie narrowed his tired eyes and smirked at Ruby.

"You'll be here another night or two, okay?" Deis cut in. "I have to make sure this plan works well enough to keep Addison satisfied, and I have to make sure you get stronger so you can go back to school. I'll also have to send FIT in to set up camp and chase off any more unwanted guests."

"What's that? Is it like the police?"

"That stands for Flu Immunization Team. It's my secret group of tiny security guards that set up barriers inside and keep yucky flu bugs from getting in. You know how castles and forts have high walls all around them to keep invaders out? They do the same thing but inside your body. Flu doesn't stand a chance against defenses like that."

"Wow!" She lit up like a Christmas tree. "Send in the crew!"

"All right, let's do it!" Deis cheered and high-fived the patient. "And, Ruby, just so you know, you'll probably be the only kid in your school with a fairy friend. Your teachers or school nurse might ask you questions when you get back. Doctors might make you explain how you feel a whole lot, over and over, but it's only because we need to watch Addison and keep her in line. Trouble-making fairies keep us grownups very busy."

"Okay, Doctor Deis."

Her optimistic smile was confident and courageous, her hand reaching for Deis'. Overwhelmed and touched, she clasped it lightly.

"Daddy said you'd help me," Ruby confided. "You did help me. You found the fairy trail. Will you stop coming to see me now?"

"Not a chance, kiddo." Deis stood with a grin, patting her hand after letting go. "I have to make sure Addison stays in line, at least until you head home."

"Okay. I like you. You're nice."

The earnest compliment warmed her. "Thanks, Ruby. You're my best patient for sure."

"And Daddy likes you too."

Charlie's head drooped shamefully as Deis giggled.

"Well, I like him right back." She wiggled Ruby's foot under the blanket. "Can I borrow him for just a second? I'll send him back when I'm done."

"I guess so," she said, turning the TV back on and settling in, slyly touching at her neck where the fairy's footprints marked her skin.

Outside the door, alone in the quiet and darkened hall, Deis giggled again, waving off Charlie's embarrassment.

"She's like a walking polygraph, that kid," he scowled.

"Most kids are honest, painfully so, but they mean well."

"So," he sobered. "Addison?"

"Yes. Unfortunately, it's Addison's Disease. It's a chronic auto-immune condition that causes a drop of cortisol production. The biggest potential complication is that Addison's can cause an unsafe drop in blood pressure. That's more likely to happen when her immune system is compromised. She needs to get enough rest, eat right and to be immunized against flu every year. I'm going to make sure she gets one today. Keep an eye on her activity levels. Other than bringing her in if any strange symptoms pop up, just keep her well."

"There's no cure, then?"

"No, there's no known cure, but cortisol supplements are our best bet. Addison's affects people in different ways. This diagnosis is extremely rare, though. Doctors will take her illness seriously and won't risk any complications. The weakness, dizziness and chills may continue until we get the dosage right, but the cortisol supplement will help a lot."

"Did I...?" He stammered, wrung his hands with his gaze turned downward. "Did I give this to her?"

Deis exhaled, reached out and took his hand compassionately. "I won't lie, it's possible but I strongly doubt it. There's evidence that it's a hereditary condition but you don't have any symptoms. It could be elsewhere in her lineage. Is her mother in the picture?"

The look in his eyes when they turned up to meet hers made her instantly regret the question. It was a cross between bitter anger and unresolved guilt.

"No, and she hasn't been around since Ruby was three. She," he paused, swallowed. "She couldn't handle it. Or so she said. The stress of the kid, of the band floundering, of my job, of all of it. It all snowballed, and one day she just up and left. I found a note in the flat, filled with flimsy excuses. She's been gone for years. No word, no letters, nothing, for her daughter or for me."

Deis released her grip, tucked her hands in her jacket pockets. "I'm sorry, Charlie, for you both. I'd wager that she's your hereditary link. Stress is alleviated by cortisol. That could explain why she was so edgy. Then again, I'm a pediatrician. 'Could' and 'should' are my go-to explanations for unworthy parents."

His eyes narrowed defensively. "Unworthy? She's Ruby's mother."

"No, not really. She abandoned that beautiful soul in there. She left a loving and devoted father behind, too. No matter the reason, it's still inexcusable in my book. There's a solution if both parties are willing to find it. But I think Ruby will learn her lessons on how to persevere and succeed from her daddy. I can't help but dislike the circumstances that got her here, but I know she's better off this way."

"All I want is for her to be a kid, to enjoy life and not make the mistakes I made."

"See? Wonderful father, case in point. She'll probably rail against you for years, daughters do that. But eventually she'll come to realize that her father is an outstanding, dedicated and loving guy. And she'll use you as a yardstick for every guy that comes later. She'll watch how you treat women and decide that's how she deserves to be treated. And fortunately for everyone, she's your princess and it shows."

Without warning and without reservation, his body moved into hers. His fingers wrapped gently around the warmth of her neck, and when his head tipped and their mouths met, fire exploded in her belly, spreading up to scorch her soul where she stood, motionless and stunned. He took her lower lip between his, masterfully exploiting the sweetness he found. As his fingers swept up into her hair, she dropped her hands from her pockets and laid them on his hips, her eyes slipping shut as bliss set in.

Finding her lips soft and giving, he shifted her against the wall and plundered. She let herself enjoy a full minute before tugging back and lowering her hands to her sides.

She was at work, in a public hallway for God's sake. What was wrong with her?

"Charlie," she purred in weak protest, opening her hazy eyes.

"I'm so sorry," he breathed, laying his forehead to hers for a moment. Before she could utter another word, he straightened up to pace away with his hands in his hair. "Don't worry. It won't happen again. I'm sorry, I had no right. I just..." He turned back to her, two strides away and with desperate eyes. "I knew better, but what you said, it was... It was brilliant."

"I meant it."

With knees weakened like a swooning girl, she leaned against the wall. Though her body desired more heat, her mind was strangely unruffled. The kiss had squashed the fear that her lust was one-sided.

"I know and it's more, she's more, than I could've asked for," he murmured, closing the distance between them. "I was nineteen when she told me she was pregnant. I was just a kid, some mediocre musician hoping for a break. And when she came, when Ruby came, life started to make sense. She was my reason. Here was my little muse. And every time I wrote, whenever I was on stage, I thought of her and it made me something else. Every time I went to work, I knew I had to come home because she'd be there. Nothing I did mattered nearly as much as whatever she was doing. I... What am I going on about? Apologies, Doctor. I never meant to worry you with all that. "

Deis beamed and took his hands in hers. "That's beautiful. And, so you know, I'm only worried that you won't kiss me again."

The truth had tumbled out like an avalanche, but she didn't have time to recoil.

With a slow, sly smile, he shifted her arms up against the wall above her head, held her wrists just firmly enough to thrill, and indulged himself again. Her body curled up against him like a kitten. Kissing her was so easy, so natural, as his fingers twisted and entangled with hers.

His grip finally released, allowing her arms to circle his shoulders and brush into his hair. It was just as silken as she'd hoped, and the scent of him, peppery and dark, swirled and confused her senses. He took his time, each penetratingly intense kiss lasting a few seconds. He swallowed her pitiful sighs as her mind went blank, the world shrinking back into the shadows while his palm tugged at her hip, kept her in close.

Undoubtedly skilled, painstakingly patient, he devastated her one breathless second at a time. When their lips parted, she moaned helplessly as her cheek brushed his coarse jaw. "My God, Charlie."

His fingers swept over her cheeks and down her neck as he watched her amber eyes spark in the dim light. His voice was barely a whisper, an inch from her lips. "Deis, you saved my little girl. You treated her like a person, not a silly child or a case study. I'll never be able to repay your kindness, your generosity. Honestly, you are amazing."

And when he pulled back to focus his deep blue eyes on hers, the gratitude and appreciation in them silenced her. She felt her heart kick once, hard, against her ribs.

With a meek smile, she nodded once and held her tongue.

As he stepped back into Ruby's room, calm and collected, he greeted her in his traditional boisterous way. And she snuck off down the hall with her head hanging.

Hope died as her mind worked overtime, analyzing his every move.

She knew gratitude and she knew passion. Her mind simply confused the two in that moment. He kissed the way many shook hands, said thanks, bought fruit baskets.

Good-looking guy, undersexed female, misplaced assumption. It was a humiliating and degrading gaffe, one she'd regret as far out as she could see.

Working hurriedly, she amended Ruby's file on her laptop and powered it down. Her SUV was headed back to Haven well after midnight and she'd be back at seven for the pre-op.

It was going to be a long, lonely and restless night.

Chapter 7

Deis and her fellows converged on the Diagnostics lounge at five minutes before eight in the morning, their coffees in to-go cups alongside a tray of bagels waiting to be decimated.

"Doctor Gordon had them brought in," Natalie explained, her candy pink dress peeking out from below her lab coat. "Butter and jam, no hazelnut spread."

"Bummer," Deis remarked, debating the carb splurge before deciding to be good. "Is Miranda ready?"

"As can be," Phil replied, nursing his coffee. "Her mum stayed the night in the chair beside the bed, but I don't think either of them slept."

"Doctor Heimer is in and April is readying the operating theatre. We'll be on the outside for this one."

Natalie nibbled at her poppy bagel. "This will go better. I have a feeling."

Deis, much less rested and cheerful than her blonde fellow, toasted her optimism with her half-empty coffee cup.

They shared an hour of relative silence, leaning on caffeine and a starchy breakfast like crutches. Deis paged through Miranda's file with a highlighter, swiping it over every recurring symptom she saw in the endless notes. Their cancer prognosis was hardly a coup, but it matched most of her ailments.

Yet, somehow, she still doubted herself. As the minutes ticked by, it became easier to.

The office phone on the other side of the glass wall rang just before they planned to join the oncologist for his post-op update. Deis threw open her office door, rushing to answer by the third ring.

The fellows watched as Deis deflated, collapsing into her office chair and clutching the receiver in her white-knuckled fist. Her eyes, unblinking, focused on nothing as she listened. When she finally hung up without uttering a word, Natalie stepped forward and leaned down over her boss.

Deis' voice was a threadbare murmur. "The nurse reports that Miranda had difficulty breathing during pre-op and seemed confused. A moment later she was vomiting blood."

"Damn it all," Natalie sighed, looking away while Phil paced.

"It's not cancer," Deis muttered. "Back to square one."

The hospital's chief gastroenterologist and the hepatologist on call met with Miranda and her mother once she'd bathed and settled back in her room. Deis stood just outside as they diagnosed cirrhosis to the shattered patient and her mother. It was a moderate case of a devastating illness.

She'd be placed on the transplant list, fortunately closer to the top thanks to her family connection, but she'd still have to wait too long. Deis had already declined the therapeutic endoscopies they'd recommended. The last time they'd tried an endoscopy, her heart stopped.

Their next move was called TIPS, and as they explained the trans-jugular intrahepatic portosystemic shunt and its insertion to mother and daughter, Deis secretly wished it had been leukemia.

The TIPS procedure was a short-term solution, an adhesive bandage over a mortal wound. It would redirect blood flow around the ailing liver and ease the burden, but the liver was still a ticking bomb inside. Every day that passed put more strain on her system, and after perusing the transplant list personally, she doubted it would be sooner than two weeks before a donor could be found. Because the transplant committee wanted a clean bill of health, aside from the liver issue, it was more than likely that she'd die before the donor did.

And it broke her heart to hear Diane beg the doctors to use her liver, to take whatever they needed for her daughter, only to be told she wasn't a match.

With no choice, the team was back to differentials. The beleaguered doctors assembled while the hepatologist prepared to put Miranda under the knife yet again.

The morning was now behind them and the afternoon sun was quickly disappearing behind the hospital. Phil was already scowling as he stepped into the lounge. "Without a diagnosis, this girl won't get a liver. We still don't know what's causing the underlying condition and now we have cirrhosis on the list."

His irritation only intensified Deis' festering heartache. She fought to focus on Miranda, her mind conflicted by Charlie and his mouth, by Myopic and her closing deadline, by the shunt that only delayed the inevitable, and the maelstrom of it all swirling together in an unrested and frustrated brain.

"Fine. Well done, Doctor Murphy, you've summed it all up," Deis seethed with drawn eyes. "We've got a time bomb in that girl's belly. The shunt will buy us some time, a few weeks, if we're lucky. We've got every damn department in this hospital on high alert and they're all waiting for our Hail Mary pass."

Natalie eyes narrowed as she looked up from her notes. "What's a Hail Mary pass?"

"American football term for a really long, last ditch pass, trying to bring a miracle about," Phil replied dryly, sitting alongside his blonde peer. "What's your plan, then?"

"Wait for the shunt, monitor changes in symptoms over the next twenty-four hours. Stop the pain meds and see if her pain is diminished. Our Hail Mary is hoping the liver was the route cause all along. And if her health improves, we can push for a clean bill of health and the transplant."

"So, our plan is to do nothing," he remarked sardonically with a lifted brow. "Brilliant. And when she crashes?"

"Blood flow through the liver, if it was tainted, could cause heart distress," Natalie suggested diplomatically.

"It would elevate blood levels, which were normal at last check," he argued.

Deis jumped in. "Have you both memorized her history?"

They both fell silent but nodded in unison.

"Then we've done what we could, so we wait. We wait and we pray some poor teenager dies in a car crash and that she wasn't the one driving drunk."

Deis paced outside the operating theatre's glass partition as the surgeons closed the incision in Miranda's torso. The shunt surgery had been a success, and as they wheeled her to recovery, Deis approached the Scottish hepatologist currently on loan from the Edinburgh Institute, Doctor Greenley.

"Doctor," she called as he strode away.

Turning back to the voice, he seemed relieved for Deis' presence. Still in his operating gown and donning a paper cap, a slow smile spread over his wrinkled face and lit his gray eyes.

"Oh, Doctor. Your patient did well. She'll recover but it'll take a few hours before blood flow is back to normal. We'll keep her in the ICU for the duration."

"I appreciate it. Did you take vitals before the procedure?"

"The nurse did," he replied, pulling the synopsis from the file he carried. "Stats normal, acceptable pulse and ox rates. Was that a concern?"

"Not necessarily," Deis bit her tongue, hiding the fib.

"Then why ask?" The hepatologist narrowed his gaze, unconvinced. "I saw in her chart that you've tried other procedures and she had adverse symptoms. Were you assuming the same would happen here?"

"I'm shocked they didn't, quite frankly. She was unwilling, in fact terrified, of anesthesia when we tried for the endoscopy. She seemed to take today's procedure pretty well."

"Maybe patient and mother had a chat after our diagnosis. This was the last option. She just resigned herself to that and handled it."

As Deis nodded limply and the doctor turned away. Tucking her thumbnail between her teeth, she made her way back to the lounge.

Alone in the quiet space, she wrote a timeline and word clusters on the whiteboard.

> *Admission Sunday, blood panel symptoms, diet, less alcohol now, self-tanner, chemical makeup, mom, difenoxin, endoscopy scheduled, stress, v-fib, off difenoxin, blood panel, rash, symptoms, cancer, CBC, bone marrow biopsy scheduled, confusion, can't breathe, bloody emesis, cirrhosis, shunt scheduled, no stress, shunt placed, recovery.*

She sat in the closest chair to the whiteboard and stared until the words melded together like an abstract painting. She tapped her feet, clicked her jaw, tipped her heart left and right.

What had changed? What was constant? Each decision they'd made, each treatment they tried caused new symptoms, but with patches of wellness between.

Hours passed and she never moved. The young fellows, upon finding her glaring at the stark black text, left her alone to stew, checking in on the patient instead and circling back hours later, only to see her studious meditation continue.

Resigned to her previous decision, the wait-and-see approach, Deis rose, threw on her wool coat and headed back to Haven, prepared to receive the inevitable phone call from her fellows reporting the downturn of Miranda Victor before she could make it back to the office with the research manual she was headed home to retrieve.

The moment she entered Haven, Anna was on her heels, aiming to sweep her coat from her shoulders. The doctor's fatigue and desperation was plain to see.

"Oh, Deis, what a sight you are. Come, let's take care of you."

"No, Chef, I'm…" What was she? She'd settle for the standard reply. "I'm fine."

"Hardly," Rai observed, descending the grand staircase into the atrium. "You look like death warmed over."

"Thanks, precious. Remind me to send you a fruit bouquet for the kind words."

"Ladies, enough," Anna chided them both cordially.

"I'll take her up," Rai volunteered. "Get some real nutrition ready for her, not that low-carb crap. And find Henry and send him up, would you?"

Anna nodded diligently, striding off to the kitchen.

"I'm just here for a manual. I have to get back to…"

Rai urged her up the steps. "No, no. Come on, stranger. It's nearly midnight. Did you eat at all today?"

"I had… a bagel, I think. No, no, I didn't want the calories. There was a salad. That might've been yesterday. Not sure anymore."

"Christ, Deis."

Rai escorted Deis to her bedroom, removing her coat and shoes as the suave, dark-haired butler rushed in, concern tinting his high cheeks.

"Henry, just in time," Rai called over her shoulder. "The doctor needs sustenance and a warm bath. Grab my lavender salts, the jar

Steve brought from Provence. And she'll need Emmi's blackout curtains hung in here."

He was gone with a quick bow and averted eyes.

"Rai, I can't sleep," Deis fought pathetically. "This kid is sick, I'm her doctor and I have fellows. Besides, I've stayed up for longer."

"Not when I was around," Rai muttered, lifting a brow. "We can do this the easy way or the hard way. I've dosed one of my friends before, and not that long ago. I'll dose another."

Deis sighed, surrendered and allowed her friend to remove her doctor's coat.

Rai readied her bed, turned down the blankets and found her pajamas. "Charlie was here this morning to sign some forms. He said you really helped his kid out. I had no idea that he even had a kid."

That name and the memory of their time in the hallway made her wince. She swallowed back the bitter taste that came along with it.

"Ruby. She's eight. Sweet as can be."

"Ruby Tuesday Marie Taylor. Isn't that cute?" Rai snickered, setting up a table at the foot of the bed as Henry delivered a tray and carafe.

"She's a gem," Deis murmured, sidling up to the steaming plate.

"Did you tell him he's the subject of your nonexistent dreams?" Rai mocked, sitting on the vanity's stool.

"Oh, shut up, Rai. Jesus."

Deis lifted her fork, poked listlessly at the long beans and pork roast.

"It won't eat itself," Rai quipped like an irritated mother. "And besides, if you can't talk to me, who can you talk to?"

"Oh, I don't know," Deis dropped the fork with a clang and glared at her band mate. "A folding chair, a cactus, something more compassionate?"

"Oh, you love me."

"Like a persistent skin rash. Look, I'm really not in the mood to..."

"I know, to deal with me. But I'm worried about you. Really."

Deis' expression was lackluster curiosity and sarcastic doubt as she grabbed the fork again, pointing the tines at her friend menacingly.

Rai's smile drooped into a sorrowful apologetic frown. "For real. We've known each other forever. I know you take work seriously, and I know this Miranda girl is sick, but what's got you so ruffled? Usually stress does your body good."

"It's not Miranda," Deis admitted with a sigh, pushing the plate back a few inches. "It's Charlie."

"I figured. He was a little off today, too. Tired like you, but quiet, detached."

Deis cradled her forehead in both hands. "I wish I could be detached. I can't afford to be detached. I'm bobbling my first case in this country."

"It's a tough one, one the hospital couldn't figure out, either. Don't forget that. And Emmi would be just as stumped."

"Not a chance in hell. She'd have had this closed and cleaned up by now."

"You can always ask for a consult. I've seen enough medical shows to know that."

"I hate needing help on this. Stupid pride, I guess. But I'm just... I'm at a loss. I'm never at a loss. I've stared at that girl's file for days. I know every nuance. I know every symptom, but not the base cause. And I think my staff is following blindly instead of volunteering alternatives."

"You said they were young and a little green. Are they intimidated or just unsure?"

"Both. They stayed away from me, let me simmer all day instead of pushing me. They don't know me well enough to push me.

Normally teams work together under less strenuous circumstances for a while before a girl's liver fails."

"Her liver failed? What happened to the leukemia?"

"False alarm."

"Good God. Her mother must be..."

Thankfully Rai saw Deis' expression, the silent but pleading demand to halt that sentence, and stopped instantly.

"Even if you don't have faith in yourself or your team right now, I have faith in you. You'll figure this all out." Rai shrugged simply. "I don't know how I know, but I know. The universe always provides for you, doesn't it?"

"Things have been working out all right for you, too, you know."

Rai beamed. "I heard from Kara today. She's still on house arrest, so to speak, but her grades have improved as has her outlook. She's switched her gang of friends out for a different crowd and the meds seem to be helping."

"Glad for some good news. Emmi emailed to tell me Carlos enjoyed his visit. She donated to the hospital's hospice foundation while she was there."

"Who's Carlos?"

"Oh, I forgot to tell you. He's a cancer patient back home. He's barely twelve with a medulloblastoma. He's got serious love for Second and superheroes. In exchange for letting me come here and leave his diagnostic team, he demanded to a visit from Emmi."

"And that was your favor in return? You're such a softie. You could've held out for your own Haven. Hell, your own hospital wing or something."

"I don't need that," Deis scoffed sourly. "I can barely handle the one patient I've got."

"You handled a different one very well. Ruby Tuesday, with a fairy named Addison living in her, from what I hear. She's actually excited to have, what is it, an auto-immune disease? Only you could diagnose that kid in two quick visits and actually have her excited about taking pills and getting shots for the rest of her life."

Rai rose, stepping over to the beaten and exhausted shell of her friend. The look on Deis' face, full of shame and insecurity on the normally headstrong woman, rattled her more than she cared to admit.

"Look, I don't know what's going on with Charlie, but it can wait. If this girl needs all your attention, then that comes first. Let him think about you a bit longer. Detached or not, his vocal practice today was all power. It's good for him." She laid a kiss on the crown of Deis' head and stepped back. "Now eat, get washed up and rest for a bit. I'll send Henry back in twenty to start your bath and get your empty plate. It better be empty, you hear me?"

Deis watched Rai flip on her flat-screen TV, some sitcom with an obnoxious laugh track on display, and then walk off without a glance back.

She finished her dinner and tea, breathed in the lavender-laden steam while bathing, and crawled into bed in the thick pajamas Rai had chosen in about an hour's time. She fought the urge to check email, to message her fellows, to do anything work-related. Gazing up at the white canopy over her queen bed, she pictured his eyes, staring right through her with that intense blue glow that stirred her soul.

He was undeniably striking, the ideal front man for an arena rock band. Anyone with that intriguing smile, bright eyes and confident style slayed females in the crowd. He'd be fighting them off with sticks.

Ruby. If they toured, as Emmi planned to have them do, where would she go? With her mother gone, who watched her while he was in pubs singing?

She wore his shoes for a moment and realized how tough they were to walk in. Everything was a debate, every move a choice

92

between want and need, her benefit and his, her future and his present.

A single dad. A damn good single dad. Jesus, could anything possibly detract from his appeal?

She huffed at herself, flipped angrily under the cotton sheet and chenille blanket. He had her riled up with a few kisses. At this rate, she'd be undone by breakfast.

Day shifted to night as she stewed. Finally, at her wit's end and with the sun peeking through the trees, her eyes winked shut and stayed that way.

Chapter 8

Myopic finished their set in Haven's studio at four in the afternoon, thanked Deis for her continued help and departed on a natural high. She waved as their car drove off Haven's property, glad to be making their music sound its best again.

She felt competent and in control when behind the soundboard. These guys were phenomenal, dedicated and talented, making the work easy. America was in love with the two talented Brits in hoodies and jeans, and Deis would keep them delighted with this next studio effort.

She found that her style favored, unsurprisingly, hot bass riffs and heavy percussion. It got the ear's attention. It made the audiences stop and take notice. When heads turned and ears perked up, videos went viral and albums went platinum. Fresh off their first album's success, both Myopic and their producer were excited to get started again and the day's session flew by without a hitch.

The day before, she'd arrived at Haven from her hospital visit just as the guys were setting up. Her fellows had peppered her cell phone with text messages since early Sunday morning. Overall, they were good reports. And when she'd arrived at the hospital and saw the progress for herself, she'd finally unclenched enough to take on Myopic's workload.

Miranda's pain was gone and in her own words, she felt great. Doctor Greenley's notes showed how pleased he was with the shunt and her improvement as a result. She was much more comfortable and willing to wait for the organ transplant in this condition. She'd added her own notes, updated vitals and the improvement in her skin rash, emailing Doctor Gordon before heading back to Haven after two quick hours at the hospital.

As her day rolled on, after completing a yoga routine and the shower that followed, she made her way to the studio to work on Second's next album. Emmi's vocals were finalized, Rai's guitar perfected, and Destiny had fine-tuned her drum lines, so it was up to her to begin the mixing and post-production sound check. Marilyn would finalize and blend the tracks after Deis' perusal but the deadline was impending, and Emmi was demanding quick progress. She was ready to arrange and plan their next tour.

Deis imagined the cramped bus, the long days on the highway from Maine to California, the bellyaching Rai would do at being worked so hard. She hated the idea of going on tour this time. Other than the little bit of producing work that she considered fun, and the few hours of sleep she'd managed since the Wembley concert just before her residency at the Eastern Shore Children's Institute, she'd had no real break from work.

But, in truth, she'd decided to take the hospital rotation back home. Her priority had been the experience, responsibility and accomplishment rather than a vacation.

With a shrug, she toiled over their first single to be released, the second track on the album. Bringing up the percussion and dimming the vocals made it perfect for the club scene. It made her snicker and she instantly switched it back. They weren't making an album for the Mirandas of the world.

With patience and meticulous calculations, she tuned the bits and harmonized the vocals into a radio-ready piece. Accomplished, she sat back to email Emmi the results.

An incoming text interrupted her typing.

Doc, the arrhythmia's back. Doctor Greenley is taking the shunt out in a half-hour. Too risky. Heart can't move blood fast enough.

Doing EKG and CT once shunt is out. Doctor Gordon suspects heart damage. Need her charge doc signoff. – P.M., M.D.

She launched from the studio, tossed her briefcase and doctor's coat into the front seat and was on her way to the hospital inside three minutes.

It was after nine by the time she arrived at Miranda's room. The patient was out cold, anesthesia still in effect from the shunt removal.

So much for the Hail Mary.

Deis pulled Diane from her motionless daughter's side, out into the hall and away from other visitors. The mother was holding her chest with both arms, her eyes heavily ringed with red but her mouth alive with never-ending questions.

"I thought the shunt was supposed to be the best option! How is this better? The doctor said there might be heart damage. Was that from the endoscopy prep? First, it's her heart. Now her liver? How is this better? All you're doing is making things worse!"

With a deep breath, Deis listened to the frantic mother grieve aloud and hurl insults and skepticism her way until she finally winded herself. Covering her face with her hands, she broke down into a mass of quivering tears.

"Miss Victor, we're doing all we can. Her liver is deteriorating, and has been, even with the shunt in place. As the hepatologist said before it was inserted, it was a short-term solution. She still needs a liver transplant."

"And now what? She's on the transplant list, but she's not well enough to go through another surgery. She's barely made it through your testing! How much longer are you going to prod her and give us these temporary fixes before she just…"

The tears continued as Natalie stepped up, with Doctor Gordon on her heels. With grace and compassion, the director escorted

Diane away from the room and spoke in gentle tones as the mother continued her spiral downward.

With a deep breath and crushed morale, Deis turned to her female fellow. "Tell me you have good news."

"I have news but it's not good. Tests confirm pancreatitis, and her fever's thirty-nine Celsius. The pancreas is shutting down, too."

"Back to the lounge," she commanded bluntly, sending a nurse in to administer ibuprofen and antibiotics to their weakening, desperate patient.

"New plan, Doctor?" Phil asked with a sardonic lilt from the other end of the long table.

Turning back to the whiteboard, still covered in symptoms and repercussions, she added the latest additions.

Heart arrhythmia, shunt removed. Pain. Pancreatitis. Fever. 39°C/102°F, Ibuprofen, antibiotics.

She underlined arrhythmia everywhere it appeared, stepped back.

"I need to make a phone call."

Leaving her staff with the whiteboard, she retreated to her office and opened her laptop. After opening the video chat program and typing in her friend's number, Emmi's face appeared in a pop-up window. She donned a prim red suit with her blonde hair curled into tight spirals, and was perched on a leather highbacked chair in Spire's office.

"Hey, Doc, I need a consult."

"Shoot," her boss and best friend replied easily, sitting back.

"Female, age seventeen, presented with weakness, dizziness, lack of appetite, sporadic but intense pain and diarrhea that loperamide didn't fix. We added to her file, detailed her history. I administered fluids and difenoxin IV, scheduled an endoscopy, but pre-op, she went tachycardic and into v-fib. I paddled her back, took her off difenoxin because of the atropine, and reran her blood panel. The diarrhea came back, but the pain died down for a few days. Then it came back big time, along with an itchy rash, eighty percent of skin affected. I ordered a bone marrow biopsy, but pre-op, she vomited blood so I ruled out leukemia. Cirrhosis diagnosis, put her on the transplant list, but need a clean bill before they'll proceed. Hepatologist installed a TIPS. That was just removed. Her heart couldn't keep up. Now she has a fever, pancreatitis and her pain's back. The clock's ticking."

Emmi jotted down notes while she spoke, creating a circle of symptoms that mimicked her friend's whiteboard doodle. "Got it. I'm following your logic. Infection in bowel, then maybe paraneoplastic syndrome from leukemia, but the cirrhosis doesn't fit. Tell me her history. I'm clearly missing something."

Deis lifted the file into the camera's view, watched Emmi's jaw drop. "This is it. I have details of every tooth she's ever lost and every bad decision she's ever made. I know her shoe size and her first crush's name. Single mom Diane. She's absent, overworked, so Miranda's on her own. She's a vegan with an extremely restricted diet. Obsessed with self-tanner and cheap makeup. Decent student, drinks occasionally but hasn't in weeks. And it's certainly not enough to cause the cirrhosis. We can't prove ataxia. The pain seems to be worse now than ever."

Emmi sat up straight, eyed her band mate through the camera. "And her absentee dad? What do we know about him?"

"The file says he left them both six years ago. He was a trucker, rarely home anyway. A month into a cross-country haul, he contacted and said he'd fallen in love with someone on the road and wasn't coming back. Miranda saw a counselor for a while, but the only medical thing I know about him is blood type. He's mentioned in Miranda's birth records. Why? Do you think it's hereditary?"

"It's a possibility. Did you do a good history?"

Deis lifted the file again. "Hel-*lo*. This is her life in Times New Roman."

"No, I asked if *you* did a good history. Not your fellows, not the other doctors. *You*."

Deis considered. "I did a history on my first day here, compared it with her file for consistencies."

"So, no, then," Emmi surmised with a smirk. "You said her diet's restricted. How restricted are we talking?"

"Citrus, spinach, very little fat aside from peanut. I've seen her mother sneak in black coffee and she's been on fluids. That's about it."

"You said self-tanner. When's the last time she used that?"

"Um, it's been at least a week. She's been here."

"Is she still tan?" Emmi's brow rose.

"A bit," Deis shrugged. "Her skin's more olive in tone than her mother's."

"I see. And her CBC? Any abnormalities? Antibodies?"

"None, and tox came back clean. No adverse blood levels in any of the numerous draws we've done, no evidence of environmental toxins, and like I said, she's been here circling the drain for over a week."

"Did her father drink? Was that in the file?"

"No real details. Like I said, he was away a lot and hasn't seen Miranda in years."

"Gotcha. How's her menstruation?"

"She hasn't since she's been here. First recorded, and in extreme detail, mind you, at age twelve. The following spring, her mother scheduled a gynecology appointment and put her on birth control pills. She had her first boyfriend at the time."

Emmi chuckled and shook her head. "That is one detailed file you've got there."

"You're telling me. She's been off the pills since admission. No extra meds are permitted right now."

"Did she menstruate each month while she was taking the pills?"

Deis sat back, her eyes narrowed. "I don't think that's in there, strangely enough."

"Seems like a good piece of info to know. Her blood's affected. Start there. And we need more on dear old dad. If he's passed on unfavorable genes, it could be part of her illness, too. Talk to mom. These symptoms are typical of a few conditions but I'm particularly curious about her periods. Deis?"

"Yeah?" She looked up from perusing the file yet again.

"Keep digging. Dig deep on this one," Emmi implored, her violet eyes intense on the screen. "I know that file's a handy little history, but there's something missing. Alone, the details don't make sense. I have a hunch but what you've told me isn't enough to confirm it. All I know is that every ailment is caused by one of two things, either an underlying condition or the treatment for it. If you've removed all the treatments, all that's left is the illness. You'll have to eliminate some possibilities and really drill down."

Deis exhaled, looked to her lap.

"She's older than your normal patient, and teenagers hide things," Emmi continued with a knowing smirk. "We did, they all do. Assume she's hiding the diagnosis right along with the skeletons in her closet. You've described her mental state and how it's changed but there's something else there. Find it."

Deis took a deep breath, nodded once.

"They have the right doctor on the case. If it were me, I'd be browbeating her to within an inch of her life by now. You're patient, reasonable, analytical. You're the Sagittarius. Let the hunter loose."

"I'll start over."

"Good. Keep me posted. I'll keep thinking on it. And I forgot to ask before, but how was the cheesecake?"

"What cheesecake?"

Emmi's brows nearly touched. "The New York cheesecake I sent you for your birthday. I had it shipped from Brooklyn, from that bakery you fell in love with on our last tour. I got the delivery confirmation last Tuesday."

"I never got a cheesecake. Henry would've served it to me on a silver platter."

"Well, I paid for it," Emmi argued. When her eyes softened and her frown turned to a scowl, she added dryly. "Check with your darling roommate. She has a soft spot for chocolate, and I made the mistake of ordering the cookie dough one, not the sugar free one."

"Damn that thieving bitch," Deis glowered.

After administering a medication that finally eased her patient to sleep, Deis retreated to the hospital's drab and deserted cafeteria. She sent her fellows home, with strict orders to rest and return renewed first thing in the morning.

Fortunate to find relatively fresh coffee in the pot and an employee in the beige-tiled room to take her money for it, she helped herself, added too much sugar, and sat with the file and her notepad.

Paging through, she looked for missing details. It was easy to see the facts, but it took real effort to find the holes in between. Emmi had named two or three of them on their consult, and those were listed in her scrolling penmanship already. The rest of the omissions, she'd have to find on her own.

How did the relationship with her dad end? Was he unstable? Was she abused?

She wrote then circled Munchausen, then crossed it out. No one could self-inflict v-fib. Scarlet Fever undiagnosed as a kid? Nope, she would've been dragged into the hospital and it would've been documented in this giant file for sure.

Thinking back, she analyzed this girl seven days ago and this girl now. What stayed the same? GI symptoms. Difenoxin plus atropine equals heart. Weakness. Lack of nutrition. Pain. She underlined that twice. It was present everywhere except in intermittent periods after procedures or med changes. No two procedures were the same. Endoscopy, biopsy, shunt. Shunt removal. Sick again.

She sat back, exhaled and stared at the baffled ceiling.

Every time they touched, prodded or tested, they improved then drastically weakened their patient. Were the procedures to blame?

Hours passed with the fretful doctor stewing over the file, reading between every line like invisible ink would appear in the gaps. She underlined, circled, and then crossed words out until the page looked like a physicist's first attempt at explaining relativity.

Coffee kept coming, the sugar keeping her blood flowing. Her intense focus on the words continued until they blended together into a blur. Her eyes dimmed as the words grew farther away. When he gray closed in, her heavy head collapsed to the notepad below.

Imagine his surprise to seek out caffeine for himself in the wee morning hours, only to find his daughter's savior and his idea of female perfection passed out on a stack of medical notes with an uncapped pen perched limply in her fingers.

Chapter 9

Her eyes fluttered open as the bright midday sun peeked through the barely drawn khaki shades alongside the bed.

The smell of dark coffee and laundry detergent had her popping upright with a start.

This was wrong. It wasn't Henry's cleanser, Anna's tea, Haven's linens. Fear and confusion swept in instantly.

Still dressed in her trim black trousers and matching V-neck sweater, but with her kitten heels on the floor beside the bed, she hopped to her feet. The bedroom, though impeccably clean, was all simplistic browns and blues. A polished walnut armoire stood beside the door, a well-worn navy rug under her toes. The open door at the far end revealed a modest bathroom, with a razor, a cobalt bottle of cologne, a dwindled white bar of soap and a washcloth on the counter. Alongside the bed, on a stout armchair of worn brown leather, her purse sat open on her folded lab coat. Upon inspection, her keys rested on top, but nothing was missing, not even the cash in her wallet. There were no missed calls or messages on her still-present cell phone.

She was sleeping on a man's bed, she assumed, slipping her shoes back on. And he hadn't tried to rob her, assault her, imprison her. Nothing was apparently wrong aside from her presence here.

This type of guy was no run-of-the-mill kidnapper. He was, what, a Good Samaritan?

She perched on the foot of the bed. She remembered watching Miranda slip off to sleep after her IV, remembered going back to the office to retrieve her things. She remembered the bland cafeteria coffee, the notes, the...

My God, I fell asleep in there, she realized, humiliation creeping in. I fell asleep in that café. How did I get here?

On her feet again, she looked around for her kidnapper. A search of the master bathroom came up empty. Well-used towels in basic black hung on brass rails. Taking a moment to fix her hair and wash her face, she examined the toiletries on display. Lifting the cologne, she removed the cap to sniff.

The familiar oak and black pepper nuances wafted up, grabbing her viciously by the throat. With a broad smile and incredulous headshake, she replaced it and stepped more confidently into Charlie's bedroom.

How he'd gotten her here, she wasn't sure. She didn't even remember a car ride or leaving the hospital at all. But stepping out in the hallway and seeing a smaller bedroom alive with pinks and purples confirmed the identity of her captor.

Ruby's room was perfect for her, with a pillow-quilted headboard and a brass vanity topped with a mirror-backed brush and pretend makeup sets, and violet curtains dotted with sparkle keeping the sunlight at bay. Like her father's space, it was well-kept, with no clothes on the floor and no toys out of place. She giggled at the contrast of alpha male and dainty female, true dichotomy across the hall from each other.

Deis bent at the waist to examine the oval mirror of the vanity. Tucked between the frame and glass was a photo of Ruby, two or three years younger, with Charlie on some pub stage. She was on his hip with the microphone in her tiny hands. His eyes were fixed on her.

Here was his inspiration, and her hero, respectively. She replaced the photo carefully, exactly as she'd found it, and sought out the coffee she smelled.

The kitchen, immaculately white and stark, reminded her of her childhood home. It was meticulously organized, with scrubbed appliances and ingredients tucked into glass-front cabinets. Bare countertops and a serious lack of décor made the space feel industrial. She spotted a percolating coffee pot on the stove, thirty years old at least. She lifted the lid, saw half a pot waiting inside, and hunted up a mug.

As she poured, she heard a key twist in the front door in the adjacent room. Stepping into the doorframe between kitchen and living room, she waited with her mug, narrowing her gaze sternly as it opened. She was ready and eager to confront her captor.

In walked Charlie, as expected, but in the pale-yellow cargoes and jacket of a firefighter. A dingy helmet was tucked under his arm. He was well past the threshold before he realized he had an audience. His azure eyes turned up at the corners as their eyes locked.

She hadn't prepared for such a hard punch to her gut, seeing him in uniform. There a bit of dirt, maybe soot, under his bright eyes, and his uniform had seen better days, but he was magnificent. As he shifted the heavy coat off, revealing a white Henley pulled over firm shoulder, she couldn't help shifting her attention to his narrow waist, dirty hands, and then the carpet under her feet as her cheeks turned excruciatingly red. She sated her suddenly dry mouth with coffee.

"Hey, good morning, Doc. Well, afternoon now." He hung his jacket on the hook beside the door, resting his hands on his hips. "Sorry to come home all out of sorts, but I couldn't bear the trek back to the station house. How long have you been up and about?"

There were a few seconds of silence, her mind desperately seeking words that wouldn't bring more shame. After another sip, she was able to finally respond in an even tone. "Just long enough to find the coffee you left for me."

He nodded with a smirk. "I meant to have it, but I don't decide when fires kick off. You just got there first."

"Well, thanks for nothing, then."

He laughed, stepping up and looking over every inch of her face. "You're a sight now. Last night, I checked for a pulse."

"I'm," she began, pausing with wide eyes as he swiped the coffee from her hands and drank it all in one scalding gulp. "I'd have worked there. I never meant to need saving."

"No one does, but you're embarrassed over being knackered?" He asked with a lifted brow before muttering, "Women."

With another damnable smirk, he swept by and into the kitchen. He left the heady scent of his cologne and smoke behind him.

Alone, she finally had a chance to exhale excitedly and fan her face with a damp palm. Nothing could've prepared her for that sight. He was gorgeous, an ideal physical specimen in her mind. A musician, and a firefighter, and a great dad.

God help her.

She turned the corner with a deep breath. He'd refilled her mug and found a second one, filling it, too. He handed her mug back as she approached.

"Enough for both of us." He tapped his mug to hers. "Did you take a tour of my humble flat?"

"A quick one. Imagine my fear waking up in a strange man's bedroom."

"You slept like the dead. I had to carry you through the back alley to your car. I didn't want to risk the media catching sight of that."

"You," she nearly choked on the scalding hot caffeine. "You... You carried me out of the hospital? The hospital that sponsors me. The hospital that depends on my professionalism. Oh, that's just *fantastic...*"

"No worries, no one saw me, and you're light as a feather. And, what, you'd have me leave you there for the director to find?" He leaned back against the counter, crossed one ankle over the other smugly. "I'm just glad you had your purse with you and that I found

106

your ride. You were too exhausted to fight me off like some of my rescues do."

"You didn't rescue me, you kidnapped me. I didn't consent."

"Oh, you were out cold, but I did a quick vital check. I think it would hold up in court. Besides, I'm a first responder. You were unresponsive. I win."

His conspirator's grin made her squirm.

"Okay, okay, I was tired. It's been a long week full of surprises." She set down her mug on the counter, then lifted it again. "Wait, that reminds me."

He eyed her curiously, "About?"

"This place. Your flat. It's immaculate. I don't want to put anything down. And that's saying something, coming from me. I'm retentive, but this place is spotless. I can't believe an eight-year old lives here."

He shrugged, taking her empty mug from her and setting it next to his own on the top rack of the dishwasher. "We rarely entertain, and she's a little obsessive like her papa. I came from nothing, pretty much nothing, anyway, so I'm trying to instill a sense of ownership in her. It's working so far."

"It's amazing," she admitted with a head shake. "I work with kids, and even with hospital maintenance and environmental services, they tend to destroy a space at Mach One. I wasn't sure where I was when I woke up, but your place wasn't my first guess."

"And why is that?" He set his hip against the counter, crossing his arms. "Did you expect a bachelor pad or a nursery school?"

She chuckled. "No, that's not what I meant. I just figured you'd have music equipment or lyric sheets all over. But I guess you're more than that."

"I know how my band mates live. If I get my way, my girl will have a manor like Haven and a butler for herself someday. In the meantime, it's just us slumming it in East London."

"That's what I meant."

His dark brows furrowed.

"I mean, you're more than the musician. I keep forgetting." She turned away with a sigh. "I have this mental block for some reason, and I just can't wrap my head around all the Charlies I've met. The dad, the singer, the guy that fights fires. Not sure what Brits call firefighters."

He laughed heartily at her flub. "We're firefighters on this side of the Atlantic, too. In fairness, I joined the East Side Brigade because of Ruby. I was a father before the job came about."

"And you perform because of her, too."

He shrugged. "And because I enjoy it. I always have. If I could afford to do music exclusively, I would. Once the album's out and we're selling out venues, I can skive off the dirty work for good."

She took his tea towel from its hook, wetted a corner with tap water and rubbed at the soot on his cheeks. "Speaking of dirty, this is driving me crazy."

"A little obsessive, are we?" He stood still, his thumbs tucked in his pockets as she doted on him.

Oh, you have no idea, she thought with a hidden grin, keeping her eyes on her work though his examined hers intently. The blue was a little darker today, deeper, like the center of a still pond.

He took her wrist in his hand and lowered her arm. "Thanks, but I'll get properly washed. I probably look like I rolled about in ashes."

She lowered her nose to his shoulder, inhaled. "You smell like a forest fire. Is that cedar?"

"Well done," he replied, impressed. "A manor house with a massive cedar closet went up in about five minutes flat. I had to run out just before dawn, after a sleepless night, mind you."

"The exciting life of a firefighter. Did they page you? I didn't hear a thing."

"About a half-hour after getting back with you. I'm glad it didn't wake you. It's like an air raid siren in my pocket. I always wake Ruby up no matter how stealthy I try to be. Oh, and she's supposed to come home tomorrow, if the doctor discharges her as planned."

"I spoke with Doctor Howards briefly. He was pretty upset with my intrusion and coercion, but he ran the test anyway. And my only reply was that, if he had any more questions or issues, he could contact the now-informed director or find someone else to bitch to."

Charlie took her cheeks in his hands, met her gaze intensely. "You saved her. You did that, not that worthless prick."

"I just found the fairy."

His lips, warm and full, touched to her forehead as her eyes fluttered closed. She froze in place, in his grasp and against his chest. When his eyes met hers again, the gaze was genuine, sentimental, alluring.

"You gave her her life back. And she's motivated to work with Addison, to keep her in line. It's such a gift you have, relating to them so simply."

"She's a great kid," Deis replied, taking his wrists and lowering his arms to his sides before releasing them. His touch was too intense to deal with. "Any victims in the fire this morning?"

"That's a doctor question," he snorted, tucking his thumbs back into his pockets. "Jennings had to run in after a housecat, but fortunately the family was on holiday. We assume there's someone inside until we're sure otherwise."

"So, standard procedure?" She added, crossing her shaky arms. The spot on her forehead burned where his lips had touched, singeing her skin like a lightning strike.

"As standard as they can be," he murmured, tipping his head with narrowed eyes. "You all right? You seem a bit put off."

"Just thinking about my patient," she fibbed, suddenly anxious. Slipping past him and back to where her purse and jacket rested in his room, she found and lifted her phone. There were still no messages to find.

Damn it, her fellows should've had an update to her by now. Maybe they didn't show up, either. Director Gordon would be hunting her down shortly to chastise.

Two palms landed on her hips, turning her around as she inhaled sharply. Face to face with him again, she couldn't hide the panic, so she clutched the phone to her chest in both hands and squeezed for dear life. His stare was penetrating, analytical, and one she recognized as diagnosing.

"Deis, you're worrying me." His hands released her as she fought to step back out of reach. "Did I upset you? If I did, I didn't mean to."

"I just..." She blew out a breath, closed her eyes on a long blink.

Lying seemed so stupid, so childish, but the truth was mortifying. She remembered Emmi's encouraging words, Rai's sisterly praise, the admiration of Natalie O'Leary. Pressing her lips together, she mustered up her mettle.

"Fine. I'll tell you. It is you."

His face twisted in shock. "What did I do?"

"Oh, come *on*." She flung her phone peevishly and paced away. "Jesus, Charlie. You're not that dense."

"I'm pretty dense," he confessed, scratching his head. "I'm a standard guy and I, like the majority of my gender, never got a copy of the Guide to Womankind."

She turned back with a glare and he lifted his palms in surrender.

With a huff, she plopped down on the foot of his bed. "Fine, fine, apparently it's not obvious to you. You're absolutely perfect and it's not fair."

He froze for a moment, with pensive brows lowered over distant eyes. He was thoroughly unconvinced. With his arms crossed, he stepped over slowly.

"I'm sorry, but do you want to run that by me once more?"

"*Damn* it, Charlie!" She leapt back up to her feet, forcing him back a step. "You're hot, first off. When you look at me, it's like I'm burning on the inside. Which is ironic, since you're a firefighter, so you'd just have to rescue me anyway. Take my pulse, since you know how, and you'll see it's racing. Hell, you probably know CPR, too, so if I drop out of sinus rhythm, that's even more reason to lock lips again. How disgustingly cliché is this? Ugh."

Collapsing back to the mattress with her hands over her face, she lost herself in red-faced shame. There was no layer of hell deep enough to escape to now.

In a daze, he stumbled to his armoire. Hearing him digging around, she watched him fish out a magazine from the top drawer. On the cover of the American music magazine, she and Emmi glared intensely at the camera. Between them stood a microphone stand and they wore little more than leather bands across their laps and chests. Hair blown out, eyes fierce, their bodies contorted like the photographer requested.

Charlie tried to hand it to her. "I'm just a hapless fool, but um, this is *you*, in case you've forgotten. Let's discuss perfection, shall we?"

"I know who I am and what I really look like," she replied dryly. "Three hours in a makeup chair isn't perfection. Everyday Charlie is perfect. Everyday Deis isn't."

He dropped the magazine to the floor with a thud. Pulling her to her feet by the wrist, he tugged her toward the bathroom. She stumbled behind, curious but humiliated.

He spun her, standing over her left shoulder so their frames were front and center in the broad mirror. "Look at this face."

She gazed up at her reflection with a sigh, her head tipped. "You're planning to argue about who's perfect?"

"No," he replied quietly, close to her ear but meeting her gaze in the mirror. With a slow finger, he lifted and tucked her hair behind her ear, then traipsed the curve of her jaw, the long line of her neck. "There no argument. This is perfection. Not to mention what's in here." His fingertip tapped her temple. "Peerless musician, accomplished physician and a beautiful face, all at once. I'm worthless compared to that."

His fingers swept through her thick wave of chestnut hair to her shoulder as her eyes fluttered in slow blinks. "Lovely, more so than mine."

With slow fingertips, he turned her head to face him, the pad of his thumb settling by her right eyelid. "And these, they're like honey. The golden bits in them catch the light. There's depth in them that words can't quite describe. And when you're eye to eye with your patients, they just trust you without fear. It's remarkable. "

His voice was so gentle, so serene, that she went to putty in his grasp. When his arms pulled her back against him comfortingly, she acquiesced without a word.

"Deis, you know you're every man's dream. Smart, challenging, accomplished, talented. Not to mention wealthy in more ways than one. You've got perfection in spades. I'm just an eager onlooker, a lucky bastard at best."

"I don't want to be every man's dream," she admitted in a whisper, her gaze fixed on his in the mirror.

"What do you want to be?" He asked in a murmur, helplessly drawn into her siren call.

"Yours, Charlie."

He closed his eyes for a moment and swore his ears deceived him.

Damn it, he realized. He was right where he'd sworn he'd never end up.

"Deis," he began in a murmur, his rough fingertip passing over her cheek. "I…"

She took the disbelief, the hesitation and his self-loathing smile as a compliment and as an invitation. She turned on her heels. Unapologetically pressing herself against his chest and wrapping her arms around his neck, she poured every bit of unrequited lust she felt doctor route. I have enough bodily functions to figure out. I don't have time to worry about anyone else's."

"True enough." Deis rose with a stretch. "If the endoscopy goes well, I should have my diagnosis by dinner. If not," she smirked, flicked Rai's nose. "Don't wait up."

Rai rose to chase but Deis was gone in a flash. With a grunt, the guitarist flopped back on her chair as Anna cleared her place setting with a chuckle.

At the hospital, fifteen minutes before noon, Deis was prepping Miranda for the procedure. Draped in a sterile gown with her dark hair hidden by a cloth cap, her patient listened with clenched fists.

"We'll escort you down to the suite, administer the medications and you'll slip off to sleep while the procedure happens. We'll wake you once we've completed the process and you'll go back on fluids."

"I'm going under?" Miranda's jade eyes opened wide. The dark circles under them weighed on her physician's conscience. "I can't be awake? I don't like this."

"It's an invasive procedure, Miss Victor. It helps to have you as relaxed as possible. It's a routine procedure, done here multiple times a week. And you have the best care team I've ever worked with."

"Yeah, that one doctor in your group, what's his name? Doctor Murphy. He's dishy," the teenager replied with a lilt.

"I assume that means he's handsome, and I'll take your word for it." Deis winked playfully and noted her mental faculties in the pre-op notes. Sharp, alert, aware but concerned. She added situational stress to the pre-op condition and noted her vitals as her fellows arrived, also in white drapes.

"Miranda, are you ready? They're ready for you," Doctor O'Leary smiled encouragingly. "It'll take less than an hour."

into a smoldering, demanding kiss that had him stumbling back against the wall.

Unable to rail against her assault, unwilling to deny himself, he selfishly enjoyed, the fire of her passion consuming him alive.

She loved his calloused hands in her hair, his eager mouth as it devoured hers. Her fingers itched to tuck under his shirt, to possess flesh. She could feel his heart pounding and taste his sharp incisor against her lip.

A helpless moan escaped from deep within his chest. He hadn't prepared for the assault, but her needy gasps clawed down his throat, ripped open his belly and left him defenseless.

In a flash, he lifted her up and set her on the bathroom counter as her legs wrapped instinctively around him. He cradled as she reclined against the mirror, his lips and teeth sliding over cheek and neck with a hunger she felt in her bones. More moans escaped as his nails abraded flesh under her sweater, unable to control the tiger inside begging to escape its cage.

There was fierceness, virility in his assault and she felt alive at long last. It'd been too long since she'd been the reason for such utter surrender. He couldn't assault her fast enough for her taste.

He pulled her back up to sitting and buried his fingers in the hair, his fingers twisted fiercely in the silk, tugging to make her gasp. He swallowed the pitiful noises with his eager mouth.

The thick muscle of his biceps pulsed in her grasp as she slicked her tongue against his. With his hands grasping like a vice and his body straining against hers, the thrill of his need spiked as the heat of her middle pressed against his belly like a branding iron. When he pulled her hair again gently, separating their lips, they both panted.

Winded and exhilarated and with eyes closed, she rested her brow against his.

"Deis," he wheezed, his hesitation and thrill gripped tenuously. "Mercy. My heart's about to burst."

She grinned, unwrapping her legs. With her palms on his forearms for balance, she hopped down to stand before him. "Now we're both filthy." With a quick motion, she tugged off her onyx sweater, revealing the red lace below. "Now bathe with me."

He lowered his arms, pitifully outmatched. There was no point in denying the primal urge for her flesh, and the thought of her standing wet and soapy in his tub sped his pulse up all over again. Desperately searching for some retreat into his self-made promise of prudence, his mind could only come up with one excuse. "I'm overdressed."

Stepping back to his chest, she tugged his tee from the waistband, dragging it slowly up to reveal smooth skin and tense torso. On the right side of his chest, below his collarbone was a tattoo of a fine scrollwork letter R in crimson ink. She traced the line with a fingertip.

"Ruby," Deis murmured knowingly.

He nodded once, staying still while she unhooked his belt and fly. He watched her deft fingers in silent reverence, swallowing hard with clenched teeth. His blood burned as it rushed south. Her tempting fingers brushed over his lap before pulling away.

"You can handle the rest," she grinned, stepping back to the shower to start the water.

"You're cruel," he muttered, watching her slip her trousers down over curved hip to reveal even more red lace.

He was torturously methodical as he lathered every inch of her skin with soapy palms. When she turned her back to him, he reached around to exploit every curve and valley. His fingers stroked through her hair as the water sluiced down, her eyes closed with head tipped back against his shoulder.

When he finished rinsing her skin and met her gaze, her look was wistful, inviting. It took every bit of restraint to keep his caresses gentle and excruciatingly slow. His libido stretched to the limit as her arms encircled his neck, rising to her toes to assault his mouth with tongue and teeth. The warmth of her, the steam around them, tried his threadbare patience.

When she broke the kiss and stepped back to soap her palms, he watched with apprehension. He was already too excited, too anxious to be with her. It would be so easy to bury himself inside and let go.

But he'd made a promise, one he intended to keep.

Her palms slicked over his chest, shoulders, arms while he stood like a soldier, shutting his eyes and willing back his betraying thoughts.

She spun him so his front received the warm spray, her palms moving from strong shoulder blade to narrowed waist and over hip. He released a slow breath as her lips neared his ear, nipped the lobe. She washed his raven hair, rinsed the soot from his chiseled face and turned him back to face her.

"You shaved," she cooed, rubbing her cheek to his.

"Finally thought to," he murmured in reply. "You like?"

She pulled her head back, her eyes dreamy. "I like the scruff, too. Makes you look sinister, dangerous."

I deserve a damn medal for not being dangerous with you already, his mind screamed with disdain.

He reached back to turn the water off before the temptation could continue another moment, but he couldn't resist her skin as she stood dripping in the basin. He lifted her against him, stepping from the tub as her legs wrapped around his waist. Her body curved, curled around him as she released a sigh, melting his heart as he cradled her delicate frame.

Laying a towel over her shoulders and tucking another against his lap, he carried her to the bedside. On her feet again, he secured his towel before using hers to pat away the drops of water at the base of her neck, in the valley of her collarbone, under the curve of her breast. Working his way down, he dabbed down her back, over thigh and down her shapely legs, lifting each foot as he knelt to dry each toe with a surgeon's precision.

She snickered as he stood to towel the ends of her hair. When she snatched the towel away playfully, he grasped her hips and deftly tossed her to the bed like a ragdoll. She laughed as he slid beside her, propped on one arm to take in her serene, undecorated face.

"You're stronger, I get it," she admitted with a sigh. "Will you admit that you're handsome now, tough guy?"

"You said I'm perfect," he replied with a brow raised. "That's a high bar to clear, Doctor. I've got plenty of shortfalls, ones you haven't seen. If you say I'm handsome, I'll take your word for it, but perfect? I respectfully disagree."

"You're both."

When he looked deeper, read the glimmering flecks of gold in her eyes, he saw gentle compassion and genuineness. If she'd asked for anything in creation in that moment, he'd have spent his life questing for it. But he also saw illicit desire and impatient lust. The promise he'd made years before was so much more important than a few moments inside her would be today.

"Deis," he breathed, hiding distress as best he could. "You're here. That's enough for now."

"I'm with you," she whispered, curling up against him. "Take me."

"This is enough. You're here," he repeated with a little more force this time. He knew his message hit home when her jaw clenched and her palms pulled away.

To ease her mind, and his, he craned down to steal one more kiss.

Their naked bodies nestled together, the evening's silence only broken by breaths, as the sun disappeared over the neighboring building beyond his window. Sleep stole them away in intervals, but when his fingertips skimmed her belly or traced the line of her shoulder, thrilling ripples awakened her senses. He nuzzled into her hair, his lips swept over her forehead and his fingers curled around hers from time to time. The caressing combined with the pound of his heart against her skin dissolved her stress into the air as she passed into and out of a dream world for hours on end.

Once night fell, his face moved to hover over hers. "Hey, beautiful."

The familiar greeting, now directed at her, brought a winsome smile to her face. "Hi, handsome."

"I'm starving to death. I'll order takeaway from over the road. Thai okay?"

Deis' eyes brightened. "My favorite, and you worked today so you must be."

"I could murder some noodles right about now," he replied, sitting up to stretch. Marks on his chest showed where she'd laid on him. Elation tickled her soul.

"Before you go," she murmured, propping herself up on her elbows. "I have to ask. Why didn't you take advantage of me?"

His gaze narrowed at her. "That's so terribly brash. Is that all you think you're worth to me?"

"No, but you had the opportunity. I'm not upset about it, but here I am, naked and apparently beautiful..."

"Unbelievably and undeniably lovely," he corrected.

"Okay, as you say, and yet unspoiled."

Toughened fingers swept her jawline and under her chin. "Deis, you are far too precious to spoil by being so hasty. Having you here with me, being with me like this, it's more than I could ask for. And, for the record, it's enough to last me a lifetime or two. I won't ask for anything else and I'll expect nothing more after today."

He laid a sweet kiss on her lips and retreated, pulling on a pair of shorts he found in the armoire before stepping out into the hall.

She sat up, her brow raised skeptically. His sudden chivalry raised a serious red flag. She'd been around long enough and knew enough fibbers of all ages to see through the ruse. She found a thick gray robe in the closet, tied it on and followed close behind. He was hanging up from his cell phone call in the living room as she emerged.

"I'm sorry, but I can't take that for an answer."

He tossed his cell phone on a sofa cushion. "Take what for an answer?"

She crossed her arms. "That more-than-I-could've-asked-for stuff. I want the truth."

"That is the truth," he retorted, his hands on his hips to steady himself. "I have no reason to lie."

"I wouldn't think so, but that's certainly not the whole truth. Maybe you'll deign to be honest with me since I've already spent so many hours naked in your arms."

She stepped to the fridge, glad to find Ruby's lemon fizz in supply. She took out two, laid his on the counter and opened her own with a sharp crack.

He exhaled sharply, turned away with his head bowed. Guilt swept in fiercely. "All right, it's a half-truth."

When he turned back, stole and drank her soda instead of his own, she crossed her arms again. "I trusted you enough to stay here all day. Out with it."

He handed back a much lighter can and met her stare. "It's been a while. For me, I mean. Like, years."

She narrowed her eyes, set the can down. "Charlie, how can that be true? You're good looking, all dark and dangerous, and rock guys tend to live pretty fast."

His attention diverted to a picture on the fridge door, of him standing alongside a carousel horse with a sweet girl perched atop it, holding the reins with both tiny hands.

It dawned on her suddenly as she followed his gaze. "Ruby. I see."

He shrugged apathetically. "Just not worth the risk. I've kissed a few, necked with a few others. I couldn't bring myself to give them more. She's my priority. She's always been my priority, and she'll always be. I won't allow competition between her and another. Not now, not ever. I hope that's crystal clear because it's the full truth."

Deis nodded, her lips pressed together as her heartbeat slowed to a crawl.

"Sex complicates things," he continued, his voice gentler. "It makes loads of women needy. Maybe not all of them, but enough of them to make me reconsider my life choices. I've been close a few times. But nothing can or will mean more to me than she does. She's my constant, my center, my everything. She's all I've got. Casual dalliances aren't worth drawing her up in, and how can I leave her to go off gallivanting, to be so selfish? Until she loves someone completely and with her whole heart, I won't either. I made that promise, and I certainly won't go back on it now that she's got Addison's. She needs me now more than ever."

Her heart stalled, dropped to her ankles like an anvil. How could she argue, insist, when this precious, angelic and chronically ill baby girl was his whole world? It was egocentric, arrogant and destructive to violate his wishes, no matter how much she wanted to.

Defeated and deflated, she exhaled resolutely and stepped past him, back down the hall to look for her clothes on the bathroom floor. There, where she'd assaulted him so shamelessly, she tossed on undergarments with a sigh. She was pulling on pants when, from behind, she heard him murmur. "I wish you'd stay."

She turned, sweater in hand. "I will, to eat, since you've already ordered. But I need to get out of your clothes, out of this situation and back to the hospital where I belong."

He withdrew with a pert nod, closing the door behind him.

119

Dressing in his bedroom, with the woman of his dreams doing the same behind the nearby but closed door, he pondered his life's path. Promises, sacrifices, conditions. Across the hall, his daughter's room waited unoccupied. He stopped in her doorway, took note of her girly belongings, of all the glitter and sweetness.

Life, he knew, wasn't always so pretty.

Everything I do is for you, he thought, turning away with leaden shoulders.

Chapter 10

Thursday, December 11

She dozed on the chaise settee in her office, bunched uncomfortably and in the same black outfit as the two days before. No pillow, no blanket, just a thinly cushioned seat and a sore back. The hospital had been closer to his place than Haven. She was too frustrated and hurt to deal with Rai. Plus, she'd been away from her patient far too long, distracted and belittled in her barely existent personal life. She'd lick her wounds, get over him and head home once Miranda was better.

As day broke, she headed down to the cafeteria for coffee, then out to a local department store for new, unwrinkled clothes. It was one thing to have insinuations fly over going to work the next day in the same outfit. It was quite another to know she hadn't enjoyed the usual reason for it. Plus, cedar soot and cologne tangled in the fabric, keeping the memories of humiliation fresh in her mind.

Arriving back at ten in the morning, with light snow falling over the historical urban landscape, she parked her SUV in the adjacent lot and made her way through the main entrance.

Finding Doctor Gordon at the nurse's station, she approached with butterflies in her belly. He'd been watching the front door intensely and his gaze was far from welcoming.

She swallowed hard, decided to take a high road. "Good morning, Doctor."

She watched his eyes narrow at her as she fought for confidence. Knowing the shoe was about to drop, she released a deep breath and vowed to accept accountability for her unscheduled time off.

"Doctor, I was looking for you."

She followed him to his office and watched him close the doors. As he moved behind his desk, she sat across from him, waiting for the atomic bomb to drop.

"I met with the transplant committee yesterday afternoon," he began staunchly, opening the glossy folder on his desk. "Miss Victor is number three on their list for a liver. Due to her blood type and profile, the committee is optimistic that, when a prognosis is delivered, she'll receive a liver within weeks."

"Fantastic," Deis answered, swallowing back the bile in her throat.

He said when, not if, a prognosis arrived. The Board was speaking through his mouth and she knew it.

"Has the status of my patient changed?" His eyes stayed down on the folder, his fingers tapping on the desk blotter impatiently.

His patient, not hers. The wording drove daggers into her soul.

She'd familiarized herself upon arriving the night before. There hadn't been any change in her condition during her absence, her fellows administering medications as directed and handling her symptoms as best they could.

"Nothing of note has changed. Her symptoms are well-managed. I've ordered a few tests this morning, including a blood panel to reanalyze levels, pancreatic and lymphatic functions. Her pancreatitis is under control, and her fever is reduced, as is her pain. I expect to find answers in the analysis."

"I expect that, also," he added bluntly, closing the file. "It's been nearly two weeks and this child's family is rewarding your team with an abundance of patience. I've read over all your notes, your differentials and findings, and am on your side, but this cannot wait. I expect your diligence until she is diagnosed and this case is resolved."

"Yes, sir," Deis replied somberly.

With nothing left to say, she sat in silence while he ordered more tests and reassessed every lab finding. His second-guessing her choices, the presumption of incompetence on her part, was a very real and very painful punch to the gut.

Back in her office an hour later, she paced on modest heels, waiting for her fellows to return from the lab. She'd pushed her tests to the front of the line, using her celebrity to shamelessly jump over the other doctors. These tests were her only hope.

Doctor O'Leary carried the results to her while her male peer waited alongside with folded arms. Deis' heart sank as the blood work came back within range. Evidence of medications, of the pancreatic bacteria she'd expected, and normal levels of heavy metals.

She unapologetically thrust the paper back in her fellow's hands. "File it. I'm talking to her."

Phil and Natalie tagged along at her heels like puppies, sharing concerned looks as Deis strode down the hall, her face fixed and her frustrated mind racing. Doctors moved aside as her heels slammed on the tile, her arms fixed at her sides. Nurses snickered as the trio flooded into the patient's room like a tsunami.

She found Miranda perusing on her cell phone, her face drawn and pale. A yellowish hue tinged her skin, drooping loosely on her face and neck. Fluids still flowed into her IV, but she was sallow, sickly and exhausted.

"Miranda, I need your help," Deis pleaded, inhaling deeply to find calm. "I'm missing something."

Her eyes narrowed over the phone's display as her mother rose from her chair alongside, on the defensive already. Despite Deis' efforts to keep neutral, a sharp impatient edge was clear in her tone.

"I can't diagnose if I don't know all the facts. I'm missing something because no prognosis matches the lab results I just received. No prognosis matches all your symptoms."

Stepping to her side, Deis gripped the bed rail, intensity blazing in her eyes. "I'm going to ask questions until I get the answer I need, and when I run out of questions, my fellows will ask any they can think of. I'm not a good loser. I *don't* lose. So no matter how long it takes, I'm not leaving until we've settled this."

Miranda's eyes sobered, widened, as the cell phone tumbled from her palms onto the bed below.

Natalie tried to interject, but Phil touched her shoulder, shook his head to silence her. His eyes glittered excitedly. His attending was beginning a descent into some brilliant form of diagnostic madness.

"Help me," Deis demanded, white-knuckled and fierce. "You're my patient and I won't fail you. But I need your help here. We need to win this, come hell or high water. Can I count on you?"

Miranda eyed her mother before her gaze returned to Deis. "But I've told you everything."

"Then we'll start over," Deis countered, taking out her notepad and pen, sitting alongside and crossing her leg. "Full name?"

"This is going to be a long day," Phil muttered from the footboard.

Deis stepped away to catch her breath sometime between Miranda's first kiss and her fifth-grade finals. She'd emptied two felt pens scribing every detail, and as of yet, nothing struck her as being wildly different from the file's passages.

Outside the lobby's front doors, she gazed up to the gray sky. The wind smelled of snow, a whiff of winter and solace that made her dream of the American northeast and its ski hills. She loved that scent in her youth. It so often meant freedom from school for the day.

But with the patient's prognosis still unknown and the director's ultimatum hanging in the air, the snow seemed foreboding. She'd called Rai before heading downstairs, alerted her of the current happenings and apologized for leaving Myopic in the lurch. Rai had cozied up to them, filled in the gaps and assured her that they'd survive in her absence, but she felt the dull ache of guilt for that, too.

Yet another responsibility shrugged off because of an inability to find the prognostic needle in this girl's haystack of symptoms.

Leaning back against the stone wall, out of sight of the entering and retreating patients and families, she checked her watch. It was just after two in the afternoon. Four long hours had gone by since her little meeting with the director, and more would pass while she interrogated her patient to the edge of both their sanities. Her fellows scribbled down their own notes so they could compare for further inquisition, which she hoped wouldn't be necessary.

She had to give herself a little credit, though. She hadn't dwelled on Charlie. Too busy diagnosing the dying, she thought with a pathetic chuckle.

He'd known more about female tendencies, and had given it more thought, than she'd expected. She'd felt her pulse race when his hands brushed over her skin, knew the need that would develop if that became a habit. He'd nailed that on the head. He was wiser, more controlled than she despite her being five years his senior. Reliving his dismissal of her affections made her teeth clench and jaw ache.

I'm never the fool, she thought self-deprecatingly. But she'd been chastised twice in the past day, and in two areas she normally felt confident in.

With a huff, she headed back for the lobby, passing through the door and nearly running over the director.

"Oh, Doctor Deis," Doctor Gordon began, adjusting his gait to free up space between them. She took a small step back to match. "In a hurry, I see."

"Indeed. I've got to get back to the patient's room."

"I'm surprised you're not there already." He shot her a judging look before brushing past her, buttoning his coat and heading outside.

She winced, trying her best to ignore the admonishment. At the nearby nurses' station, she regained her bearings, paging through the admission binder for anything she might have missed in Miranda's intake documents the first three times she'd checked them.

"Come on, Daddy!" Ruby called from the hall outside her hospital room.

Charlie followed behind with her stuffed animals, favorite blanket and half-empty can of lemon fizz in his arms. Her discharge orders, prescription instructions and post-hospital checklists were shoved in his pocket.

"You can handle your drink, eh?"

She plucked it from his fingers, and he almost bobbled the whole lot.

"Thanks, darling. So glad of your help."

She narrowed her eyes in a knowing, taunting look as he chased her to the elevator, wildly cackling to make her scream in laughter. By some minor miracle, his daughter was going home symptom-free and with a legitimate diagnosis.

He took a moment in the descending elevator to picture Ruby's diagnostician's face, the tender smile she showed his daughter, the sultry smile she'd shown him the night before.

With a quick head shake, the image faded. There was too much at stake to be fixated on some farfetched fantasy. He'd been forthright, at least enough to chase her off. Now, if he could just forget the feel of her body against...

The doors slid open with a ding and Ruby launched into the lobby with the energy of ten cheetahs. Tomorrow's school day would tire her out but until then, she'd be tearing around their flat like a twister.

When his gaze settled on the dark beauty at the nurses' station, he froze two steps off the elevator, still laden with his daughter's necessities. But Ruby, free and unencumbered, flew to her with a high-pitched squeal. "Doctor Deeeis!"

Ruby clipped around the counter and threw her arms around the doctor's neck as she knelt to obediently accept the embrace. With an easygoing smile, the doctor lifted the eight-year old to her hip and followed her gaze up to Charlie.

His heart sank. Two beauties in each other's arms. His daughter ran to her, straight into her arms, with a broad smile and genuine affection.

Control yourself, his mind chided.

"Hey, Doc," he remarked as casually as he could manage, stepping up to the pair. He glared playfully at his daughter and she hid her giggling face in Deis' neck.

With a protective hand on her back, Deis shifted Ruby's weight up higher on her hip. "Looks like the discharge order went through. Headed home at long last, are we?"

"And I'm going to school tomorrow!" Ruby sang before pouting dramatically. "Just for one day, though, then two more days of lying about."

"Oh, kid," Deis sighed. "You just wait a few years. You'll be begging for a few days of lying about."

With a tickle and squirm, Ruby was back on her feet, attached to her father's leg. He patted her head. "She'll be a terror tonight with all this pent-up energy. So much for my clean flat."

"You could stand a little disorder," Deis replied coolly with her arms folded and a hip leaning against the counter. "Call me right away if anything happens with her."

He understood that calling for any other reason was not advised.

Lowering to a crouch, Deis murmured to Ruby. "And if you don't feel good, even if it's a silly thing, make sure somebody knows about it, k? We can't take our eyes off Addison for one second."

"Got it."

Charlie gladly accepted a tote bag from the triage nurse. After packaging up her belongings, he took Ruby's hand and walked out the front door. Her little body took off down the sidewalk once she cleared the entryway. He gave chase, hollering unheard commands at the fleeing child beyond the glass door.

"They are too precious," the nurse behind the counter breathed. "The perfect father-daughter duo, they are."

"Perfect," Deis repeated distantly, stepping away. "Perfection's so overrated."

Back upstairs in the ICU, relieving her fellows for a long overdue coffee break, Deis sat with her notepad and a fresh stock of pens. Miranda's body laid limply on the bed, her palms up and her eyes heavy. The doctors kept their patient awake, sedated with painkillers, so the inquest could continue.

"At thirteen, you started taking birth control pills. Did you switch pills at all?"

"No, that first brand is the one I'm still on. Some generic I can't pronounce."

"I've got it written down. How many periods did you have before you started oral contraceptives?"

"Three, maybe four. When Mum found out I had a boyfriend, she rushed me to the doctor. I wasn't having sex and she knew it, but she was young when I was born, so she didn't want the same mistake for me."

"You were no mistake," Diane interjected. "And you know it."

"Move on," the teenager told the doctor with a sigh.

"And when did you become sexually active?" Deis asked, looking back to the notepad.

There was hesitation and a glance to her mother.

Diane scowled. "You'll tell the world you were a mistake, but you won't tell the doctor that you shagged him in the backseat of my car the following month? For heaven's sake, Miranda."

Miranda's mouth dropped open. "How did you...?"

"I'm your mother," Diane replied simply, petting her daughter's waxy, unwashed hair.

Deis jotted down the detail. "So, thirteen. Do you take your pills religiously? Same time every day for all these years?"

"As a saint. I even tucked it into the lid of my lipstick when I went out at night. The doctor said skipping pills made it less effective."

"That's true. Is that the only contraceptive you use?"

"My first boyfriend, he wore a johnny. The next one, we went to a clinic together, the one at school, and we both tested clean. So just the pills after that. We broke up a few weeks ago."

"Fair enough. Are you getting normal periods on the pill? Five to seven days long, flow changes from heavier to lighter toward the end?"

"I did for a few months, but they stopped by the time I was fifteen. In the packet, it said that sometimes people skip periods or they're so light that people don't notice them. I just figured it was a normal thing."

"It can be. You started reporting increased symptoms during those years. You'd come to the hospital, get tested for all sorts of illnesses, feel good enough to go home only to end up back here. Is that right?"

Her patient nodded. "Seems like it. I didn't have liver, pancreas or heart issues then."

Deis rose to pace at the foot of her patient's bed. "No periods, no periods." She chanted, tapping the pen to her lips as the fascinated fellows and the Victor family watched. "Birth control can cause blood clots, a host of other issues, but none that fully explain your symptoms."

Her mind raced. Random phrases and facts whizzed through her brain. They were all tempting little glimpses of a diagnosis. Emmi's questions returned to her mind, illuminating the bulb within.

Maybe. It was a long shot, but maybe.

When she turned on Diane, her face was a demanding glare. "Your ex, Miranda's father, did he drink? Occasionally? Often?"

She gaped at the doctor's intensity, averted her eyes for a moment. "He'd drink every day, some more than others. He was on the road a lot. I only saw him well and thoroughly pissed a few times in all our years. Why?"

"Blood. It's the blood," Deis breathed, exasperated and excited, grasping the footboard with both hands and squeezing until her knuckles ached. Her head hung and swung side to side as she snickered pitifully at herself. "Damn it. This whole time. It was right in front of me and I missed it. Damn it."

"Whose blood?" Natalie asked, stepping in with Phil behind.

"Hers, and her dad's," she murmured, still clutching the board with her head hanging. "I've been wringing my hands, torturing myself over why this kid gets better when we open her up. It's not the surgery making her feel better, it's the damn procedure."

With a self-critical chuckle and a palm on her forehead, she turned to Miranda. "We drew blood every time anyone had any questions. It's a test that even a lying teenager can't fake. It's one we get answers from. Every time we draw blood, you improve a little. Every time you go under the knife, you get a little better. And you're still tan after all this time without that cream of yours."

Doctor Murphy's eyes lit up like a Christmas tree topper. "Son of a bitch! Sorry," he added as Diane Victor glared.

Deis nodded to her fellow before turning back to the patient, her palms slipping into her jacket pockets. She dropped onto the chair alongside the bed. "Miranda, you have a disease called hemochromatosis. It means there's too much iron floating around in your body. Iron, potassium, magnesium and a bunch of other minerals are critical in maintaining normal health. They support cellular development and organ function. Their levels are just as important as they are, though, and if they're too high or too low, there are dangerous side effects."

"Of course," Miranda replied confidently, more engaged than she'd been in a week. "Too little potassium causes heart issues. We learned that in health class."

"Absolutely. So iron, then. Iron's another mineral with devastating consequences. Excess iron destroys the liver, heart, pancreas, and leads to toxicity. We tested for it, multiple times, but we must've done the tests too close together to allow the iron to build back up again. And because of your surgery, you lost even that much more blood. A common treatment for hemochromatosis is phlebotomy, removing blood from the body. We were doing that, that's been happening all along, so we were treating your condition without even realizing."

Diane took her daughter's hand. "You said it's a disease. So, there's nothing to be done?"

Deis' eyes lifted to the concerned mother. "It's a genetic disorder, and one she'll always have, but symptoms can be managed. It's a rare diagnosis for someone her age because menstruation would cause normal bleeding. You'd dispose of that extra iron naturally if you bled as nature intended. Those pills kept the iron in, kept the level too high, but alcohol, pain meds and your limited diet affected the iron in your blood. It was the perfect storm of conditions to hide the diagnosis from us."

The exhausted doctor rose from her chair, turned to her fellows. "Order a serum ferritin test to confirm." They both nodded and headed out into the hall without a word.

When Deis turned back to Diane, the mother's eyes were hopeful for the first time in weeks. "You said she'll have to have blood drawn routinely, right? If she does, she'll be okay? She won't need another surgery or pills or anything?"

"She'll need phlebotomy two or three times a week until we get it under control, then maybe twice a month for the rest of her life. Certain sicknesses, viruses and behaviors will exacerbate the symptoms, but I'll give you all the information you need."

Miranda spoke in a hesitant tone, sitting up for the first time that day. "Wait, you said it's genetic. Does... Does my mum have it?"

Deis shook her head. "I doubt it. We'll test to be sure, but I'd bet it's on your dad's side. Drinking thins blood, so it's possible he was self-medicating. Not partying so much lately is part of the reason why your symptoms increased over the last few weeks. It's a delicate balance in there."

Diane sat down, her head in her hands. "And the transplant? She's got a chronic condition. A blood-based one, no less. She'll never get a liver now."

Deis stepped over to lay a palm on the mother's trembling shoulder. "Actually, she's a good candidate. This is good news. Hemochromatosis isn't a death sentence, and it's a much better diagnosis than leukemia. We'll get her symptoms under control. The heart arrhythmia is manageable, so is the pancreatitis, and the iron will be, too. In a matter of days, she'll be in much better shape than she is now. You'll see."

Miranda took her mother's hand and smiled over to her. "See, Mum? I'll be fine."

"You'll get your liver," Deis added confidently, stepping to the door. "I'll see to it myself. I'll go see the director now and share the news. My team will be in shortly to administer that serum ferritin test, then I hope you'll rest a bit easier."

The weight of two lives lifted from her shoulders as she traversed the hall, rounded the corner and headed down the wooden staircase.

Both Ruby and Miranda were on the right treatment path. And Diane could begin to put her life back together, too.

At the bottom of the steps, she grasped the rail, stopped. With the first genuine smile of the day, she threw her head back, felt her confidence flow through her like a roaring river and strode past her naysaying peers to the director's office.

Chapter 11

For the first time since day one, pulling into the London hospital's parking lot wasn't foreboding, intimidating or humiliating. There was no differential diagnosis hanging over her head, no crying parent to console, and no patient to interrogate.

Arriving in the late afternoon after spending a few hours on producing work for Myopic, she strode into the lobby in business black. In a trim suit jacket and trousers over heeled booties, she was invincible. Her hair was down, flat-ironed pin straight, rather than in the dowdy bun or ponytail she'd donned over the past weeks. With light makeup applied, feeling professionally understated, she approached the nurses' station to page the director.

She'd completed her notes on Miranda Victor's case the night before, adding ongoing treatment recommendations and follow ups for her fellows. Her condition was improving gradually, as expected, and Doctor Gordon, as physician in charge of her maintenance plan, would be delivering an imploring speech to the transplant committee Wednesday morning.

Today was her handoff to the director and the official closing of the diagnostic case. With her name signed on the bottom line, she was free to produce music exclusively and consult medical cases only when necessary. And hopefully for younger kids, and not for Emmi. She'd paid her debt.

"Doctor Deis," the director called from across the lobby, waving her over. "I received your update this morning."

Following him into the office, she made her way to the familiar guest chair. "Yes, sir. She's improving at the gradual rate we expect. Frustrating as it may seem, it's the best sign of a correct diagnosis."

"The ferritin test was conclusive. Mother's negative. Dad must be the culprit."

"There's no fault here. It's a condition that no seventeen-year-old girl should have. Her menstruation should return to normal now. If she has another condition, like polycystic ovarian disease, and her menstruation doesn't restart, that'll have to be dealt with quickly."

"As your continuing care notes stated," the director concurred. "And, Doctor, I've also recommended a varied diet of natural protein sources and healthy fats for our patient. Our chief dietician was in with her this morning, answering her questions and assuring her that being vegan doesn't mean being boring or unhealthy."

"Fantastic," she nodded, crossing her leg. "And the fellows have their instructions. Are they both staying in diagnostics?"

"One of them, yes. Doctor O'Leary will remain. But Doctor Murphy, it seems you left a strong impression on him. Offering diagnoses only to be proven wrong and seeing the patient deteriorate encouraged him to explore other opportunities. He'll be returning to school to specialize in laboratory analysis once he's done his fellowship."

"You know what they say about the best laid plans. Doctor O'Leary, once she finds her footing, will be a valuable diagnostician. She was more confident than I was sometimes."

"If you'd pardon an old man's musings, I'll say that when anyone's under that sort of pressure, it's tough to see the end of the tunnel. But it's always there. What finally clued you in? You never did tell me."

"Blood," she replied. "It all came down to blood. Her father's, hers, what they had in common. How alcohol affects it, how her diet changed it. It suddenly dawned on me that the blood I took and that she lost during procedures had a lot more to do with her condition than we realized. I received a valuable consult last week from a certain blonde physician friend of mine. She brought up a few things that no others had considered, issues that weren't documented in that giant file. That helped point me back in the right direction."

"Ah, there's always a clue, always a starting mark, and sometimes we need a little help to find it. And our board member was very pleased to hear that his niece is headed down a brighter path. He's eager to see improvement. He'll be in attendance for my address on Wednesday. I expect it will attract a great many onlookers. It's to be held in the grand theatre, not the board room as I'd suspected."

Her pulse skipped up a few beats. This case had already caused enough speculation and gossip. Beth, the band's social media manager and reputation recovery specialist, was already elbow-deep addressing emails and messages about her involvement and eschewing any negativity and speculation from the world outside.

"Doctor, is that necessary? That room seats three hundred. Surely a smaller venue would be best for such an intimate subject. I can't imagine the family's comfortable with such a public display."

He merely shook his head. "It wasn't my choice, or theirs. The Chairman expects quite an audience, like I said, including board members and the committee itself. My peers from the other area hospitals will be in attendance as well."

With a sigh, she looked away. What a scene it'll be, she thought with an eye roll, especially if she made an appearance. "I'm very sorry this had turned into such a spectacle. I'm sure my being on her diagnostic team only stepped up the public's interest."

"No doubt it did, but we both have our crosses to bear," he replied amicably. "I received the memo and made the necessary precautions. I'll make the address as eloquently and imploringly as possible and Miranda will receive the transplant she deserves."

"Fair enough, Doctor. I'm going to clear my scattered notes out the office and ready it for your next case. I'll be here in London for a bit longer, should a pediatric case arise. Emmi will be returning just after the new year to continue work. I'm here in her stead until then."

"Wonderful, and we owe you a great debt for being so flexible and dedicated. Touch base on Wednesday before the conference so we can consult. I'm interested to hear your opinion on my finished draft."

She contemplated and thanked the heavens that she didn't have to make the address herself as the narrow elevator ascended. In the diagnostics office, she tidied and gathered, placing her notes and summaries in Miranda's file. She logged in to check email, responding and setting up her out-of-office replies with a personal email in case of emergencies.

Turning and heading back to the elevator, she rounded the third-floor medic station. Several young nurses, with stethoscopes and clipboards as accessories, waved and smiled as she passed. The radio buzzed to life as she returned the gesture. Her ear perked up at the shrill voice exploding from the radio:

> APB, incoming emergency, three on route via ambulance. Pediatric male, age eight, Caucasian, and pediatric male, age twelve, Caucasian, both with smoke inhalation, suspected first-degree and second-degree burns. Adult male, age twenty-eight, Caucasian, fire rescue, with smoke inhalation, unconscious, CPR underway, second- and possible third-degree burns. ETA ten minutes.

She doubled back to the nurses' station after hearing the word pediatric, her palms slamming down on the counter. "Ten minutes?"

"Go," the nurse implored, lifting the radio transceiver. "Emergency bay one, first floor. Now."

Deis was off in a flash, down the steps on clattering heels to the admission bay with her heart in her throat.

"We've got two minutes," she called out to the trauma nurses as the emergency department's attending physician stepped up alongside. "Two pediatrics, unit B, beds three and four. Start fluids ASAP, burn unit eval first thing, intubation only if necessary. They're breathing without assistance per the radio alert, but they'll need lung capability testing once they're stabilized."

The attending physician spoke aloud in a strong British accent when Deis' voice stopped. "Unit A, bed two, for the male rescuer. Burn evaluation once basic life signs are confirmed. Burn Unit techs are on route, ETA ten minutes. Stabilize, fluids, then evaluate. Everyone clear?"

The nurses and physician's assistants hummed and nodded in recognition.

A moment later, the galley doors swung open and paramedics rushed in with wheeled gurneys. One pushed a tiny towheaded boy inside as the nurse rushed along, directing the medic to the proper unit and recording vitals and conditions. An older boy, a dark-haired kid busily wriggling in his restraints, rolled by seconds after on his own gurney.

A paramedic stopped at her side. With a grin, he pulled down his narrow-fitting coat over a burgeoning belly. "Christ on a bike, you're really here. I figured that was a rumor."

"We can catch up later," Deis replied dryly. "My patients?"

"Oh, right," he regained his bearing with a grunt. "Eight and twelve, both breathing but labored. Found in the paper warehouse on the East side, suspected arson. Flash burns from the looks of it. Pulse and pressure within range."

"Okay, and the adult male?" She asked, accepting his file and noting her first observations while the nurses began treatment in the next hall.

"Male, twenty-eight, Caucasian, first responder. Brigade Fourteen, East Side. Ran in to rescue the younger after the older ran out, left him high and dry. Got caught in the blaze heading back out. Fire suit prevented severe burns on the legs, but he's torched at neck and shoulder. He used his coat to shield the kid. CPR is underway. Too abraded to intubate on the way in. It's a damn miracle he had those fire pants on. He was a roman candle on legs."

"Wait," she looked up, her eyes wide. "Twenty-eight years old? Eastern brigade? Dark hair, about six-foot?"

The medic nodded, handing over his file. "Taylor on the tag, no first name and no ID on him. Rushed him here straightaway."

The doors swung open once more. Raised voices flooded the hall as another wheeled bed came into view. Nurses ran alongside, analyzing injuries and squeezing air from a blue vent bag into the lifeless patient's lungs. A whoosh of air pungent with acrid smoke and singed skin blew past as the eager rescue team continued toward his prepared room.

His pant legs were gone, shredded, blackened bits of fabric barely hiding the irritated but intact flesh below. The white Henley was stained with sweat and soot, the dense brows dusted with ash, but his sapphire eyes were lifelessly closed, terrifying her down to the soul.

"No, no, no," she pleaded, tossing the files to the nearest nurse and commanding her to the pediatric patients' side as she ran along after the last arriving gurney.

Her emergency room autopilot turned on as the gurney paused in the bay. Stealing a rubber tourniquet from the med cart, she tied back her hair and ripped off her suit jacket, revealing the narrow white tank underneath. The monitors blipped to her right. Threadbare pulse, elevated temperature. Fluids by IV had begun but he was unresponsive as the nurses continued chest compressions.

"He's not breathing. Airway, damn it! Airway's first!" Deis shouted, moving the nurses aside to get in close and feel his chest. With the stethoscope she snagged from a nearby aide's neck, she listened closely amid the hubbub.

"No good, the lung's collapsed." She tossed the scope around her neck, turned and hollered at the closest nurse, stationed at the med cart nearby. "Ten-gauge syringe, dry, now!"

Scared by the normally cool doctor's tone, the nurse froze with a gape. A second nurse dashed to the med cart, tripping over the first.

Left without options, Deis exhaled sharply, asked silently for his forgiveness and shamelessly climbed on his lap. Stunned medical staff stepped back as she straddled his middle, tearing off his stained shirt with a quick, fierce tug. Scarlet burns grinned angrily back at her, blisters already forming on his shoulder near Ruby's tattoo.

The nurse handed over the syringe. Using her teeth, Deis pulled the plunger out, spitting it to the side. With blunt precision, she thrust the pointy tip into his chest, deftly landing between his ribs.

A gasp of the staff around her drowned out the whoosh of escaping air as she listened with the stethoscope. As lung decompressed and expanded, his pulse strengthened, but no breath sound accompanied the beat.

"Come on, Charlie. Come *on*," she sweet-talked tersely, tugging out and tossing the syringe to the floor before continuing chest compressions. "Come on, come *on*. You got this. Damn it, Charlie!"

She pressed down a few more times with both palms as the ED doctor rushed in. "What the... Doctor! Get off the patient!"

Deis continued her compressions, ruthlessly and methodically, ignoring everything else as she frantically fought to maintain life. One, two, she counted in her head. Pause, one, two, pause. She felt ribs crack below like thin branches in a hurricane, but she continued, panting and fighting like her own life depended on it.

I'm not stronger than you. Prove me wrong!

Ruby's face flooded her mind. The photo on his fridge. The one on her vanity mirror.

The coffee that waited for him in the percolator. The lemon fizz.

The thought of telling Ruby that her father gave his life to save a stranger, some stupid kid he'd never met. Knowing for the rest of her life that he did that reckless thing, that unbelievably senseless thing, for the decorations in her princess room and the roof over her head.

It felt like an hour, but only mere moments had passed before she cried out in frustration, tears streaming down her cheeks. With a sharp, downward punch, she struck his left chest, over the ailing lung, with the side of her fist once as the awestruck attending doctor dashed up and grabbed her wrist.

She watched Charlie's face with fervent expectation, her eyes fixed on him as the emergency team pulled her off the gurney with brute force. Succumbing to the onslaught of tugging hands, she slid off his chest, her damp palms clutching for his palm to feel for a pulse.

But when his eyes burst open and his torso bent up with a sharp gasp, stunned shouts erupted from the crowd. Their hands fell away as Deis swept to his side, taking his cheeks in her palms with grateful and breathless weeps.

He met her gaze first with fear, as if the fire still surrounded him. Calm took fear's place when he recognized his savior. His lips curved slightly. She was a welcomed sight. The tears rolled down her cheeks, but he knew they were joyous by the subtle flash of her dimples.

Fear swept back into his eyes as he wheezed, his breaths hoarse and erratic.

Wiping her teary eyes on her forearm, turning to the closest nurse, she hollered again. "Intubation kit!"

The nurse staggered back and grabbed the tubing. The emergency physician dashed in to assist, lifting Charlie's chin and popping open his jaw.

"Hold on, Charlie. Just hold on. This is going to suck really bad," she murmured, inserting the tube. She found her way down the narrow, swollen windpipe into his trachea before hooking it up the breathing machine.

She stepped back with shallow, frantic breaths and shaky hands as the nursing team surrounded the gurney and went to work stabilizing the patient. Backing up until she pressed against the wall, her head tipped back as tears burned her quivering cheeks. Her arms were smeared with makeup, her camisole damp with sweat. Terror ebbed as the rhythmic pulse of the heart monitor grew steady.

Dropping with a grunt and sitting among the discarded gauze pads and gloves, with legs numb with pins and needles, relief and devastation swept through her in undulating waves.

After pulling herself and her makeup together at the restroom mirror, she slipped her suit jacket back on and made her way to the pediatric burn patients. Nurses had started fluids and the twelve-year old was already sitting up while the burn team examined his ankles. Blisters formed where his sock cuffs had been.

Deis stepped up alongside the charge nurse in the doorway and spoke in a muted tone as the burn tech asked diagnostic questions to the cagey juvenile.

"Daniel," Deis read from the whiteboard beside the patient bed. "Vitals are under control?"

"Yes, Doctor," the nurse replied, handing her the clipboard file. "Sammy, age eight, has burns on his legs up to the knee, some spots of second but mostly first-degree. Techs say he'll heal well enough with silver sulfadiazine cream and fluids. Smoke inhalation was minor. It seems the responder removed his oxygen straightaway, put it on him during their escape. Could've been much worse."

This kid was the same age as Ruby. Charlie had had a guttural, knee-jerk reaction, no doubt, one that could've easily killed him. Instead it saved this child and landed the rescuer in the room across the hall.

With a sigh for the first responder's selfless bravery, Deis read over Sammy's evaluation. It was standard fire-induced complications. He'd be on supervised recovery for his burns, but no surgery or grafts seemed necessary for either patient.

The younger boy eyed her curiously as she approached, smiling comfortingly to ease his fears. "Hey, Sammy. I'm Doctor Deis. I'm just checking you over. Do you want to tell me what happened?"

He looked away as Deis applied gloves and carefully turned his knees to eye the scalded skin. He winced when she touched a peeling area. "Sorry about that," she murmured. "I know they hurt. Burns are nasty but these should heal nicely if you don't scratch. Don't feel like talking right now?"

He laid back, crossed his arms over his chest. "Not really."

"All right, I won't make you. But I'm glad you got through the fire okay. It was a bad one. You know the guy that ran in to grab you, the firefighter? He's really sick."

The boy glanced over to his older cohort in the next bed, who was listening actively but pretending not to. Guilt tinged the younger lad's face.

"He'll be all right. He's here. You'll help him." He replied in a small voice.

"I already did," she admitted, sitting in the chair between the two beds, her focus on Sammy. "It was really sad. He wasn't breathing because he gave you his mask. Did you know that?"

143

Sammy nodded, regret and panic sweeping over his little face like a sandstorm.

"His lung was collapsed, like a popped balloon. Too much smoke got in. And he has burns, too, way worse than yours."

Sammy shifted on the bed, his eyes on his lap. "I... I know."

"Did you know he wouldn't have been in there if you hadn't? He went in to get you out."

Daniel's voice ran out from over her shoulder, his tone defiant. "Sammy, go ahead and nark. I know you want to. I set the fire in a stupid energy drink tin. The coppers already know. We're already in for a tonking from the parents, so might as well fess up."

Deis didn't turn, didn't acknowledge, instead reaching out a hand for Sammy's arm and setting her chin on his bedrail. She kept her eyes soft. "What happened?"

The nurse took notes as the younger boy confessed everything in a whisper. Daniel had challenged him, called him names and bullied him. He went along even though he didn't want to. An online video showed them how to set up the can fire, but it got too big too fast. The factory was full of boxes but there was no one around to help. Daniel ran, called for Sammy, but burning boxes fell and trapped him.

Deis sat back with a slow exhale, listening to the boy's story and knowing it was, for the most part, truth. He claimed to not remember all the details of the rescue, but he felt the strong arms, the lift and the retreat. He breathed in the oxygen from the mask, closed his eyes and shielded his face in the firefighter's coat. When the rescuer got outside and collapsed, another yellow coat grabbed him and carted him off. He looked back, saw his savior on the ground and watched the other guys pat out the flames burning his coat with their palms.

"Thank you, Sammy," Deis replied, standing and touching his shoulder companionably. "I'll be back to check in. In the meantime, I'll be meeting with your parents. They'll be here soon."

"Mine already are," Daniel said behind her, despondent. "I'm so dead."

Deis lifted a brow as she strolled out, satisfied that this situation was under control. Her nerves, on the other hand, were not.

Imagining the bravery, his reckless dedication to someone else's child, made her knees tremble. The image of him being on fire, of the rest of the crew rushing in to save him, was one she'd never be rid of. She sat at the nurses' station, waiting for Sammy's parents and pretending to inspect his file, but her mind was hopelessly preoccupied by him.

Two hours later, Charlie was admitted to the second floor ICU, his internal recovery underway while the burn unit treated his surface injuries. He was breathing with assistance from a respirator, but a CT scan showed lung damage from the smoke and subsequent collapse. He would recover in time as the damaged cells died and were replaced, but the burns kept him in critical condition. If the topical treatments didn't work as they hoped, he'd need abrasion and skin grafts, but the lungs needed to heal before the burn unit could begin that process.

Deis waited outside the private room until the ICU physician emerged. Doctor Jefferson Ivers was a slight man, thin and aged, with octagonal glasses and an obnoxious gold paisley tie. Trying not to fixate, she crossed her arms and refocused on his pale eyes.

"Doctor Deis," he began in a slow Tennessee drawl. "He's in critical condition. The burns are a concern, as you know, and we'll evaluate further as the skin cools and cell regrowth begins. His pulse is stable and the pain's managed. It'll only get more painful from here, though, I'm afraid. And that cracked rib will complicate things. His airway constricted around the vent tube so the next few hours will be critical. His recovery hinges on his progress through the night."

Deis nodded, lowered her gaze. She already knew most of that from eavesdropping. "And his prognosis?"

"At best, a day or two here with us in the ICU to improve lung function, before a few days under the burn unit's care. If the burns heal as expected, he won't need grafts. But the prime concern is that, if the lungs don't improve, he won't survive the grafts or any other burn treatments he may need. He'll stay intubated while we medicate, as a precaution. By this time tomorrow, we'll have a better idea."

Deis took the doctor's hands, her eyes pleading. "I hear about it, whether it's good or bad. After his family, I hear next."

"On the contrary, you're to hear before the family. I'm following his instructions right now, in fact. It seems you've made quite an impression on him and the staff downstairs. And he's making you his medical proxy, assuming you sign off on it. The forms are being drawn up by legal as we speak."

Deis gasped with wide eyes.

"I guess you're as astounded as we are," Doctor Ivers snickered. "I'm off to contact his folks. He wanted to see you, so head on in."

As he strode off, she turned her gaze to the doorway and took a deep breath. He wanted her to be his proxy?

That was... Well, it was crazy, to say the least. It was advisable and smart to have a proxy be a doctor, but it was still insane in this case. They weren't related. He barely knew her. But she knew him better than her hospital peers. She did understand him, she did treat him in the emergency department, and she did care.

She shook her head, clearing those dangerous thoughts as she stepped over the threshold.

He was propped up forty-five degrees with an oxygen mask covering the bottom half of his face. Wiped clean of soot and with his burned and ripped clothing removed, he turned his gaze sluggishly to her as she perched in the doorway. His eyes brightened instantly, easing her broken heart.

Both his legs were bare, his hospital gown riding up on his thighs. The hair was singed from ankle to hip and his skin glowed silver from the burn cream. Bandages were stuck to his shoulders and upper arms with thick, clear tape. A gown in dull blue draped over his chest, covering his middle, and an IV inserted into his neck delivered fluids at a slow pace. Drowsy and weak, he lifted his hand to take hers as she approached.

Her fingers wrapped around his as she sat beside him, grief haunting her face. When he shook his head and patted her hand impatiently, she sighed and tried to brighten her eyes with a lackluster smile.

"Hey there," she murmured, holding his hand in both hers. "I shouldn't say this but, my god Charlie, you scared the hell out of me."

Shaking his head again, he squeezed her hand. When he tried to speak, only a gurgle emerged. A wince darkened his eyes.

"No, don't talk. You've got a breathing tube in and your airway is swollen. Your lungs..." She sighed, rethought and replaced her technical wording. "They're damaged. They'll heal with time, but for now, it has to stay."

He lifted his hand to point at the foot of his bed, where a whiteboard and marker rested on the fitted sheet. She nodded and stretched for it. Uncapping the marker and slipping it into his fingers, she propped up the board so he could write.

The penmanship was slanted and haphazard but legible.

Hey beautiful.

"Hey, there. I was better looking when I got here a few hours ago."

She erased the writing while he balanced the marker in his slow fingers.

How am I really?

"You're going to recover. It won't feel great, and it won't be easy, but you'll get better."

He managed a nod, his blinks slowing as the morphine pump hummed to life.

"I should let you rest, but I need to know. Where is Ruby?"

His eyes shifted to her, widened in realization. He wrote with a shaky hand.

Babysitter. Our flat. Go get her.

"You want me to go get Ruby? I won't bring her here, Charlie. This will scare her too much."

He wiped away his words and replaced them with desperate scribbles.

Haven. Please, Deis. Sign proxy, take her to Haven. Watch Addison. Please.

"But I can't be here as your proxy and at Haven with her at the same time."

Rai, Anna, Henry. My parents are old, sick, can't handle her.

Deis sat back with a deep breath. She'd be taking control of father's health and daughter's life at once and with zero prep time. But she was Ruby's doctor, and no one else would be a better medical proxy for her father. She'd have to convince Haven to help out.

"All right, I'll take her. I'll relieve the babysitter, but I need to know you'll be okay until I get back in the morning. I have to make sure she's settled at Haven and understands what's going on, and where you are, before I can come back here. You have a capable medical team here. She's alone, Charlie."

He smiled exhaustedly, laying his palm over her hand.

"Damn it, Charlie, you scared the *hell* out of me." She repeated shakily, her tone threadbare as tears threatening again. Despair squeezed her heart until it burned.

He lifted his hand, picked up the marker and wrote again in haphazard letters.

Don't cry. You saved me.

Deis shook her head after reading, meeting his gaze. "I just did what I had to do. You're not allowed to leave Ruby yet."

He erased his words, replaced them.

You punched me. Broke my rib.

He drew a winking smile emoji alongside.

With a pathetic chortle, a salty drop rolled down her cheek. She clenched his hand, holding it to her lips as her forehead dropped to the mattress at his side.

With his hand drenched in her tears, he looked to the ceiling and prayed for the strength he'd need to fight his way through, to do right by this incredible woman.

Deis arrived at Charlie's flat a few minutes after eleven, only after he succumbed to the morphine-induced sleep his body so desperately needed. He'd struggled against the narcotics long enough to text the babysitter and to send his family messages to update them. Before walking away, she'd signed on the bottom line, taking responsibility for his care decisions for the interim.

She was now charged with transporting his treasure to Haven.

Christine opened the door as she approached, putting her index finger to her lips. The teen girl, neighbor and impromptu sitter was barely five-feet tall, with a thick mass of brown curls and dark eyes. Her eyes brightened as she recognized Deis, still in her business suit and with her makeup deftly reapplied by the light of the hospital's parking garage.

"Hey!" The babysitter whispered excitedly, covering her cheeks with both palms. "Holy... You're Deis. This is amazing!"

"Guilty," Deis smiled as best she could, sneaking into the kitchen for the coffee she smelled, waiting in the ancient percolator.

Bless his neurotic heart for always having coffee ready.

While Christine fetched and loaded Ruby's suitcase and favorite toys into the SUV's trunk, Deis sorted and stashed the Addison's medications into her purse. Both passed through the halls with muted steps, double-checking cabinets, dressers and cupboards for any stray items an eight-year old couldn't live without.

"You have it all, even the bathing suit," Christine murmured in the hallway outside Ruby's room. "And if there's something else she begs for, I have a key and can let you in."

"Thank you, Christine. I appreciate your help. I'll probably have her a few weeks."

Her eyes turned somber, fearful. "Will Charlie be okay? I kept the telly off but saw the report on my phone. It was a horrific fire."

"He should be fine. He's young, strong, and the ICU is the best in the country."

"He's got loads to live for," Christine added, peeking through the cracked door to the girl, bundled in blankets. "And he's so gifted. It would be a damn shame if he couldn't sing anymore."

"One step at a time," Deis encouraged. "Grab her up and lay her across the backseat. I'll drive slow and maybe she'll just sleep the whole way."

The teen nodded, stepping inside and lifting the girl up against her torso. Ruby's head dropped on her shoulder as she tiptoed to the door behind Deis.

When she pulled into Haven's front circle, Henry dutifully emerged. He cradled the gently snoring girl in strong arms, his white gloves handling her like priceless art as he swept her up to the guest suite closest to Deis' room. She murmured in sleep and cuddled her stuffed white tiger with both arms as Henry tucked the tiny houseguest into the periwinkle linens he'd chosen specially for her.

Chapter 12

Monday, December 15

The next morning, as the sun began to crest over the hills outside the window, Deis took a seat alongside Ruby's bed. It dwarfed the sleeping angel with its ivory down comforter, flowing canopy and frilly roll pillows. Cradling coffee desperately in her hands, she waited for the child to wake up, wondering if it would be in time for school.

She hadn't slept a wink, so she had plenty of time to educate the staff and Rai on the evening's happenings. And, as if they'd looked forward to this for years, they immediately jumped on board. Anna filled the fridge with lemon fizz and Rai laid out the pool towels just in case. Her book bag and lunch were packed, waiting by the front door, and Henry was ready to drive her to school when she finally came to.

Deis doubted the kid would ever wake up. The beds here were fantastic and she herself had enjoyed many hours wrapped in their marvelous linens. The child deserved to sleep, and she knew that, as soon as she woke and learned her father's fate, she'd likely hesitate to sleep again.

Sitting back, enjoying the peaceful sound of her shallow breathing, Deis contemplated how she'd explain everything. She had a knack for twisting tales, turning negatives into positives for her young patients. Only this time, she'd have to dream up ways to keep Ruby informed of the facts but also calm despite them. Her father's condition wouldn't be resolved with a simple diagnosis and medication. It would take weeks, possibly even months, for him to recover and she, at eight, needed the patience of a saint to wait out his slow progress.

And heaven forbid he didn't recover. Then what would she say?

With a grunt and yawn, Ruby's eyes opened as the hall clock chimed seven. She sat up slowly, her little head of matted hair on a swivel as she realized she was no longer in her princess bedchamber in East London.

"Morning, Ruby," Deis spoke quietly as Ruby's cerulean eyes focused on her. "Did you sleep well?"

"Uh huh. Where am I?"

"You're at my house."

"Your house?" Ruby slid to the edge of the bed, narrowing her gaze. "Why?"

"I came and picked you up last night. Your daddy asked me to." Simple responses, she'd decided, would be the best course.

"Daddy. Is he back from the fire? Where's Christine?"

"I sent Christine home when I got there to pick you up. You were sleeping so I didn't want to wake you. Your daddy's done with the fire but he's at my work."

"Your... Your work? The hospital?" She asked, fear edging up her tone.

"Yes, Ruby. He's okay but he needs to stay there for a little while, just like you did."

Deis saw the panic clouding her eyes. "Does he... Does he have a fairy, too?"

The doctor stood and approached, setting her coffee down on the nightstand and easing herself onto the mattress alongside. "No, your fairy is a rare thing, remember? Your daddy, his situation is more common, and a real risk for firefighters."

"Oh. Did he get burned?"

Deis nodded, glad he'd discussed this possibility with her before. "On his arms and shoulders, and he breathed in some smoke. He's sleeping now, and I'm helping Doctor Ivers with his treatment so he can get better as soon as possible."

"You're a good doctor. You're my doctor. But Daddy... How long's he got to be there?"

Deis exhaled, patted Ruby's hand. "A little while, probably. But he asked me to help, to keep you safe and happy until he can take you home himself."

"You... I have to stay here?" Ruby's tone turned defensive, edgy. "I want to go home."

"Maybe we can do that a couple nights coming up, but I'll need you to help me out a little, to be patient with me. Christine's busy all day with school and I have to be at the hospital, so I've asked my friends here to get you to school, to make sure you have yummy things to eat, and to show you all the fun things we've got. My friends are good cooks and helpers. They know all the secrets of our big house. It's like a real castle here, you know."

Her cherubic face tipped up curiously with glittering eyes. It was only then that she noticed the giant upholstered bed and majestic window curtains.

"Have you got a tower like Rapunzel?"

"No, not exactly, but we have lots of other fun things to explore, and Henry's decorating for the holidays. He'd love some help."

She considered with a lip tugged to the side and averted eyes. "If Daddy needs you, I better stay here."

Deis shot her a conspirator's smile. "Thank you, princess. I'll show you around, introduce you to my friends, and we'll work together to get him better. How's that sound?"

"Okay," she replied with a little smile. "I'm starving. Who's your friend that makes yummy stuff?"

Henry was meticulously organizing Ruby's clothes in the cedar boxes under her bed as Deis toured her through the upstairs wings. She loved the pictures on Rai's walls, the big desk in Emmi's office and the plush furniture tucked into each space. Deis' room had the princess vanity and the tallest bed, which she jumped on like a monkey for a few minutes while the pediatrician-turned-babysitter changed in her walk-in closet. The girl peppered her with questions about the house, many of which Deis had trouble answering. She'd done precious little of the design or planning for Haven and it showed.

As she led Ruby down the grand staircase and into the marble atrium, the girl's mouth dropped open. With a gasp, she ran to the entry's central fountain, dipping her hands in. "You've got a fountain! And angels up there!" She pointed to the cherubs hovering overhead in the arched ceiling.

"We have lots of little surprises, and a huge, warm pool that you and Rai can enjoy together. It's a pretty amazing house, huh?"

She nodded excitedly, traipsing a finger up the fountain's climbing ivy until it escaped her reach.

Anna-Lena, clad in a crisp white chef coat, toddled into the foyer, her hands perched on her hips. At Deis' side, she watched the girl dance in spins across the marble until she wavered, dizzily collapsing on the edge of the fountain in a billow of giggles. She began an intense search for fish of the shallow waters.

"What a beauty," the chef murmured. "It'll be a real pleasure having her here. Good morning, doll baby," she called to the guest.

Deis smiled as Ruby ran back to her. Pressed against the doctor's hip shyly, she peered up though her dense lashes at the stout woman. Deis' fingers slipped down comfortingly over Ruby's mane as Anna crouched to her level.

"Hey, I'm Anna, and I'm the cook here. You ready for breakfast?"

Apparently, the stout and boisterous Austrian woman wasn't so scary after all, because Ruby detached from her leg with a bright grin.

"Uh huh. I hear you make scrummy stuff. Whatcha got?"

With a burly laugh, the chef stood back up. "Whatever you like, doll baby. Come with me. The rest of the house is already enjoying."

Deis followed as Anna guided Ruby to the kitchen and to the table where Rai was elbow-deep in a pile of thin waffles. Ruby analyzed her tablemate with the same sidelong stare she'd given Deis at first, one of uncertain recognition.

"I've seen you before," she declared. "You play guitar on telly with the blonde lady and Doctor Deis."

With a lifted brow, Rai set down her fork. "That's me. I'm Rai. Who are you?"

"I'm Ruby Tuesday Taylor."

"Nice to meet you, Ruby Tuesday. Are you going to have breakfast with me?"

She climbed up into the chair at the end of the table, eyeing Rai's cloyingly sweet morning mountain. "Uh huh. I want that."

Anna laid her palms on the counter and lifted a brow. "So many? That's a big breakfast. You sure?"

"Uh huh! And a pile of bangers and brown sauce!" She confirmed brightly, gripping her fork like a sword and thrusting it high.

Deis refilled the mug she'd toted all morning, watching Anna as she readied more batter in a broad metal bowl. The pixie was already babbling into Rai's ear, keeping her friend's fork frozen above her plate as she waited patiently to reply. Watching Ruby make fast friends eased her stress about leaving. She was impatient to see Charlie's progress, but Ruby's comfort came first.

"Hey Rai, can we swim in the pool later? After school and homework since Daddy always says I gotta do work first. And you have a secret, right?"

"I have a few. Which one are you talking about?"

"Doctor Deis said it's a ruby, like me."

155

"Oh," Rai chuckled, slipping the platinum from her left hand. The cobalt diamond twinkled in the light as she turned the ring over and held it out to Ruby. "It's right here. See it?"

Squinting, she spotted the little red dot nestled in the bright metal. "Wow, yeah, it's like a little rosebud."

"You think so?" Rai asked, moving her chair closer to their little houseguest.

"Yeah, it's lovely. Who was it that gave it to you? Doctor Deis said but I can't remember."

"His name's Steve. He's thoughtful and funny. He writes TV shows and movies. He'll be my husband one day. This ring proves it."

"He must be brilliant," she retorted, handing the ring back with a wise nod.

"He certainly thinks so," Rai admitted with a smirk, slipping the ring back on. "Did you meet Henry?"

"Yeah, upstairs just now. He's folding up my clothes funny, in those smelly wooden boxes. He looks like a penguin."

Deis snorted, almost launching a mouthful of coffee across the polished flooring. "He just dresses like one. It's part of his job to look like that."

"He said he had to wear that big coat and gloves, but he wouldn't tell me why," she declared as Anna served her a platter with three sausages and a mountainous stack of caramel waffles, as high as Rai's but a third the diameter, ready to enjoy.

"I'm going to love it here," she proclaimed with wide eyes as she dug in.

Deis thanked Henry for his diligence but decided to take Ruby to school on her way to the hospital. She watched her leap from the backseat and join the barrage of youngsters, decked out in their anoraks and knit caps, huddling through the towering front doors of the primary school. The raven-haired tot didn't turn back as she joined the others, falling in line like dominoes.

She watched her little body disappear through the entrance before driving off. She'd included a note to Ruby's teacher, complete with all the phone numbers and facts she was able to share while carefully redacting the details of his prognosis. She ended with instructions to contact her instead of her father until further notice.

The news that morning had detailed the accident, the firefighter's ailments, but not his identity. Ruby knew not to spread information, but she knew there'd be gossip. Deis of Second was some sort of surrogate parent in an impossible situation after saving her father's life in the emergency department the night before.

Emmi had Beth working on suppressing and controlling the rumor mill online. Fortunately, Deis' affiliation with the hospital, in addition to Second representing White Light professionally meant their relationship could be construed as strictly business. But emerging reports of her behavior at his bedside and her taking his wellness a little too seriously raised gossiping folks' brows.

With a sigh, she made her way through the tangled streets to the hospital. Henry and Dante, the massive yet somehow tender Caribbean bodyguard on loan from Emmi's entourage, would pick up Ruby in Haven's new black Town Car after school, drawing even more attention. But she trusted the diligent sentinel and the servant and needed their help. She was suddenly, inexplicably and unbelievably burdened with family life. She needed the full artillery to make it through.

Her cell phone chimed to life with an incoming call. Switching on speaker phone, she answered aloud. "This is Deis."

"You're driving," Emmi's voice rung out inside the cabin. "Off to check in on our downed hero?"

"His attending texted earlier, said his lungs are still labored. I doubt there's been much progress."

"Smoke is rough on soft tissue," Emmi confirmed dimly. "Beth's released our statement to the press. I just approved the draft. It says Charlie's been in an accident and is in excellent care, his family is being taken care of and asks for the public's understanding and for some privacy."

"I just dropped Ruby off. She made fast friends with Rai, Anna and Henry. If they keep her busy, she should be fine. She's adjusting better than I thought she would."

"I'm sure he's told her about the risks before. She's, what, eight?"

"Yep, as everyone in Haven now knows, along with her shoe size, her breakfast preferences and her favorite numbers."

"Hah, sweet. I just hope he's done with all this. Running into fires? That's a liability nightmare for us."

"Selfish request, considering he only does it to keep food on the table until Light makes it big. And that depends largely on us, doesn't it? Rai's arranging a few press junkets in London to promote. How's their tour plan?"

"I'm working on it. Myopic's ready to headline, and Light will open for them for a few hometown shows I've ironed out in Britain. Here in the States, I'm trying to get the Fighters to take them on as openers. It's a tough sell."

"They're unproven. I just hope he'll sing again."

"He has to, Deis."

"Yeah, I know. No pressure," Deis rolled her eyes, pulling into the parking garage. "I'm here and I'm going in. Keep up with the press on this, especially the British smut mags. They're going to hound that poor girl, and Dante showing up at an elementary school's going to draw a lot of curious eyes."

"Did you ever hear the phrase, there's no such thing as bad press? It's not a fallacy."

"You're heartless," Deis replied sourly, eyeing her phone as if Emmi was there in person.

"I have to be sometimes. I'm the ringmaster in our little circus."

Upstairs, Deis met with Doctor Ivers in his office. Aside from two drooping potted plants and scratched mahogany desk, the Doctor's space was unsettlingly barren. He handed over lab work and test results as Deis shrugged out of her wool overcoat.

"He made it through the night, which was our prime concern, but he's still fragile. His fluids are running around the clock, and his temperature's stable but low. The burn unit's charge doc checks in every few hours, changes the bandages, but the damage is unchanged. It's too soon to do a full analysis, but pain is centralized to chest and arm. Legs and torso aren't as big a concern."

The photo enclosed in the file made her gasp. His shoulders and upper arms showed blisters and scales, caked thickly in silver cream. She'd seen plenty of burns before. These looked particularly vicious.

"My God," she breathed. "It must have been an inferno in there."

"Paper burns hot. Some would say it's a miracle those kids escaped real harm. I don't typically believe in such things, but that firefighter makes me think twice about that."

"I checked up on Sammy and Daniel before I left last night. They're in big trouble but they'll be back to normal in no time."

The aging doctor nodded, sitting back. "Charlie Taylor's another matter, Doctor. I have his medications up high enough that he's out most of the day. The less strain on his body, the better for his recovery, but it can't stay this way for much longer."

She handed the papers back, the images lingering in her mind. "I imagine the prognosis is the same as yesterday."

"Mm, and we'll keep on course through today and tonight then reevaluate in the morning. He's on antibiotics as a precaution."

"His daughter, Ruby, is in my care until he improves enough to be discharged. She'll be tended to, will attend school and be a part of my household so he can focus on recovery."

"That's very generous," the doctor replied with lifted brows. "She was discharged recently with an Addison's diagnosis, correct?"

"After an impromptu differential diagnosis on my part, yes."

"Please understand, Doctor." He sat forward, resting his forearms on his basic desk. "I won't allow this patient to have visitors until his prognosis improves. I even checked to make sure your immunizations were up to date before letting you set foot in there. His body is traumatized, and I doubt his immune response is capable of fighting anything off. And with Miss Taylor's illness, it would be unwise to subject either of them to unnecessary risk. Surely you agree."

Deis gaped. "You can't be serious. She's his daughter."

"Doctor, be logical, please."

Her eyes clamped shut as she sunk back to the chair. "You're right. Damn it. How will I tell her that her father is okay but not let her see for herself?"

"Let's give it another twenty-four hours," the doctor cajoled. "Let's have another day of treatment, of fluids, of recovery. Her seeing him in this condition, and him seeing her while he's so vulnerable, that'd be too much for either of them anyway."

"That's the main reason I'm not arguing," she muttered, crossing her arms.

"And I have to know, if his condition doesn't improve, if his lungs don't respond, you're on board for more... unorthodox treatments?"

"You should know I don't care about decorum. But what are you thinking, a transplant? He wouldn't survive the surgery."

"No, but there are other options to help improve lung function and to heal wounds. Back in the US, treatment was modest, even restrained. But here in Britain, and in this facility, we use whatever tricks we can get away with."

With a grin, Deis sat forward. "Doctor, you do what you have to. I'll sign on the bottom line if he can't."

"I certainly hope so."

She sat beside his bed through the afternoon, paging through old magazines until the lines blurred. Switching to modern entertainment, she flicked through her phone while he lay still on white linens.

His room in the ICU was undecorated, stark and antiseptic, utterly devoid of comfort or warmth. Glass walls separated his corner room from the rest of the wing, their curtains open to let the nurses observe from their station. Warnings posted on them forbade any unauthorized visitors. His ventilation unit puffed every three seconds, breathing life into him, and his IV fluids drained along with the morphine through a narrow tube into his neck directly into his heart. His pulse blipped across the monitor, reassuringly stable, as she waited for him to wake.

She replied to the occasional text from Rai and Emmi while the hours passed. Both band mates questioned her motives, her sentiments. To Emmi, she stayed professional, cagey. He was merely a patient, a nice guy and an investment to Second. And his daughter was his muse, so it was in Second's best interest to help. To Rai, she confessed more private thoughts. She admitted to lusting after him, thinking about him, stewing over his rejection.

Rai suggested using her own strategy, overbearing tactics and manipulating ploys, to get him into bed. Knowing it was a waste to argue with her, she simply poured her heart out into the phone's writing app. It made her feel better to admit that Charlie was a fixation and nothing more. She'd thrown herself at him, admitted that she wanted to be his, only to be told he wouldn't belong to anyone.

His kisses spoke differently.

Imagining their escapades in the shower, on the bathroom counter, in bed, in the halls here, made her pulse spike and her palms sweat. Regaining composure with a deep breath, she kept typing with furious thumbs.

He better have some aces up his sleeve. I hope he knows he's in deep already. I see him when I close my eyes. Every blink, every dream.

There were song lyrics in there, she realized with a smirk. Damn good song lyrics.

She began the editing process, replacing certain passages and rhyming loosely as she went. Using some British slang she'd heard since arriving, she continued the entry until the chorus was complete.

With a sense of accomplishment, she emailed it off to Emmi. She knew it would raise eyebrows, the subject matter being so obvious, but she was willing to take the ribbing for a number one single on their next album. If it wasn't too late to slide something else in.

Stirring in the bed grabbed her attention. His eyes fluttered as he groaned, winced. She eyed the morphine pump, noticed the dosage was a little lower than the day before, and as she stood to increase it, his hand snatched her wrist with impressive dexterity.

When she eyed him, surprised and startled, he shook his masked head weakly and motioned with his fingers like he wanted to write. She retrieved the whiteboard, nestling the marker in his curved hand.

Easy on the meds.

"You're in pain. There's no need to be."

She swiped the words away. He replaced them.

Less pain today. I swear.

With a sigh, she eyed his bandaged shoulders. "I don't know how that's possible, but I'll believe you. For now."

Good girl, he wrote, and drew another winking smile for her.

"You're remarkably cheeky," she replied with a brow raise, erasing his jots.

I'm a wreck. Where's Ruby?

"At school, and you're not allowed visitors, so it's just me for now. You're at risk for infection. Please tell me you're done with running into fires?"

162

Want to be. Will I sing again?

"You will," she breathed, laying her palm on his forearm. "Your lungs will recover. You'll sing again. I know it."

Optimism, he wrote. *Much obliged.*

"It's the truth. And I'll make sure it happens."

My baby girl? How'd it go last night?

"She's fine," Deis answered, wiping away what he wrote. "But I must say, she's no baby, Charlie. She's adept, smart and settling in just fine. She left Haven this morning with a lunch from a pro chef. Henry's over the moon with her already, and he'll give her a princess ride home in our new Town Car. Dante will go with her whenever she leaves the manor. As you can imagine, the media is circling."

He shook his head with an eye roll.

Monsters. I was nobody before.

"I know, and I'm sorry, but Ruby's settling in so well. She's a gregarious kid. She called Henry a penguin this morning. I very nearly sprayed coffee all over the kitchen."

Charlie drew a smile again, using his remote control to incline his head to sit up at a sharper angle. Deis stood to dote on him, adjusting his pillows and fluffing them around his head.

He wished he could smell the honey and spice that so often fragranced her skin. Lush, mink hair swung forward and brushed his knee as she tucked his blanket under. Golden eyes focused on his collarbone bandages as she retied the gown's strings. When her fingers swept his hair back from his forehead, tucked it behind his ears, he looked up to her, hoping his upturned expression showed his appreciation.

"I'll find some dry shampoo in this place. It looks like the nurses cleaned you up a little, but you won't enjoy a real shower for a while."

His eyes diverted to the whiteboard, his fingers taking up the marker. She sat as he wrote.

Bummer. Enjoyed ours.

"I did, too," Deis admitted with a smile. She rested her elbows on his mattress and propped her chin on her fists. "I wish it was easier for you to talk. I have so many questions and we have all this time to kill while your lungs catch up."

He drew a question mark on the board.

"You'll need more markers," she warned lightly.

His brow lifted in challenge and she chuckled.

"Okay, what's your favorite color?"

Really?

"Yes. Humor me. I'm watching your kid."

Blackmail, Doctor. White, I guess.

"White's not a color."

He tipped his head and wrote, *All of them.*

"It's the presence of all light waves, yes. Is that a feeble attempt at dodging the question?"

He shook his head. *Not scared. Vermillion. Mauve. Puce?*

With a chuckle, she erased his mockery.

"Fine, smart ass. Okay, how about... When did you start performing on stage?"

His eyes flashed, and she imagined the grin he couldn't show.

Twelve. School play.

"Really? Were you Oliver?"

Sod off, twat. Judas.

"At twelve?" She asked incredulously. "Your elementary school did *Jesus Christ Superstar*?"

His chest rose and fell as he tried to chuckle. He could only wince with his free hand over his broken rib.

No, 2ndary school. I'm a prodigy.

"I should say. So, you tried out for the high school play and got the lead? Well, he's basically the lead."

Close enough. Loved it.

"Wow, good for you. I was too timid to do stage drama."

His brow rose as he drew a bold question mark then underlined it.

"I know, I know, it's ridiculous. Being on stage with just my friends, that's fun to me. It always has been. But I was more bashful when it came to scripted stuff. And my parents expected so much from me grades-wise. I was too scared to even ask them if I could audition. School was too important for silly distractions like that. By the time we were ready for talent shows, I guess I'd convinced myself that playing music and performing in musicals were different things."

His gaze saddened as he watched her expression shift in recollection. Her whole demeanor changed from confident, headstrong female into some timid, unsure child before his eyes. He tapped her hand, brought her attention back and watched her regain dignity in a well-rehearsed move.

He erased the mark and wrote again.

You inspire me. You did, do still.

She puzzled over his words. When she met his stare again, she murmured, "I don't understand."

She imagined that he sighed as his shoulder slumped.

Second, you all, strong, successful. You, a doctor, skilled, thoughtful. Makes me want better for Light, for myself.

"We do our best to keep it together. That's a lovely thing to say, err, write."

He shook his head and pointed the marker at her emphatically.

"Me? I'm what? Lovely?"

His eyes rolled as he chucked the marker at her. Her laugh echoed in his room and down the hall.

Chapter 13

Deis visited Ruby's bedroom in the morning and sat with her while she readied for school. She excitedly recounted the fun she'd had swimming with Rai, how delicious Anna's roast dinner was, and how much bigger her Haven bed was than her narrow one at home. Cradling her coffee mug, she watched the junior whirling dervish bounce from dresser drawer to closet to television and back while she chattered endlessly. It was more entertaining than any show.

Deis replied to the endless questions before hurrying her out to the waiting car when Henry honked the horn. The penguin was on chauffer duty today.

Back inside, she retreated to the studio and uploaded Emmi's vocal track to the sound board. Her sultry singing rang out in the booth, the exact lyrics Deis had texted the day before.

It was hauntingly and beautifully intense. Her influx, the brightly pitched highs and scowling lows, the power of unrequited lust in the almost begging vocals, and the combination and shifts between them gave Deis chills. Singing along with Emmi's track, she recorded the backup vocals in breathy whispers. The tale of desire and fixation, desperate and all-encompassing, was going to be huge. And she was fortunate that Emmi had agreed with that assumption and had poured effort into it immediately.

Not only would it be included on the upcoming album, it would be their first single released in two weeks' time. With the Grammys looming, Emmi was overjoyed to have such an inspired, passionate tune to present during their first live award show performance.

Deis began work mixing Myopic's second album. She adjusted vocals, tweaked bass riffs and fine-tuned percussion. It was so powerful to her ear that at times, her eyes closed to better absorb the pounding in her chest. That reverberation had bounced off the walls of the Wembley arena months before when they'd opened for Second, and she'd been enamored with it ever since.

Her mind ousted Myopic from that massive stage and replaced them with White Light. Charlie was out in front. Low-slung jeans, heavy boots, with his wide shoulders squared to the audience. Behind him, Liam rolled his head over his shoulders with eyes clenched as his guitar sang. Devon's bass kept the crowd pulsing. Robbie destroyed his drum kit with manic, fiery beats as the crowd chanted their lyrics back to them. As the house lights rose, illuminating the onlookers, screaming applause erupted and the band responded with their first single, sweeping up the mob of local fans in a whirlwind.

Her eyes reopened from the daydream, and it dawned on her that she missed that unabashed adulation and overwhelming excitement from their fans. They shouted lyrics back, pounded their heads to their songs, memorized every word she wrote. And it was an absolute rush to see that worship transfer to newer musicians and to see them awestruck by it, too.

The sound of the studio door above swinging open and Rai's voice echoing through the stairwell snapped her out of her daze. "Come on down. She should be done by now."

She quickly sent the track back to Emmi before powering down the board and rising with a stretch. Charlie's bandmates, the ones she'd just envisioned, emerged from the darkened hall into the studio space with Rai close behind. Liam, tall and trim in holey jeans and a black tee, looked exhausted and sickened by a night of partying. Devon, a dusty redhead with a buzz cut and scar on his cheek, sauntered in next with his thumbs tucked in his khaki pockets. Robbie had the short dark Mohawk and fierce eyes she'd expected, looming large over the other two at six-foot-four. Rai moved alongside, no larger than a marionette in his shadow.

Her respect quotient for the petite band mate doubled, knowing she'd stood up to and strong-armed the giant into submission at least once before.

The three sets of male eyes focused on Deis as they edged closer. She examined each rough face, equally fixed and masculine as they questioned her without words. It was the same scared, suspicious expression she recognized from patient families. She responded by stepping forward with the million-watt smile of a practiced extrovert.

Devon reached out for her hand first.

"Hi, I'm Deis," she beamed as he gripped her hand. "It's nice to put faces with names. You're Devon."

He nodded once. "It's a real pleasure. Your riffs are spot on."

Deis bowed her head in silent thanks as Liam approached, his eyes taking in every inch of her. His head tipped to the left as a brazen grin spread over his unshaven cheeks.

"You are extraordinary," he admired gruffly.

"You must be Liam," she retorted, laying her palms on her hips instead of risking touching him.

"Aye," he confirmed with a stately bow, arms out to his sides. "The one and only, here to please."

"Oh, bollocks," Robbie quipped behind him. "My stomach heaves at the sight of you."

With a lifted brow, Deis accepted the drummer's immense hand. His eyes were hard, judging. She held her tongue and so did he.

"The guys wanted to come by, get the doctor's recap on the patient," Rai explained, commandeering the rolling leather chair at the soundboard.

"The chat's got us worried and the hospital's turning away visitors," Liam explained. "I got a hell of a load on, the only thing I could do for my fallen comrade."

Deis stepped up instinctively and peeled opened Liam's right eye with her fingers. She spotted his tiny pupils before he winced, swatting at her as she stepped back with a chuckle.

"First, he's not dead, and by 'load on,' I assume you mean you drank yourself sick. Probably a foreign substance or two in you as well. You've got the telltale signs of a hard night."

"Seriously, Doc," Devon interrupted, crossing his arms. "With the smoke, the burns, will he be fit for performing again?"

Deis raised her brow as the three rockers formed a tight semicircle around her, their faces grim and bodies staunch as if ready for battle. If this was his gang, it was a loyal, tough and steadfast one to have. Her words were careful, conservative.

"I can't give you many details, but I'll tell you what I can. I'm going in to see him soon, but when I left last night, he was awake, lucid and stubborn, which are all good signs. The first twenty-four hours is always the hardest and he made it through. The ICU and burn unit are the best, and if anyone is dedicated enough to see it though, it's him."

"I heard he's on a ventilator. Are his lungs that knackered? His voice is going to be wrecked, isn't it?" Devon asked.

"That's like life support," Robbie commented, passing a spinning drumstick between his fingers. "He's a goner."

"Sod off," Liam snapped, leaning against the wall with a grunt.

"Ventilators aren't life support," Deis corrected, holding out both hands for peace. "It's a breathing aid. The ventilator helps takes the load off while his lungs rehabilitate. Once he passes a test called RSBI, he can be weaned from the ventilator and will breathe on his own again. The burns will take longer to heal but the lungs have to come first."

169

"And the news also said his legs are destroyed," Robbie added grimly.

"Not 'destroyed,' they said 'devastated.' Devastating injuries," Devon interjected.

Deis shook her head with a sigh. "I'm not sure of their sources, considering he's not allowed any visitors. His legs aren't the issue. The burns on his chest and shoulders are worse. Fortunately, where the fire suit protected, the skin is intact. The lungs are the worst of it. It could be a long road back, but like I said, he's alert and stubborn, so I'm optimistic."

Devon stepped up, laid his huge palms on her shoulders. "Doc, you gotta save him. He's White Light. We're just the blokes on backup. And his little girl..." he paused, looked down with a scowl. "He's all she's got. They mean the world to each other."

"I know," Deis exhaled. "She's here and healthy, and she'll be immaculately cared for. Emmi has been working around the clock, she's got our social media manager on it, and we," she paused, gestured to Rai, "We'll do all we can. And I know it's frustrating to not be able to visit, but he's at risk right now. Once he's recovered a bit more and can speak, I'm sure the doctor will lift the hold."

"You gotta fix him, Doc," Devon implored again. "You just gotta. Light means too much, this shot means too much, and he... we can't go on without him."

Liam thumped a hand on Devon's shoulder and guy-hugged him with one arm as Deis' phone chimed.

Incoming message from Natalie O'Leary.

Doctor, update on Charlie. RSBI isn't up to snuff. Dr. Ivers is recommending ECMO. Ninety-hour duration at most. Patient is looking for you, wants to ask your opinion. – Nat, MD.

The doctor's heart sunk like a stone.

"I have to go," Deis announced abruptly, darting to the door with her eyes on her phone. "I'll send an update when I get there."

The studio door slammed as her friend climbed from the plush seat. The rest of White Light looked over to their petite producer with raised brows.

"She's the decision maker. There must be a decision to make. That's progress, in one way or another." Rai decided with a shrug.

The guys shared depressed grimaces.

A brisk wind carried more flurries through the London streets as she arrived at the hospital's garage. She rounded the corner of the long hall, headed to the ICU as Doctor Ivers stepped from Charlie's room, removing thin gloves before accepting the patient file from a passing nurse. The senior doctor's eyes turned down as he read the pages on the clipboard. The curtains were drawn and the door was closed, obscuring her view inside.

"Doctor," Deis called out, winded from her run in. "ECMO? What are you thinking?"

"Come with me," he answered, leading her off the floor and to his office. With the door closed behind her, he sat and leaned forward on his desk.

"Yes, ECMO. That's where we're at, Doctor."

"With all due respect," Deis implored, taking the seat in front of his desk. "That's way too risky. It's not even sanctioned for adults yet."

"His lungs are recovering too slowly. He can't stay ventilated forever. The goal was to have him breathing on his own in five days, but at this rate, we're looking at a month. He's still abraded, swollen. If we wait, he'll decline before long. I've seen this many times before."

"But my guess is you haven't sentenced someone to death by ECMO yet," she grunted peevishly.

Breathless, she sat back, her eyes on her lap as her heart ached. There had been no progress, no improvement. She'd so desperately hoped for a little something. With labored breathing and a lack of organic oxygenation in his body, ventilation became life support, just as his band mate had feared.

But ECMO was a ludicrous idea. Typically used for premature babies whose lungs hadn't developed completely, adult patients faced a whole myriad of other risks during the process. The only studies she'd read had been done on livestock, and those trials only had a seventy-percent success rate. Research facilities refused to take a chance on human trials and only worst-case patients received it as a last-ditch effort.

"ECMO," Deis repeated, dumbfounded. "Seriously? I figured you'd try more established paths first. Steroids, medications, something."

His tone was gently insistent, like a parent to an unruly child in public. She watched urgency scorch his normally cool expression. "We both know what'll allow the fastest lung regeneration. I'd mentioned having to do the unorthodox, the crazy, if need be. You said you'd sign on the bottom line. We don't have much time here. I'm going to need a signature on this before long."

Deis rose to pace, only getting five steps away before having to turn and double back in the tiny office. She covered her face with her hands, wracked her brain over how to explain this risk to Charlie, his friends, his daughter. This was a true long shot. And this decision was one she'd ultimately make for them both and the future of his career, his family and his life.

Deis exhaled in defeat, her hands resting on the back of the chair, her knuckles white as she hunched forward, much the same as she'd done to Miranda's footboard. "Seventy-percent, Doc. The tests top out at *seventy-percent* improvement. That's what we're going with, seventy-percent?"

"Seventy or zero, as far as I can tell. I'm asking for ninety hours max. Ninety-six is the longest ECMO's approved for and I'm not getting too close to that. I will medically induce coma, administer heparin and begin the process by nightfall."

"And *heparin*?" Deis argued incredulously. "That's just asking for trouble. Compromised breathing, thrombocytopenia. This just keeps getting better and better."

"His dosage of heparin will be minimal, just enough to thin his blood enough for the machine, and the chances of thrombocytopenia in only four days' time is exceedingly rare. It takes much longer for platelets to break down, as you well know. He's already having trouble breathing. He's a normally healthy and vital patient, by no means high risk for excessive bleeding or heart attack. His burns are well-managed. ECMO's his best chance at full lung usage and recovery. It's tough to be logical here, but think it through, Doctor."

"Ruby," Deis fought weakly. "He needs to see her before we start. To hell with your clean, sterile, controlled room conditions. He needs to see his daughter before we put him under. He needs to know she'll be waiting on the other side."

"I'll allow a short visit under these circumstances, no more than thirty minutes, but it must be before six this evening. We're on the clock."

"So, I guess we're going ahead with this. God help us."

Taking the clipboard and signing the bottom of the consent form in a jagged loop, she resigned his fate to the wisdom of the aging yet progressive physician.

She returned to his room to find him propped up, clutching his chest as it rose and fell. The ventilator struggled to keep up with his panting. His blinks were slow, fierce as his toes curled in the sheets.

"Charlie," she murmured, approaching slowly with her hands behind her back.

Exhaustion and agony were clear in his eyes as they shifted to her. It was chilling, terrifying, to see the headstrong firefighter lying in bed, laboring just to breathe. But he clutched her hand tightly and smiled behind the mask as she brought his knuckles to her lips.

"Hey, I'm here. It's going to be all right."

Sitting alongside and trying to maintain composure, she helped him lift the whiteboard and marker.

ECMO?

"Looks like it," she confirmed, vowing to keep her voice calm. "It's an unorthodox approach, Charlie. It's an experimental treatment for adults. It shows promise in tests but isn't a completely safe option."

How's it work?

"I'm sure the Doctor explained it."

His head shook as he wrote. *You.*

She sighed, unwilling to divulge the riskiest details. "It's like a portable, exterior lung. You'll be given a medication to thin your blood and you'll be knocked out for a little over three days. While you're out, your blood is piped away from your heart, oxygenated through the ECMO unit, and then pumped back in. It helps your lungs take some time off work, so to speak. It's a tried practice in premature newborns, but adults don't have the same lab tests to fall back on."

He pushed his torso off the mattress with a grunt, turning onto his side to eye her directly. They were dim, tired, but such a pure blue that she couldn't help but fixate. And for the first time, she saw real fear in them, the kind that weighed on her soul like an anchor. She knew the terror, had seen it in her young patients' eyes many times in her years in diagnostics. But on the grown man's face, in the fascinating cobalt eyes she coveted, it was a horrifying change from the casual confidence she'd seen before.

He dropped the marker, taking her hand in both his and closing his eyes with the ventilator bag rising as he inhaled deeply. She slid her chair closer to the bed, easing her fingers through his hair, back from his forehead and over his ear. Her eyes followed her fingers as they stroked his cheek, down his neck and over his bandaged chest.

"You're in no immediate danger. We have some time. I'll bring Ruby by after school," she whispered, her fingers traipsing back into his hair again.

His eyes snapped open, gripping her hand as his head shook.

"Yes, Charlie," she insisted with argumentative nods. "Yes. I'm bringing her here. I'll explain it to her, and I will help her understand, but you need to see her. She needs to see you, in case..."

She trailed off, looking down. She'd vowed not to bring up the consequences, the thirty-percent failure rate, but it haunted her.

He took her hands, opened her palms and traced them with his thumbs. As her fingers curled around his and their eyes met, he nodded once before looking away.

"Okay. We'll be in around dinnertime. I'll make sure to answer her questions but be ready for her chatterbox routine." Deis managed a smile. "She's been busy at Haven. She's got plenty of new things to tell you about."

He nodded once more before pulling her toward him. She laid beside him on the narrow mattress as he silently commanded. His chin rested on the crown of her head as her legs shifted beside his, edging into his embrace as the incessant monitors blipped above them.

She felt his heartbeat, heard his tired lungs force shallow breaths through the clear tube, and absorbed the warmth of his lingering blisters as she held her ear to his chest. He smelled of salt, talc powder and metallic salve. Her eyes closed as she prayed, holding back tears that threatened to rip her soul to pieces.

Deis escorted Ruby into the hospital lobby just as the evening shift began in triage. Staff nurses who recognized them both waved as they passed, on their way with quick steps to the east elevator bank.

Inside the ascending lift, Ruby turned her face up to Deis. "Hey, you said Daddy's gonna be awake, right?"

"He should be. If not, we'll wait until he gets up. They're going to hook up the machine at six."

"Right, that lung machine. And he'll sleep for three days or so, right, like Snow White?"

"Like a tough manly Snow White, but yes," Deis snickered.

She'd spent the last hour in traffic with Ruby, breaking down the incredibly intricate and risky procedure into kid-friendly anecdotes and metaphors. It was exhausting, but she was amazing again by Ruby's adept mind and innate understanding.

Ruby's little brows furrowed. "But you said that he has a machine on to help him breathe now, right? How will he say hi to me if his face is covered up?"

"He writes on a little board, like teachers do at school." The door dinged and slid open as Ruby reached for her hand. Deis took it easily, smiling down to her before leading her down the hall to the corner room. "You're great at reading, so you should be able to read his chicken scratch."

"I'm usually all right at it. He leaves me notes when he heads out to fires."

The thought lifted Deis' spirit like a hot air balloon. After a deep careful breath, she turned to Ruby, stooping down to her level. "This is his room. Be careful with him, okay? He's got blisters and loads more stuff stuck to him than you did when you were here."

She nodded solemnly, noting the concern in the doctor's eyes and grabbing hold of her fingers tightly.

Deis brought her inside the doorway as a nurse finished hanging a new bag of fluids. When Charlie's gaze shifted to his daughter, it brightened instantly.

"Daddy!" She waved frantically as the nurse headed out with a smile.

He tilted the bed up fully, holding out his arms.

"Remember to be careful. He's got bruises and burns," Deis murmured, releasing Ruby's hand as she tugged to go free. She instantly climbed onto the chair and hopped to the mattress as Deis slipped out of her coat and scarf. Charlie's arms closed around his little girl, her head resting on his bandaged chest, her scrollwork tattoo hidden underneath.

"I missed you, Daddy," she purred, playing with the ties of his hospital gown. "But don't worry. Deis, she lets me call her Deis now, she's nice. She painted my nails today. And Henry, he's good at maths and he draws with me, even though all my people are all sticks. And Anna, she's the best at making proper tea and roast dinners."

Charlie shook his head with an eye roll as Ruby giggled.

"Tell your Daddy about what Rai got for you." Deis remarked.

"Oh!" Her eyes lit up. "She bought me a bike! It's my size, with a matching helmet, and she's teaching me how to ride, but I keep crashing into the hedges and getting scrapes on my arms. It doesn't hurt but it makes Henry scared. He watches me from the front step with loads of bandages shoved in his pockets."

Her little laugh echoed in the barren room.

Deis sat beside the bed and watched Charlie relax for the first time in days. His fingers swept through Ruby's raven hair while her dreamy eyes focused on the gown ties, twirling them in her tiny red-tipped fingers. His love poured silently into her as he rocked her in his arms.

Deis' heart swelled at their reunion. And she knew that, no matter how hard it would be, no tears were permitted now. She fought them back mercilessly as Ruby prattled on about Haven's pool, her vocabulary words and how Henry drove too slowly.

Ruby, on the other hand, wasn't sad. She wasn't scared or worried. She was her usual brilliant, affectionate and comforting self.

177

Deis kept underestimating the child, only to be wowed by her all over again. And her father was no doubt the one responsible for her outlook, her opinions and her capability. She kept her room at Haven tidy, ate her meals at the family table without argument and knocked on doors when she wasn't sure who was beyond them.

And Deis knew damn well that no eight-year old was that conscientious without rigorous observation and coaching.

Ruby laid little kisses on her father's cheeks and forehead, giggling at his mask and eyeing his bandages. When she kissed the white gauze, Deis sat forward, watching carefully for a pained response, but Charlie's eyes just closed softly.

"I kissed them, and it'll make them better, like you do for me. Are you scared, Daddy? Deis said it's okay to be a little scared of sleeping for so long."

He smiled a little under the mask as Deis handed him the marker and board. He wrote in big print and showed Ruby.

A little, but you help.

"A little, but you help," she read aloud. "I do? Deis, he said I'm helping!"

"What did I tell you? I had a feeling that if you were here, he'd perk right up. You have five more minutes, okay?"

"Okay," Ruby griped, her fingers curling around the ties of his hospital gown a little tighter. Charlie's fingers reshaped her mouth, pulling up the corners of her pout as he winked.

"Daddy? I don't want you to be sick anymore. I don't want Deis to cry anymore. I can hear sobbing through her door, and it's awful. I know she's so sad because she doesn't want us to be sick anymore, and Addison is no big deal, but your burns and all, that's worse. She acts like she's all right, but I know she's not, so I need you to wake up in a few days and feel better, okay?"

"You're an eavesdropping little tattletale," Deis grumbled with an eye roll.

Told you, Charlie wrote and showed Deis.

As Ruby hugged her father and waved goodbye, Deis showed her into the hall. Reddened and humiliated from Ruby's blatant gossiping, she snagged a nurse to keep Ruby in tow for a moment while she went back for her forgotten scarf.

Charlie grabbed the board and wrote quickly as she passed through the doorway again.

Can't thank you enough.

"She makes it easy," she replied, her cheeks cooling too slowly. "But she is a little gossip, isn't she?"

Like a little hen.

Deis turned at the sound of the marker on board, chuckling at his words while her trembling hands slipped into her coat pockets. She wanted to touch, to comfort, to do something other than abandon him. It was time for truth, and as Ruby had already started the ball rolling, she couldn't leave the matter unsettled.

"I am scared, Charlie," she sighed, stepping up to his side with her voice hushed against Ruby's overactive ears. "I'm afraid for selfish reasons. I don't want anything to happen to you, and I don't want to see that little soul suffer. She's been a bright spot at Haven. It's been a pleasure watching her and helping her, but she needs her daddy to stick around a while longer."

His eyes turned up, sorrow and unspoken apology filling them.

"I need you to *fight*," Deis commanded sharply despite his guilty stare. "It's going to get dark in there once the meds start, and it's going to feel like you could fall forever, but I need you to rail against it. We all need you. Not just Second, not just White Light, not just Ruby. The world needs you here. I'm being selfish and demanding, but you *can't* leave us, not now, not like this. You've gotten this far with mettle and strength. I *need* you to go a little farther. Got me?"

His palm reached out and squeezed hers tightly. Sets of azure and golden eyes fixed and narrowed intently on each other in understanding.

"You hold on," she demanded in a murmur. "I'll take her to Haven then I'll come right back. I'll be here, watching and waiting on you the whole time. And you'll come back to me, to us, on Saturday, right?"

He nodded once and drew a narrow heart on the board.

She lifted the marker and drew a broad one alongside his.

Chapter 14

Saturday, December 20

The days of his coma passed too slowly, the seconds ticking by painfully on the sluggish clock. Days turned to nights as she sat at his bedside, living on stale coffee and watching his monitor blip rhythmic patterns across the screen. Doctor Ivers came by personally twice a day to monitor his heparin drip, antibiotics and vitals while nurses came and went on their respective shifts.

Aside from trips to the restroom or to the coffee machine down the hall, she didn't divert her attention for a moment.

The ECMO unit's pumps hummed, the red stream escaping and reentering at his collar. Random blips and the bright LED display kept her weary mind alert, off-center and on panic's doorstep.

He was deathly still, so unbearably vulnerable, with tubes, machines and equipment keeping him alive as each terrible moment bled into the next. Keeping the constant terror at bay, maintaining an optimistic outlook despite his body lying lifelessly beside her, was by far the hardest part.

Each morning, she did calisthenics with him, lifting and bending his legs and arms, and when the medical aides brought dry shampoo and wipes, she insisted on bathing him herself, rolling up her cuffs and caring for him as she would a much younger patient. She stepped in boldly, tending his wounds when the burn unit did their rounds, rewrapping the blistered skin and applying cream with precision.

The burn specialists' prognosis was the high point of her week. They were convinced he'd heal without grafts or surgery. Skin would scar but he'd progressed beyond their stipulations. Avoiding the pain of skin resurfacing and the brutal healing afterward was a coup.

To pass the hours between medical visits, she spoke to her silent roommate. She told him her childhood hobbies, relayed the story of her first performance with Second, of her first shift at the hospital back home. She needed to believe he could hear, that he could understand though he couldn't reply.

Nurses came to hang more fluids or check his vitals each morning, but few stayed long. Deis watched them work like a guard dog on patrol. They scurried off hastily once they finished their assigned duties, no words spoken between the caretakers.

She hadn't had the wherewithal to consult with Doctor Gordon, but Wednesday's conference pertaining to Miranda's transplant had gone well according to her fellows. Natalie came to visit after the hubbub had died down, glowing at how well Deis' notes assisted the director's campaign. She would remain on the transplant list and the Board supported the ongoing treatment her diagnosis would require.

Rai stopped by, visiting Deis for a half-hour each night. She reported progress for Myopic, the touring dates planned for them, and that Marilyn's newest prospect band, the same one that Emmi had flown home to meet, had as much natural talent as an untoasted bagel. Marilyn's faith in that lost cause of a band had cost her manager a week's unnecessary labor, and as Simon's shooting schedule was finished stateside, she'd be headed back to Haven way sooner to work on White Light's tour and Second's Grammy performance from her plusher London office.

Deis heard every word Rai said but knew her mind would soon dump them like a wrung-out sponge. Rai hugged her each day, kissed her dour cheek and left with a sigh.

Henry didn't stay long when he visited, either. He brought her changes of clothes, packed lunches, magazines, a laptop and books to keep her busy, but once she carried them upstairs to the ICU, they sat idly stacked on the chair beside her own.

Her life had become nothing more than restless expanses between opportunities to nurse him. Everything in her life was on hold until Doctor Ivers returned to disconnect the unit, and everything following that milestone was up in the air until she saw his eyes reopen. The ongoing flux, lack of control and caffeine dependency kept her heart pounding a little too fast.

When her sanity was pushed to the brink, Saturday morning appeared outside his window. The day began with gray skies over a freshly fallen blanket of snow. Her phone buzzed to life in her pocket, rousing her with a start.

Less than three hours sleep. She'd survived on less before. She glanced to the phone display. The text notification showed Emmi's name.

Hey, stranger. How's the patient?

Deis stretched, slid her finger across the electronic keyboard and prayed autocorrect would do its job properly for once.

Still under. He's due for resurrection at ten this morning.

Deis folded the blanket she'd pulled on, shoving it onto the adjacent chair. It rested atop the ignored periodicals and uneaten sandwich Henry had dropped off the night before. The coffee she'd purchased still sat on his side table, room temperature but drinkable, so she downed like a double shot of vodka. Emmi's reply arrived as she tossed the rumpled cup in the bedside trash.

Ruby joined us on our web conference last night in your stead. We missed you.

Sorry I wasn't on the call. I did get the notes, though. Rai's been keeping me updated.

She knew it wasn't a worthy excuse, sitting alongside an unconscious man while he bled, but she also knew Emmi to be equal parts considerate and demanding. She doubted the blame would go farther than that text, though guilt now tugged at her conscience.

If Simon was in the hospital, I'd be right there. Are you still insisting that he's just a patient, just a friend and just an investment, or are you going to confess to wishing he reciprocated your undying affections?

The winking emoji at the end of the text taunted her. She typed and sent her reply before she could quell the steam pouring from her ears.

I'll admit, and I think it's clear, that I have a vested interest in this man's wellness. I have temporary custody of his daughter. I am relying heavily on my friends and employees to care for her while I'm here making his medical decisions. I'd appreciate a reprieve from speculation. I'm shouldering two lives and totally ignoring my own.

With a huff, she tossed the phone on the side table and retreated to the bathroom to splash her pale face with water. She barely recognized the long, dim eyes glancing back at her. Her full face of makeup had disappeared sometime between Rai's last visit and the crying fit just after midnight.

When she returned from the vending machine with hot, murky water masquerading as coffee, her phone light blinked with a waiting message.

Easy, killer. I know you have responsibilities, ones he foisted off on you in a pinch. But I also know who I'm talking to. Responsibility's your middle name. I know you enjoy caring for children. I also know being a stand-in parent for one is different. All I was texting for was a check-in, not to start WW3.

You're right, but I'm tired. My brain's fried. Too much hospital coffee. Swill.

Deis yawned hugely, checking his bedside clock. It was nearly eight. Rubbing her sore neck, she lifted her phone to see Emmi's reply.

Ick. I've been there, and recently, too. Look, if you care, which you obviously do, I hope you've told him about it. I know he's got

184

baggage but he's reasonable. I worked with him. And I know few men can resist your charms. If you've been playing coy, it's time to insist.

It was time for more honesty. Rai had been a better and more reserved confidante than she'd assumed, and Emmi knew less than she'd figured. Deis cleared her throat and typed with thudding thumbs.

We circled the runway last week, before his accident, when Ruby was still an inpatient. He took me home when I fell asleep in the cafeteria over Miranda's notes. But nothing happened. He had me naked, he kissed, touched, but that was it. I wanted more. I made that clear. He's avoiding sex and relationships, avoiding competition between any woman and his daughter. I was dismissed, plain and simple. So, I can care, I can be here, but he's not interested and I'm learning to deal with it.

With a snort, she pulled her knees up under her chin. She'd considered, stewed and obsessed for long enough. She couldn't possibly compete with Ruby and she knew it. She wanted to share, but he was unwilling to divide his affections. And that was that.

When her phone buzzed a few minutes later, she wanted to ignore it. She knew Emmi's response would be sympathetic, but she couldn't bear to obsess any more. It was an unfortunate game, one Deis wasn't emotionally prepared to inevitably lose.

But her innate curiosity, the same trait that so often destroyed any normalcy in her life, had Deis lifting her cell.

DeAnna Karine Sarafian, I'm extremely disappointed.

Full named? Damn. With a brow raise and a speedy swiping finger, she replied.

What? Why?

It took a moment, but her manager's reply soon filled her screen.

Because, my dearest Deis, you are a strong, dedicated woman. You are the smartest woman I know, no question. You know a ruse when you hear one. I told you to dig deeper with Miranda and you did. You found your answer, one you both were happy with. This is no different. It's not a competition between you and Ruby. It's a team sport. No one understands that more than you, and as a proficient diplomat, you should be MORE than capable of explaining that to him. Two people care more than one, and I know you wish that kid was yours already. How could you not? I saw her. She's ethereal, cute as a button, and totally in love with you. And she trusts you. I don't know where the mom is, pretty sure it doesn't matter. When he comes to, take a minute and show him how important Ruby is to you. I know you two haven't been able to talk lately, but you need to. Don't let him steer your ship, damn it. I convinced myself I couldn't be happy on a personal level, tried to alienate a good man and I nearly lost Simon. Don't make me threaten you…

Deis laughed aloud, picturing Emmi's waggling finger and wide, threatening gait. Shaking her head, she typed out her response.

K, boss. Gotcha. Simon's made you soft. And by the way, I steer my own ship but sometimes the harbor's closed.

Emmi's quick reply made her gape and snort.

Sometimes the harbor's closed because the gatekeeper's convinced all the ships out there are full of raping and pillaging tyrants. We both know your ship is damn near dry-rotted but well-run, so get the hell ashore before the damn thing sinks.

At ten o'clock precisely, Doctor Ivers arrived with two nurses, ready to separate man from machine. Deis had cleared her area, moved the books and remnants to her car and was pacing a threadbare line in the carpet.

"Doctor Deis, mornin'," Charlie's attending physician greeted in his southern drawl. On the other side of his bed, the nurses jotted down his vitals and began detaching the heparin IV.

"Morning, Doctor Ivers. Need help taking him off ECMO?"

"You've done enough already," he replied easily, tucking Charlie's file under his arm. "We'll wheel him down to the operating theatre. He'll be back here inside of an hour. I'll do another RSBI lung capability test once he's off the unit. He'll stay intubated until he regains consciousness, and within the next few hours, we'll be able to confirm the success of the ECMO. Off we go."

At his request, the nurses wheeled his bed from the room and down the hall as Deis followed. "When can I bring his daughter back in? She'll want to see him once he's awake."

"Wait until after lunch. No other visitors until this time tomorrow. You and his daughter are the only ones allowed."

The doctor duo stopped at the elevator threshold as the nurses pushed Charlie inside. The doors slid closed and she lost control of his care for the first time in four days.

"I'm counting on you. Everything's riding on this," Deis told the doctor, her tension held back tenuously. "I'm heading back to wash up and grab Ruby. We'll be back. Call me if anything happens."

He nodded once and pressed the elevator button as Deis stepped into the descending stairway, releasing a deep breath. The next hour would be the most precarious since his arrival. She'd done everything she could and now the responsibility rested elsewhere.

Her shattered mind just had to stay lucid enough to get her home in one piece. A hot shower and a decent meal were waiting there.

Despite her fear of abandoning him, she drove toward Haven, hugging the road's yellow line for guidance.

Back in her room, she collapsed to the mattress, her mind in turmoil and her body desperate for rest. By the time Henry knocked and made his way inside, she was asleep, still dressed and with shoes on, facedown and sideways over the made bed's linens.

He chuckled to himself, setting the tray of infused water and date scones on her bedside table. Carefully, he repositioned the shattered doctor onto the pillows, slipped off her flats and tucked a blanket over her frame. Sneaking off and closing the door gently behind him, he made his way back to the kitchen.

He reported to Anna and Rai that the doctor was home and already out like a light, passed out across the bed. They shared amused and knowing glances.

Rai stepped in to entertain ever-inquisitive Ruby for a few hours while Deis slept, teaching her basic songs on the studio's piano to distract her from endless questions about her father's condition, none of which Rai could answer. Instead, she taught her a few Christmas carols from the sheet music found in the filing cabinet. Teacher watched student, fascinated, while she picked out a feeble *Für Elise* after only seeing it done once. If kids were like this, she'd have to bring up the baby subject with her studious fiancé again before long.

Upstairs after their lesson ended, Anna prepared a pasta lunch for her little houseguest, complete with the long, tender breadsticks she'd demanded every day that week. Tapping, dipping and munching, she bopped her head to the carols playing in her head while Rai squeezed in her daily swim routine. Henry polished wine glasses, rehanging them with white gloved hands as he watched Ruby enjoy, a genuine smile etched on his angular face.

"I will miss her," he admitted quietly to the chef in his rarely heard and deeply resonant Welsh accent. She was watching the youngster, too, while a teapot heated on the stove.

"She's a darling doll baby," Anna added, wiping her hands on a thin, white towel. "She's certainly brought so much joy to this place."

"You think Miss Rai will add to the manor?" Henry asked quietly, hoping to hide the gossip from Ruby's ears.

"I certainly hope so, and I think Emmi would make a marvelous mother, too. But I think Deis will be first."

Henry, agape and turning his back to Ruby, asked in a hush. "This girl? Is she staying?"

"No, for God's sake," Anna chuckled. "I think she'll win over her daddy and we'll have this one and perhaps another to spoil after that."

Henry beamed, excitement stewing in his belly as he set off to retrieve the girl's cleaned plate. He'd never served a more beautiful and jubilant soul in his life.

"All finished, miss?" He asked, leaning at the waist with the bread-wiped dish in his open palm.

"Yes, Mr. Henry," she replied, hopping off the chair and over to Anna, who had prepared her wooden stool by the sink for her customary post-meal hand wash. "Chef Anna, it was scrummy. Even better than last night."

"You are a pasta monster," she replied, tickling the little girl's middle playfully as she squirmed. The chef's and child's laughter, equally bawdy, echoed through the kitchen. "I'll make it until you turn into one long noodle yourself."

"Deis told me I'd turn into lemon fizz back when I was in hospital, but I'm still Ruby."

"Indeed," Henry chimed in, handing her a nearly empty can of her preferred soda. She finished it in a swift gulp and handed it back.

"Can I go ride my bike? I'll tell Rai so she can watch me."

Anna nodded and the child dashed off, out the back door and into the pavilion. Both caretakers watched her with proud smiles and eager hearts.

Deis roused herself at one, coming to in her bed but still in her overcoat. With a chortle, she hastily ate what Henry had left and bathed just as quickly. In the clean black trousers and the green cardigan the butler hung nearby, she grabbed her purse and made her way downstairs, the nap and snack doing wonders for her spirit.

She found Anna in the kitchen, stirring a massive pot with a wooden spoon shaped like an oar. When the immense lid was set back on, she turned to her with a welcoming smile.

"Good afternoon, Doctor. Stew's on, but I've got shepherd's pie and peas made if you're hungry."

"No, I'm all right, Anna, but thanks," Deis replied, sitting at the table. "Henry left me something upstairs. I'm sorry for foisting Ruby on you all week."

"Tish tosh, she's been an utter joy. It's an extra person to cook for, and an extra heartbeat in this huge place. It does a soul good to have a young one at home. And a sweeter child, no one could find. Such an angel, she is."

"I'd like to talk with her a moment if you know where she is."

Anna delivered a steaming cup of strong black coffee, a few drops of which Deis would have killed for the night before. With a pat on the bassist's shoulder, the chef retreated to find Ruby.

Deis lifted the mug, smelled the South American stimulant waft up and rejoiced in it. The conversation she was about to have, on the other hand, would likely be much less comforting. She'd realized in the shower that she couldn't avoid coming clean with the little girl any longer. She'd have to tell her how she felt before her conscience would let her confront Charlie again.

She did care too much and it was affecting her ability to objectively deal with them both. To walk away, to leave them behind, wasn't an option. If she moved on from her feelings for the father, she'd still care for the daughter for eternity.

And if Ruby did trust Deis already, and if she wanted to keep the child's trust, she'd need to put all the cards on the table, let her see the situation and be a part of it. She couldn't sneak around behind her back and wouldn't let the truth wait. Ruby needed to know that her newfound caretaker wasn't disappearing forever, even if Charlie turned his back on her.

190

As the child ran in, headed straight for another can of lemon fizz on the bottom shelf of the fridge, Deis' breath caught. She was a miniature version of her father and it still left her breathless. When Ruby brought the can to her caretaker and doctor, Deis opened it and handed it back instinctively. She hopped into the chair beside hers.

"Hi Deis. Have a nice kip?"

"You knew I was napping, huh?"

"Yeah, you were well and truly knackered. Henry brought you scones, the icky brown speckled ones, but he left them up there and came back down straightaway."

"You're very observant and absolutely right. I was really tired." Deis reached out with a shaky hand, suddenly unsure, and tucked Ruby's wispy hair back behind her ear. "It's been a long few days. We're going to go see your daddy soon, though."

"Is he off the machine yet?"

"He's probably still sleeping, but yeah, it should be done by now."

"Brilliant," Ruby responded simply before taking a sip of soda.

"Before we go, I wanted to talk to you about something, okay? It's important."

Ruby's eyes narrowed a bit, but she stayed silent.

"I'm going to tell you the truth and I want you to tell me the truth back, okay? I'm a little afraid but I want to be honest with you. Your daddy's told you how important it is to be honest, right?"

"Uh huh," she replied, her hands moving to her lap as she turned to face Deis. "You can tell me, I'm brilliant at secrets."

"I don't think it's a secret," Deis admitted with a sigh. "But it's really important and it can't wait another minute."

"Oh," Ruby's eyes saddened. "Are you ill? Do we both have fairies?"

"No, no, Ruby. It's about my feelings for you and your daddy."

"Oh," she repeated, dread creeping in to tint her irises navy. "Are you fed up with us?"

"Oh, dear God no," Deis breathed, taking both Ruby's hands in her own. "Please, just let me explain."

Ruby nodded and waited, rubbing her thumbs over Deis' unpainted nails.

"Ruby, you are a perfect girl, the best I've ever known. When we met, I was in a bad place. I felt like I was a horrible doctor. Finding Addison and watching you get better has made me so happy. Having you around lately has made it even better."

"You're sweet," Ruby gleamed. "And you're a lovely doctor. You're Daddy's doctor, too. You've been by his side this whole time."

"It's scary to see someone you care about be sick. You understand that, right?"

"Uh huh. You're scared for Daddy."

"I have been since he first came to the hospital. That's why it was so hard to leave him there alone. And it's been very hard on my heart because I really like him, as a person and as a good friend. I want him to be better and for you two to be happy again, back home together."

Ruby's eyes narrowed in thought, her head tipping to the side as she watched Deis hold back tears. "You cry when you talk about him. If you like him, why are you so down about it?"

Deis cleared her throat, blinking back the waterworks the child so adeptly saw. "It's not that easy, Ruby. I've talked to your daddy about how I feel before, a little bit. I didn't want to leave the hospital lately because I worry about what will happen if I'm not there watching, making sure everything is okay. I feel bad for leaving you here, for not being with you, but I had to make sure he was okay, too."

"No worries," she replied easily. "Rai taught me some piano and Henry's good at remembering what stories I like at bedtime."

Deis chuckled, but it was tinged with nerves. "Well, that's good. And I really need to thank them for their help. But what I wanted to tell you is that I like you too. Very much. Even more than I can explain."

"I know. You're nice and you're sweet to me. I like you too. Do you like me like you like Daddy?"

"It's a little different, but I just want you to know that if your daddy doesn't like me the same way I like him, I'll still care about you even though you may not see me as often. Does that make sense?"

Ruby nodded with sad eyes. "Yeah, but that's bollocks. Can I still come here and swim and ride my bike in your garden?"

"Of course you can. You're welcome here whenever you like, and your daddy will be, too. But you know I'm telling you the truth, right?"

"Uh huh, and if you're gone on Daddy, you should make sure he knows it. He bad at listening. And he's lonely a lot. Mummy," she paused, looked away. "She's been gone a long time. I don't think she loved him much, but he really loved her, and he cried a lot. He cried a lot and he was really scared. And he's been on his own since she's been gone. But he likes you and thinks you're pretty. I can tell. And if you want to keep him from being so lonely, I think that's brilliant."

A hot tear spilled over as Deis reached for a nearby napkin.

Ruby frowned, distraught. "You're crying again and now it's because of me."

Deis gathered Ruby up in a hug, burying her face in the girl's raven mane. "No, you sweet girl. No, you've given me the courage I needed so much. You are my biggest helper."

Ruby kissed her cheek and tossed her arms around Deis' neck. "Then please, don't cry anymore."

A little after two, Deis escorted Ruby through the ICU halls again, holding her hand tightly to keep her from dashing. Nurses waved excitedly as they both passed, bringing out the tot's million-watt smile.

Henry crafted two bows of red satin ribbon to secure the twin braids that snaked down behind Ruby's ears and hung to her shoulders. In jeans studded with faux diamonds, a fluffy candy-cane striped shirt and new black wool coat Henry bought her so they could match, she looked ready for a holiday party.

Rested and uplifted by the girl's comforting words, Deis felt more alive than she had in a week.

Charlie was lying still with closed eyes when they arrived. The ECMO machine was missing and the bed propped him up. The IV still administered fluids between his neck and collarbone and the hospital gown still hung over his chest, but blankets were tucked around him, covering his legs. The mask that hid his mouth had been replaced with clear tubing under his nose, strung up behind his head and leading to the smaller ventilation machine to his left.

Deis exhaled a sigh of relief, drawing Ruby's attention up to her smiling face.

"What? He still looks knackered."

"Oh God, Ruby, he's *so* much better," Deis declared, lifting Ruby and stepping over to the bed, pointing at his face. "See that tube under his nose? That's called a cannula. That's a huge step up from that big mask. He's breathing easier now. I'm so happy."

"Brilliant. Why is he still sleeping?"

She dropped the girl into a chair by the bed and sat beside her. "The medicines he was on were a lot stronger than he was. He's sleeping them off. He should be up soon. Do you want to wait?"

She nodded. "He always wakes me. Now I get to wake him."

"Okay, you got it." Deis shrugged out of her coat and took Ruby's, laying them over the back of her chair. "What did you do while I was sleeping today?"

"Oh, Rai taught me some carols! She said I could sing them to Daddy to help him feel better, and that if he knew them, we could sing together when he's ready."

"That's awesome. Which ones did she teach you?"

"I know the first bit of *Jingle Bells* on the piano and she taught me a new one, but I forgot the name of it. It's something to do with Santa going down a chimney and reindeer on the roof."

"Oh, *Up on the House Top*. That's an old American carol. I think it's from back in the eighteen-hundreds. Do you remember how it goes? I sing a little, you know."

"I think I remember. Let's try."

She climbed onto Deis' lap and began a shaky, high-pitched rendition of the carol. Her impromptu guardian interjected to remind her of forgotten lyrics as they progressed. She ended with her arms lifted jubilantly and Deis wrapped her up in a victorious hug as they both laughed.

Charlie's eyes had opened sometime during the first verse. He watched his beautiful daughter sing along with his rescuer, a smile lifting his cheeks. And when the tune ended and they both laughed in each other's arms, he felt his heart kick pleasantly in his aching chest.

Nothing could've prepared him for the sight of his most precious love dressed up like a Christmas present, in the arms of the finest woman he'd ever known.

As Deis glanced up and met Charlie's gaze, she gasped with a smile and rose quickly, nestling Ruby on her hip. "Hey, stranger. Ruby, looks who's up!"

Her little arms reached out for his. As Deis placed her gently on his bed, she curled up at his side with her cheek on that bandaged, tattooed collarbone. "Hi, Daddy," she cooed, playing with his gown's ties again. "I missed you."

He exhaled with his arms around her, his voice a hoarse, strained whisper. "I missed you, too, beautiful. So much."

Deis watched from his bedrail, in the chair she'd lived in since Tuesday. After a few minutes of reverent silence, she finally chimed in. "How do you feel?"

"Sublime," he replied, stroking Ruby's hair. "And a bit nauseated. Is that normal?"

Deis nodded. "Heparin does that. You'll be a little dizzy, too, so be careful. And you're breathing on a PAP now. That's a huge improvement, Charlie. It's more than I'd thought possible."

"To be honest, I could stand a trip to the loo, but I'm not giving this girl up just yet," he grinned, laying his head back and looking to the ceiling. "It can wait."

Deis grabbed and read over his chart. ECMO had improved his lung function and recovery by seventy percent. He'd begin hyperbaric rehabilitation the next day and continue a lung recovery care plan.

"This is fantastic," Deis commented, replacing the file. "Despite my qualms, it was the right course of treatment. I guess I owe Doctor Ivers a basket of mini muffins or something."

"You don't owe me a thing," the senior doctor's voice rang out from the doorway as he entered with a nurse in scrubs. "Good morning, Mister Taylor, and welcome back to the land of the living. I see you're breathing easier, and that means we can, too."

"Yes, Doctor. Well done. You've given me my life back."

"You took it back for yourself. And we've got a fair way to go yet," Doctor Ivers added. "I'm optimistic for the first time since you were admitted, and I bet your proxy feels the same."

"Without a doubt. Come here for a second, Ruby. Let the nurse take your daddy to the bathroom a minute."

When Ruby climbed down and entered Deis' open arms, Charlie smiled and lifted his healing legs from the mattress for the first time. Deis and his daughter watched as he staggered to his feet, the nurse supporting him under his unburned arm and grabbing his IV and ventilation pole with her free hand. He clutched his head, struggling for his bearings as she slumped to take his weight.

"Dizzy? Nauseated?" Doctor Ivers asked.

"Yeah, a bit," Charlie admitted while traveling to his bathroom with the nurse's help. "I'll make it, though."

While the door was closed, Doctor Ivers turned to Deis.

"I'm sure you're aware that I've got him on hyperbaric rehab for an hour a day for the next week. His RSBI is in the normal range, and the PAP is only on to help him readjust to breathing on his own again. His lungs are weakened from a lack of use but he's on the right track. It's a true medical marvel, that ECMO machine."

"I'm awestruck, and so excited to see it work on an adult," Deis replied, cradling Ruby and rocking her while she toyed with the platinum chain around her neck. "And no skin grafts, either."

"Wasn't a need for them, and the hyperbaric regimen non-invasively heals the damaged layers of skin anyway."

"I want him to sing again," Ruby demanded, her pale eyes up on the aging physician.

"He'll sing in a few weeks, and he'll be wonderful, probably even better than before."

"I'll have to compete with myself," Charlie said, emerging from the bathroom with a pained look. "Throwing my lungs up with this thing under my nose is horrible. I'm about done with this, Doc."

"See that? He's more eager to be done than we are." The doctor winked at Ruby. "We can try to remove it, if you'd like."

"Now? You think I'm up for it?" Charlie asked, settling back in bed.

Deis rose, setting Ruby down on the chair and moving to the PAP unit. "Sure. You've got a medical team here. I can always punch you again to bring you back. Doctor, will you assist?"

With a smirk, Doctor Ivers approached and unhooked the tubing from behind his ears. "Be prepared. Breathing will be painful but try not to gasp. Your lungs had a chance to relax over the past few days, so they'll take time to strengthen like a weak muscle would."

The attending physician removed the tubing from under Charlie's nose as Deis flipped the machine off. A few seconds passed before his palms moved to his quivering chest. Deis took the nurse's stethoscope and listened for breath sounds as Doctor Ivers offered the PAP unit in open palms.

His lungs labored, fought hard as he panted, but he waved off the doctor's offer to replace the tubing. Deis propped him up, and with his chin tipped back, she heard his lung completely inflate and his heart rate pick up as oxygen coursed through his body.

"Awesome," Deis praised, removing the stethoscope and handing it back. "Your lungs are capable, just out of practice."

"Chuffed... Feels ... Great." He croaked.

Ruby's eyes were serious, scared. "Daddy, you sound horrible."

"I'm... I'm all right. Come. Listen."

She climbed back to his side and rested her ear on his chest. He breathed easier with her nearby, and the physicians were delighted to see his recovery take shape.

Rai arrived as Doctor Ivers was excusing himself. He'd insisted on waiting twenty minutes after Charlie began breathing on his own, both for safety's sake and to commend his patient's impressive recovery. Rai waited just outside the elevator bank on the second floor until Deis could sneak away.

"Hey, Doc," she as her friend came into view. She gestured to the parted curtains and to her view of the daddy-daughter reunion down the hall. "Looks like progress to me. How relieved are you?"

"Oh, you have no idea. He's so much better. Whether it's the hospital's care or positive thinking, he's certainly turned it around."

"That's great. I snuck out for a bit to come see. Steve's at the house resting. He took a red-eye in. He hasn't slept well, worried about you and Ruby, though I think it's because he can't wait to meet her in person. He loves kids."

"It's easy to love her. And having Charlie awake and recovering is going to do wonders for all our stress levels. His doctor says he'll be back at the mic in a few weeks. Visits are okayed for tomorrow."

Rai nodded. "I'll text Devon later. But, in truth, I came to steal the kid. We'll go catch a burger or something. I had a feeling you'd want to talk with Charlie now that he's up."

Deis looked down, considered with pursed lips. "He's just off the ventilator. It's too much too soon."

"No delaying it," Rai chided with a raised brow and her arms crossed. "It's been too long. And you won't survive this ridiculous obsession much longer."

"I get that. It's just been a very emotional day already."

"I heard you talked with Ruby." Rai held up open palms for peace when Deis glared. "Hey, you sent Anna to go get her, to speak with her alone. I'm just assuming it was a heart-to-heart chat, one you'll tell me about since you're in my debt."

"It was, and it went better than I thought it would. The details can wait," she murmured, turning back to watch the raven-haired pair.

"It's been a day full of pleasant surprises, hasn't it?"

Deis chuckled. "Oh yes, especially after days of insomnia in an uncomfortable chair beside a man on his deathbed."

Rai stepped up, laid an arm around Deis' waist with her voice lowered. "It's painfully obvious that you love them, momma bear. How long before you admit it's worth fighting for?"

Deis nodded, her heavy gaze still fixed on the man and his daughter. "I really do love them, more than I wanted to admit. It's so huge. I haven't even come to terms with it yet. And Ruby? She's even pushier than you. I told her that I cared about them both, and she said to tell him how I felt and to be clear about it. He's a little dense, apparently."

Rai glanced at the reunited family before turning a fiendish grin on Deis. "Then go get him, killer."

Chapter 15

When Deis woke at dawn, nestled peacefully in Haven's lush linens, a few texts were waiting. One was from Emmi's cell and two more were from numbers not saved in her contacts list. Emmi's message displayed first.

HE'S AWAKE!! SO HAPPY!! ECMO to the rescue! At least Rai thought to fill me in... I was waiting over here!

The excited capitals made her giggle as she propped herself up to read the first of the other two.

Deis, it's Simon. I haven't met Charlie, but I'm sure he's a fine bloke. You ladies have good taste. And I'm glad he's coming around. Emmi's been a damn riot over here. See you soon.

With a broad smile, she flipped to the third message.

Hi, beautiful. Thanks for charging my phone. And please come by soon. SO BORING. How did you sit here nearly four days and not carve out both eyes with a plastic spoon?

She laughed aloud again, swiping her finger across the screen in reply.

Morning, handsome. I'll be in as soon as I can. Henry is taking your girl horseback riding today. She's been jazzed about it for days, so I'll be on my own. I hope that's okay.

She rose, stretched and opened the curtains, welcoming the pleasant morning sky over the English country. The sun was surprisingly warm, the snow had melted, and the sky shone as blue as Ruby's eyes. Henry was on the entry steps, dressed in his long wool coat, wiping the glass of the front doors in slow circles.

Life was moving on as usual, and nothing pleased her more than knowing he'd be around to see it. Her phone buzzed as she rounded the bed.

Horseback riding? Christ what a life she's leading these days. Come on your own. I think we need to talk anyway, now that I can. And can you please, please bring me some coffee? Oh, good Jesus, my head is killing me. It's got to be a caffeine headache.

Sorry, dude. You're going to have to live for a few more days without it. Caffeine is a diuretic. It'll make your heparin symptoms worse. Still nauseated?

She readied dark, boot-cut jeans and a white button-down top to go with her tan leather jacket. With the clothes piled on the chair, she turned back to her cell as a message arrived.

Bollocks. And yes, other than lousy telly to keep me occupied, I've had the honour of throwing my guts up every hour. The nurse has fluids in my arm now, the site on my neck's bandaged and hurts like hell. How about a soda? Can I have that, Nurse Ratched?

It's Doctor Ratched, thank you very much. I earned my title. I'll dip into Ruby's stash of lemon fizz. See you in a bit.

She added a smile emoji to the text and tossed the phone onto the chair. Undressed and with the door locked, she began her yoga routine. Refusing to feel tension over their looming chat, she descended into the lotus position and began the relaxing ritual she'd so dearly missed.

She left Ruby in Henry's capable hands and headed to the hospital. She'd be thrilled when the panic-inducing urban building was only a distant memory.

Upstairs at the nurses' station, two techs in scrubs were readying medications and comparing notes as she passed. Both glanced to her, to each other, then back to their work, knowing they'd have one less room to worry about on their shift.

As she approached his room, the curtains were closed but she heard music coming from inside through his ajar door. It was heavy and quick like an action movie soundtrack. She peeked like a snooping child.

Propped up in bed, his head bobbed rhythmically as he wrote with a thin pen onto a yellow pad, balanced on his up-drawn knees with a blanket over them. A small wireless speaker on his bedside table was respectfully quiet though vibrating with heavy metal guitar and vocals. The IV piping swung as he scribed, immersed in the tune and his work. He looked like Emmi when she was on a wild writing kick.

She watched a few seconds, nibbling her thumbnail and grinning before clearing her throat. He froze in place as he looked up, the pen hovering over paper and his brows lifted.

"Hey there," she murmured, stepping inside and closing the door, flipping the door lock silently behind her back. "Thank goodness there's no one in the rooms around you or you'd be getting complaints. Getting some work done?"

He slid the pad and pen to the side table. "It's about time. I've been skiving off for, what, a week now? Dead lucky I'm not that important to Light, eh?"

"Your posse threatened me, said they wouldn't survive without you, so yeah, you barely matter at all," she quipped, taking the can of soda from her pocket and setting it on his side table.

As she stepped closer, his eyes passed from her leather jacket to her form-fitting jeans, then back up to her styled, flowing wavy hair and long, dangling earrings that he ached to touch.

"And you," he breathed, cooling his face with his waving hand. "Christ on a bike, turning down modeling must've broken those fashion designers' hearts."

She tucked her thumbs in her pocket, tossed her head to the side and turned slowly to give him a three-sixty view. "You think so? It always seemed a little shallow to me. I'm a doctor, after all. A little demeaning, don't you think?"

"Sorry, love, run that by me again? Pretty sure I stopped listening there somewhere."

She smacked him gently with the back of her hand as he shrugged away chortling. "Ow, ow, easy. The hurt means it's healing, right?"

She nodded. "And it'll start itching like hell soon. That's a good sign, too."

"Fantastic," he grimaced, shifting his legs to the side and patting the mattress. "Here, beautiful."

She sat obediently, her legs hanging off the side. "How are you feeling, really?"

"Better than I figured I'd be. I'm properly washed and brushed. I feel human again. And the doctor dropped in an hour or so ago, handed me a little pill and told me I'd been sick enough already. I'm headed back to normalcy but still sporting the attire of an invalid."

"I figured he'd put you on an anti-emetic if you were still nauseated this morning. The more you stand and move around, the faster you'll recover. Going downstairs for your hyperbaric treatment will help."

"A whole hour of just myself for company, sitting in a big tube and reading gossip mags. It's wasted on me. The scars add to my tough guy image. I should just keep 'em."

"You can just tell everyone that you survived an alligator attack instead of a fire. Saving yourself from the jaws of a predator versus saving the life of a trapped boy? That's manlier, more macho for the metal guy, right?"

He sighed impatiently. "You're going to make me out to be some sort of hero, aren't you?"

"Too late, the papers already did, especially when his mother's statement was added to the story."

"Damn it to hell," he glowered with an eye roll. "It's a job. What a waste of newsprint."

"No good on the fire brigade, no good in White Light. You're just a waste in general, huh?"

Though she jibed good-naturedly, apprehension and insecurity haunted her. She questioned being as outwardly affectionate as she had been. He was no longer a scared, mortally wounded soul. He was a live, energetic, downright sexy man with a serious beard started, barely dressed and on the same bed.

When she hesitated, tucked her hands back onto her lap, he reached for her wrist, pulled her hand into his. Her fingers were curved, her palm damp. His voice softened. "You're making it pretty obvious and I'd figured we'd have some things to clear up. But I have to tell you how much it meant to me, you doing what you did, abruptly and thanklessly, for me and Ruby. I can't thank you because it wouldn't be enough, and you'd just tell me you're a doctor and it's your job anyway."

She nodded, watching their hands. "Sounds like me."

He smiled faintly. "Deis, I didn't want to be, but I was genuinely terrified, not of dying so much but of leaving her behind, of leaving her here to figure out how to go on. It wasn't your job to take such brilliant care of her, and it certainly wasn't my intention to have you sit here with me all day and night worrying."

"Then you really don't know me well at all," she admitted quietly, watching his face turn sorrowful. "I can't help but take a wonderful child and her dutiful father under my wings."

He exhaled, methodically turning the smooth platinum ring around her middle finger in slow circles. "I know you care. I woke in time to catch you two caroling yesterday," he confided, glancing up to see the warm glow in her eyes as she smiled. "It was magical. I've never seen her take so readily to anyone before. She calls you Deis, she listens to you, she even walks with you instead of taking off like a shot. She doesn't even mind me that well. It's like... Well, it's like she's already decided about you. She's been careful, shy, since her mother left. But it's like she went ahead and fell in headfirst."

You sweet man, she thought with a little chuckle. You've kept her loving soul to yourself all these years, and she's been careful and shy for your sake, not hers.

"Charlie, I had to be honest with her. I told her how I feel about her. She's witty, sharp as a tack, wise beyond her years. And I was very clear when I told her she was welcome in my life and in Haven whenever she likes, no matter what happens between us. Hell, Henry has her on horseback and wearing a junior version of his penguin coat. She's got Anna making pasta and those damn breadsticks from scratch twice a day. She's been adopted by us all. And we're going to miss her when she's gone."

"It's what I was hoping for, that she'd actually enjoy the time there. Christine told me she pushes food away while I'm on a call, asks a million times when I'll be back. She insists on saving the notes I leave for her. I'm supposing she's been so busy at your place that she barely knew I was gone."

"You're her father first, the most important person in her life. She was more understanding of this than I figured she'd be. She's a considerate kid in general and that's your doing. She's given me courage a few times, including last night."

"What did she do last night? Odds are I won't be astonished."

She chuckled, looked to their hands. "After I told her that I'd always welcome her, that I'd always love her, she told me I needed to talk to you about all the crying I've done and why. And she told me to not be subtle about it, either, since you can be a bit dense, to use her word."

"Tattletale," he mumbled, imagining his absent daughter's face. "That kid's going to be the death of me. But you told her you love her? How can you? It's been what, a week? You can't possibly..."

"Don't tell me I don't love her. I can't help my heart. And she's a damn gem, so it's easy to. And I don't love her for any reason other than the fact that she earned it, so don't assume it's a ruse or I'll just punch you again."

"For the record, you broke my rib doing that. And I don't think you're someone who throws the *L* word around willy-nilly. You obviously care for your patients, but I don't think you love them. And I don't know how I feel about you loving my daughter, to be honest. She clearly adores you, though. I could tell when she climbed on your lap yesterday. She," he began, looked down with a sigh. "She's been lonely a long time. She has mates at school, but I work 'round the clock and she's come to depend on Christine as a big sister of sorts nowadays, especially on long nights."

"She thinks you're the lonely one. I don't think she's wrong about that, either. I've met your band mates. You have nothing in common with them beyond camaraderie and their dependency on you."

"I spend a lot of time in my own mind, and I do a lot of thinking, a lot of worrying, especially about Ruby. She's the most important thing in my life."

"Clearly, and she's become very important in mine, too. You both have."

When her eyes warmed and she cradled his hand in hers, he read between the lines. "Deis, I can't do this. I can't. I thought you understood."

"All I understand is that your ability to trust is damaged. Your heart's cracked, barely held together by a Ruby-shaped bandage. The idea of opening up and letting yourself care again is just too risky."

"Of course, it is," he huffed. "If I try, she suffers when it ends. I just.... I can't do that to her again. I'll never forget holding her while she cried night after night. I watched her mother stride off like we never mattered at all. Honestly, I don't care if I matter or not, but

Ruby matters, more than anything else, and I won't let it happen again."

"For the record, you held her while you both cried. She told me that, too. What happened before is regrettable, but let me clarify, you both matter a lot. And as I see it, from that tragedy came a beautiful dark-haired angel of circumstance. Think of where you'd be, of how different it all would be, if she'd never been born. I can understand not wanting to see her hurt, I can, but she sees that you're hurt and knows it could be different. She's old enough to understand."

"But she's young enough to have to deal with my decisions. I can't put her in harm's way."

Venom clawed its way up her throat before she could rein it in. She rose, pacing away, unable to sidestep his verbal gut punch. When she turned back, her gaze was like fire. With hands on her hips, she exhaled a sharp breath.

"Is that what I am, Charlie? *Harm*? I should be offended. I'm the *opposite* of harm. I'll tell you what I am, though. I am a good woman. I work hard and I've earned this spot I'm in. I have no desire to hurt you or your daughter. To assume I'd want to hurt you is a base insult to my character after all I've done for you both. It's downright disgusting to even think about."

She released a hot breath, strode back to his bedside and craned down close while his face remained solemn, blank. "I've been honest with you and acted in your best interest this whole time. You clearly trust her with me. And you should, because she is *very* important to me, more so than any child I've ever known. I do love her. I want to continue to be a part of both your lives. I think that's pretty clear. What I don't get is why the concept of us isn't even worth a second thought to you. Walking away now, assuming this is all going to self-destruct? That's just stupid and short-sighted."

He brought his face in close, his expression fierce and his tone acidic. "It all sounds so *pretty*, this promise of forever. But when it gets too hard, when a choice has to be made, you'll choose what you know. You know Second. You know the road. You don't know *us*, our structure, our sacrifices, and you don't know how to be a parent."

No gut punch this time. His words were a flaming glass-tipped arrow aimed straight for her heart. He'd clearly wanted an immediate, aggressive response. She wouldn't condescend to give it.

Resolve swept through, brightened her eyes and lifted her head high. "You're right, I'm not a parent. But I'm not incapable and I'm certainly willing. If you don't see maternal care in everything I do, in every decision I make, you're lying to yourself. Stop making this about my hypothetical inabilities. This is about you and your stubbornness, your ignorance and your fear. You're the one refusing to stand up for what you want, for what you need."

"You don't know what I need. This won't work out long term. I can't be what you need, what you deserve. And I won't promise you a forever knowing I can't make it happen."

"To say you can't make anything happen is a damn fallacy, Charlie! You've made *everything* happen. You are White Light. You got them through your manager's resignation and to a record deal. And you're working full-time, handling a household and raising a kid on your own. All with no help. You're no failure. There's nothing you can't make happen. You just don't want to risk getting hurt, to break some ludicrous promise you created to shield yourself from having to try. When will you tell me the truth?"

"What truth?" He argued with a lifted brow. "I've been pretty damn clear this whole time."

Deis whirled to the chair where the whiteboard rested. She tossed it at him with a scowl. The hearts they'd drawn days before were still there in undeniable black marker.

"*This* truth," she added viciously. "I *know* better, and you're just insulting my intelligence, saying you don't feel anything for me.

Insisting that I'm just going to walk anyway so I'm not worth your time? How could I possibly walk away now?"

Unable to quell the flames burning the edges of her heart, she paced away only to whirl on him again like a hungry tiger. "*Damn* it, Charlie, you've pulled me into bed with you more than once, you've kissed me like I was all you wanted. You signed your life over to me, handed me all your responsibilities. You gave your kid to me on a silver platter and was happy when we got along. And now you're telling me it's all been, what, a ploy? I wish I could believe you're that cruel. It might make all this easier. But if you are, and if this is just some twisted game, you have this one chance to make it clear as day, for the sake of our working relationship. Tell me you don't want me. Make me believe it. I have to leave here today knowing we're off the table. I have to believe you're that heartless."

His azure gaze shifted to the window, his lips pressed together into a thin line.

After a sigh of defeat, she wrung her hands and took a deep breath. "I'm sorry, I shouldn't be this angry. It's been a tough week for us all. But this wasn't a hookup at some club after a show. Do you really expect me to think this is just casual and to walk away because I will at some point anyway?"

Exhausted and humiliated, she laid her forehead in her palm, took a deep breath, and fought desperately to calm her pulse. Her temples ached and her eyes stung with denied tears.

His brain toiled, searching for a way out of this. He'd insulted her, lashed out, and deemed her unfit. He'd done so selfishly, hoping to avoid this very scene. The promise he'd made to himself, the commitment to a life dedicated to lonely nights for his daughter's sake, seemed silly now in the face of such vehement insistence from someone Ruby clearly loved and wanted. Deis clearly loved them both in ways he'd never experienced before.

She watched his eyes turn up in consideration, finding the strength to approach the bed. She fought to keep her tone calm. "Look, I know I'm a lot to deal with. I know who I am, and I know I lead a very hectic and very public life. But if you can look me in the eye and tell me honestly that this is all in my mind, that this isn't even worth a try, please do that now. If you want me gone, honestly and for the right reasons, I will step away and this will be over. But it needs to be now, before I fall any harder than I already have."

When he didn't move, didn't speak, she took his hands, leaning in. "Charlie, please."

But he didn't need words. He needed her. Nothing had ever been more clear in his mind.

"Deis, I can't do that," he hummed as he focused on her, reaching up and laying his fingertips on her cheek. "I can't send you away again."

"I'm right here," she whispered by his ear.

"Don't walk away again. You belong with us. Don't ever leave."

Easing fingertips tipped her head so their lips could meet. Her eyes fluttered closed as his eager palms swept up into her silken mane. The heat of promise, of potential, flooded her belly and left her lightheaded.

His hands tugged her down onto the bed. The kiss paused as she slid her jacket from her shoulders and tossed it aside.

"Warm in here," she murmured, her finger traipsing his jawline to chin, over the chiseled bone that made her mouth water. "Think you can handle a little lung stress test?"

His sapphire eyes sparked in welcoming challenge. "You're my doctor. You tell me."

"Not for the next few minutes, I'm not," she grinned, tossing her leg over his lap and sliding up to his chest. His breath caught as her hot center pressed against him.

"Doctor, the door," he gasped, wide eyed and turned on.

"It's Deis and it's locked. Enough talking," she demanded, taking his palms and laying them on her thighs.

She assaulted his mouth with the passion she'd dreamed of, urgent like a raging fever. Her hands trapised under his gown, trailing gently over his chest as he released a guttural growl, stealing her contented sighs with his greedy lips. She undid the simple knot, separated the fabric of his gown and slid eager fingertips to his neck to feel the wanton, dangerous pound of his pulse, thrilled that she was finally the cause.

Under her fingers and the scrape of her nails on unmarred skin, blood boiled in his veins. He assailed her, possessed her and coveted her with racing hands as she ground herself against him. Primal need grew so fierce that he could barely contain it. His chest squeezed as his lungs fought to keep up, but he'd succumb before he stopped her.

He'd done that once. He never intended to again.

She dreamt of this, of his rough fingers coaxing her shirt buttons open, spreading the fabric to smother the tender skin he found with soft lips and demanding teeth. Her legs shifted, wrapped around the inclined bed as she stretched back, supported by his flexing arms.

He watched her crane back gracefully, saw her core muscles tighten and silently blessed her fascination with yoga. Sweeping fingers skimmed down over trembling breasts and belly before unfastening her jeans and shifting them down over her hips. Her body twisted so he could pull them free and off the bed. She released a moan that nearly made him weep.

Sitting back up, she rose to her knees, ripping away the tiny lace triangle covering her. Tossing it aside, she pulled his lips back to her greedy mouth. In a desperate race for release, he reached down, freeing himself as she rose above him once more, her eyes fixed on his with brutal intensity. She fetched a small square of foil from her jacket pocket and opened it while he feasted on her neck. Her fingers rolled the latex down his length as his head rolled back, a breathy moan emerging from his lips. Pleased to find him so eager, she lowered her lap to his, surrounding him in one easy slide.

He dropped his face to her shoulder, trying desperately to muffle his groans. With her arms and legs around him, she pounded into him relentlessly with gritted teeth. The unrelenting pace made him pant, his hands holding her up and stroking over the skin he'd craved for years. He lost himself in the moment, in awe of her animalistic rapture. It was his fantasy coming true as the Armenian goddess tore him apart with claw and teeth.

His eyes begged for more and for mercy at the same time. As she leaned back and exposed her throat, he instinctively craned up to taste the warm, swift pulse pounding just under skin. When her body tensed with pitiful groans escaping her lips, she pressed desperately to him.

He felt his resolve reach the end of its tether as his fingers clenched. "Deis," he breathed the quiet warning.

Her eyes flashed open as she whispered, "With me."

Her body tensed in a sudden flood of heat, a flash fire streaking through her from toes to fingertips. He gripped her hips, rising to answer her demand with a rumbling groan of his own.

His body weakened as his head dropped to the pillow like a sandbag. He was spent, dehydrated, weak and gasping for breath.

Humoring herself, she checked his pulse with a sweaty forefinger to his wrist. Elevated, but in range. And he was breathing. It was labored, ragged, but stable. It made her strangely proud.

She hadn't killed him, but she wasn't nearly done with him, either.

Back at Haven, she strode through the front door and kicked it closed behind her with a wide sweep. Grinning, she practically danced to the kitchen, grabbed Anna up in a swirling hug and snagged a bottle of water from the fridge. With a contented hum, she breezed back out, leaving Anna with a raised brow and strong suspicion of what changed the straitlaced doctor's temperament so abruptly.

Upstairs, she undressed again. Kicking her boots off, she started the warm water and poured vanilla suds into the deep, porcelain tub. She'd just lowered herself into the froth when the door swung open, slamming against the wall with a sharp bang.

Prepared for her friend's inevitable interruption but too thoroughly pleased to be ruffled by it, she closed her dreamy eyes with a grin.

"Tell me you jumped his bones." Rai demanded, striding in and hopping up onto the bathroom counter.

"As always, your grace and decency floors me."

"Oh, gag me, Miss Eloquence. You practically waltzed with Anna. I saw you grinning like a psycho downstairs. Only one thing makes a sexually deprived woman dance with the staff. You boffed the hottie."

Deis pulled the curtain aside just enough to lift a brow at Rai. "I find that assumption crass, unbecoming and impossible to deny."

With a grin, she jerked the curtain closed as Rai erupted in applause and hoots.

The guitarist hopped down, whipped the curtain back and laughed. "You... Oh, thank God! I was seriously worried you'd let his devastated dad routine win out. He is obviously crazy about you. How'd you do it? Wait..." Realization swept over her face, widening her grin even more. "He's still in the hospital. You... No! You little whore!"

Deis laughed, lying her head back against the sloped tub wall and bending her knees up. "I mounted him like a taxidermy moose, right there in the ICU."

"Fuck me!" Rai exclaimed, launching in a full spin. "That's fantastic. With the nurses nearby and everything?"

"It couldn't wait. I'm sure you understand."

"You animal! I'm so proud of you. My God, it's like a miracle." Rai leaned a hip against the counter to regain her breath. "It's awesome. And seriously, the kid is great. She's a natural rider, too, apparently. Henry wants to get a stable here so she can ride all the time. Think Emmi will approve the construction?"

"Not a chance, and can Charlie and I have one real date before they move in?" She asked with a brow lifted. "I love them both, no doubt, but we have a ways to go yet, don't you think?"

"The hard part's over," Rai answered, crouching beside the tub and grabbing Deis' bent knee above the sudsy water. "Once Steve came clean, told me the truth, and once Emmi admitted how she felt to Simon, we moved along pretty quick. Just work together, be honest from here out and keep being you."

"No arguing your progress," Deis shrugged, flicking a bubble onto Rai. "But will he let me be more to Ruby? That's another matter, isn't it?"

Chapter 16

Wednesday, December 24

Their first official date would have to be in the hospital on Christmas Eve. That simple fact sent Deis into a total meltdown and to a local dress shop in search of the perfect piece.

Bernie and Steve's friend owned the boutique, purported to be the finest in London. It took some convincing, but after promising him they'd spent some serious money and give him some social media praise, he agreed to let Deis, Rai and Anna have the shop to themselves on one of his busiest days. He waited behind the counter, keeping busy on his cell phone in the darkened shop while Deis tried on every style in her size. Anna and Rai drank blush wine and snacked on sharp cheese and thin crackers on the plush settee near the closed, mirrored door.

"Dates in hospitals seem stupid. Couldn't this wait until a few days?" Rai whined, wiping crumbs on the leg of her jeans.

"Shut up," Deis snapped from behind the door. "I brought you here for moral support, not to bitch."

Anna chuckled with a sympathetic look, turning to Rai. "Let her be excited and nervous, little bird. I bet you were a wreck when Steve came by for that midnight swim way back when."

"She was in her element," Deis called out. "She and Destiny are the seductresses. I, on the other hand, need to convince this guy I'm both sexy and responsible. Does this one say that?"

She stepped out in a skim black dress dotted with subtle sparkle, cut diagonally over her legs from below the knee on the left leg to mid-thigh on the right. The neck was high against her throat. As she turned, the back was nothing but straps slanting from waist to shoulder.

Rai lifted a disgusted brow while Anna winced and shook her head.

With a huff, Deis retreated to the dressing room yet again. It was almost one in the afternoon, and she still had hair and makeup to worry about.

The chef snatched up a cube of pale cheese. "A first date on Christmas Eve, so romantic. Did you already pick up his gift? I thought you two weren't exchanging since he can't leave his bed. This one told me otherwise."

Deis' answer to Anna was muffled as she fought to free herself from the strappy dress. "He's out of the ICU so he can have guests. His band mates are dropping off something that he ordered. He told me our date was a big enough gift for him, but I ordered him a new tailored leather jacket. He'll get it in a few weeks. Are you good watching Ruby tonight, Chef?"

"Oh, it's a pleasure to. We're having a baking lesson. She wants to make her father's cake for the welcome home party tomorrow. And since my employers were so generous in giving me a holiday, and since my flight's out first thing tomorrow, I'll need her help to get it all done on time."

"Oh God, Emmi's running the kitchen for the next week?" Deis declared with a snort. "Make sure to leave meals already done or it'll take you forever to put everything back where you wanted it."

"You're running the household so Henry can have time off, too, Miss Perfect." Rai griped. "Talk about retentiveness. If I don't make my bed, you'll have me strung up by the ankles."

"How hard is it to make a bed?" Deis chided, stepping out in a red wool pencil skirt and matching jacket, trim at the waist, with a rounded collar and black buttons.

"Are you going on a date with a stud or to a job interview for a non-profit?" Rai lifted a brow as Deis turned her back and retreated to the dressing room, slamming the door behind.

"Enjoy your trip," Rai smiled to Anna. "Imagine it. The lunatics will be running the asylum." She lowered her voice to a whisper, shielded her mouth with her hand. "And the scene's all set for tonight?"

Anna nodded with thumbs up while Rai celebrated their espionage in silence.

When Deis stepped out once again, both sets of observing eyes widened.

"This must be the winner, then," Deis assumed, turning to the mirror to admire the snug blueberry-hued velvet, the abbreviated hem cut at mid-thigh, the long sleeves and laced up neckline, opened just a bit to show olive skin beneath. Slipping on the ankle-twisting pumps borrowed from Emmi's closet, black leather with a silver-pointed stiletto heel, her legs looked six miles long.

With a toss of her hair and outstretched arms, she turned to her committee. "So?"

"God help him," Anna muttered, clutching the crucifix hidden under her blouse and shaking her head.

Charlie was much more comfortable in a standard room. He was finally off IV fluids, on a normal diet and acclimating to the hyperbaric treatment routine, which would continue on an outpatient basis. Doctor Ivers transferred his case to Doctor Howards, who'd changed his opinion about Deis since her daring rescue the week before. Both Doctor Howards and her formerly skeptical fellow Doctor Murphy now spoke highly of her, but only after they'd heard of her dramatic, unabashed life-saving techniques in the emergency department.

Charlie's White Light band mates, the three rowdy Brits in worn denim, arrived just after lunch for their first visit, passing the nurses' station in rolling laughter. The recovering patient heard them and readied himself, his gait wide in preparation for their onslaught.

"There he is," Devon declared, tossing Charlie's garment bag onto his bed as he strode over the threshold first. His fierce arms grabbed him up where he stood in his tee and loose gym shorts, between the bathroom door and his bed. "Looking good, mate."

"Thanks, feeling good. Though suddenly I'm in pain," Charlie winced, gasping as Robbie tossed an arm around him. His burns, while itching like hell, were still tender to touch.

Ignoring his discomfort, Robbie welcomed Liam in for an improvised rugby scrum. Devon attempted a dog pile, but the group moved left, causing him to stumble into the bedside table.

Charlie laughed as he sat on the edge of his bed, motioning for his chums to fill the chairs around him. "Did you remember to pick it up on the way?"

"I'm the responsible one." Devon handed over a square box wrapped in light blue paper. "Posh shop. You must've dropped some serious quid on that."

"I haven't spent this much on me and Ruby combined this whole year," he acknowledged, setting the box aside. "But she's worth a ton more than that."

Liam snickered. "She's got a mansion, she's totally dishy, got killer curves, legs for days, nice... What was I talking about?"

Robbie smacked his arm and instantly Charlie felt back in the game again. It was a nice change from the somber, sterile ICU and the fear of death hanging over his head.

"You're headed home soon, mate?" Devon asked, shrugging away from the slap fight between Liam and Robbie.

"Tomorrow's it. I'm supposed to keep up with the burn treatments, but I think the scar's a good look." He lowered the neck of his tee, showing off the marred, coarse skin above his tattoo, over his left shoulder and down to the top of his tricep. "All things considered, I made out all right."

"You were nearly dead," Liam retorted, leaning back with his ankle on the opposite knee. "That bird of yours saved your bloody hide."

Charlie nodded. "Oh, no denying that, but she also broke my rib and cornered me into having it a way in my old room, as a little lung stress test of sorts."

All eyes brightened as Devon hooted and went for a high five.

"No shit!" Liam exclaimed. "The doc? Really?"

"Let's just say I left the room a little less sterile than I found it."

Charlie's grin was so wide, it practically split his face in two. The ability to finally gloat was such a relief to his soul. And from the looks of it, his band mates were too envious to argue.

"And tonight, maybe a replay?" Devon asked. "Whatever's in that box should do it."

"No, not a replay," Liam argued. "It'll have to be a whole new set. Two nights with the same playlist won't keep a bird like that around long."

The other two laughed at Charlie's expense.

"I can handle my own with the brunette, no worries. I'm good."

"Not a chance," Robbie added with a headshake, seeing through the ruse. "You're a dead man. She's... Well, Liam's already said it all. And she's taken with you, God only knows why. You should've seen her face when she was telling us how good for nowt you were. She was gutted. She's got your bollocks for baggage, mate."

Charlie exhaled, his palms resting on the bed on either side of his lap. "Probably. But there's one little thing left to handle first. It's gotta be on the up-and-up, this whole mess."

Devon's brows lowered as dim realization set in, his eyes shifting to the gift. "You smarmy git!"

"Wait, what's in the box?" Liam clued in just after his bandmate, already on his feet and heading to the table to snag it.

Charlie swept the present onto his lap, pushing his friend away. "Get back, you bloody scrumper!"

Robbie squinted. "What are you hens going on about?"

"There's a ring in that pack, mate! It's gotta be. Give us a shufti. I just want to make sure it's suitable for the likes of her," Liam insisted, hedging Charlie's defenses left and right.

"Sod off!" Charlie shouted, pushing Liam back hard enough to for him to stumble.

"Quit yer lying, you div!" Devon exclaimed at his now crimson-cheeked cohort.

"Fine, fine. Good Christ, sit down you louts."

Charlie held the box in both hands, eyed it as the cacophony around him shifted into a strange calm. Among them, there was rarely silence, but his band mates saw the trepidation, the realization of truth in their friend's expression and it hushed them like school children.

"I'm in deep shit, boys." Charlie began in a murmur. "My heart's done for. I fought her off, said some downright nasty things, made up reasons in my mind why she'd skive off. Ended up arguing myself into a corner. But she wants me, she's told me so, and she wants Ruby. She wants us both. It's... Well, it's daft, to be honest. But I'm done arguing with her about it. It's the best thing I've ever had."

When he glanced up, the three sets of eyes looking back were contemplative, patient, and shockingly adult. He saw concern and consideration on their faces as his words continued like a flood.

"She's a rock star, she's brilliant and a total firecracker. I can't pretend to not be over the moon about it. And I well and truly insulted her, genuinely tried to take the piss out of her, just so she'd back off. But she didn't. She stayed, she insisted, and I believed her. And Ruby, she's mad about her. This whole date thing is my meddling daughter's idea. And she deserves some maternal love in her life for once, right?"

Devon chuckled while Robbie and Liam, the free-wheeling lads of the crew, shared confused looks.

"Sounds like it's all sorted then, mate," Devon replied easily, sitting forward with his elbows on his knees. "Nothing wrong with that. And hell, if my girlfriend looked like that, I'd be chuffed, too."

"I'm all sixes and sevens," Liam scratched his head, genuine confusion on his face. "But if it works for you, mate, I'm pleased as punch for ya."

"And you, Rob?" Charlie asked.

"Eh," his friend shrugged. "They're all controlling twats but if she puts out and gets along with the tike, can't ask for more than that."

"Such beautiful sentiment." Devon rolled his eyes before turning back to Charlie and leaning in again. "Do what's best for you and little Tuesday, and we'll sort out what's left. Don't let these narks ruin it."

Charlie slapped a hand on Devon's shoulder as his friend rose.

"We'll get on so you can pretty yourself up," Devon grinned as he corralled his buds toward the door. "And the party tomorrow is shaping up nicely."

"Wait, what party?" Charlie gawped, turning to them as they neared the door.

"I guess you didn't get to that before you two got all rumpy-pumpy the other night," he mocked as Charlie reddened again. "But there's a big to-do in the works for the hero. Emmi's on her way back, and she put together this Chrimbo-slash-welcome-home bash for us all at Haven. Emmi and that actor Simon, that comedian Bernie and his lady friend, Rai and her other half, plus us in that stonking mansion. Brought in a keg of your preferred, she did. And Ruby's making the cake. I heard all about it from that little yakking kid of yours."

Overwhelmed and without words, Charlie just shook his head and waved them off. What a crazy turn his life had taken lately.

Reclining in his bed, he couldn't stop the wicked grin. He had a few surprises of his own planned for the evening.

At six precisely, Deis returned to the hospital in her new dress and heels. Covered from chin to ankle in a long wool coat, she shielded herself against the bitter, snowy wind outside and snooping eyes inside. She was going for shock and awe and wouldn't have the hospital workers gossiping before she made it to his room.

She hadn't visited since Sunday and had only called him twice in the interim. Ruby, off school for the rest of the year, required more attention than she'd bargained for, as did her producing projects. The chef and butler babysat Ruby while their employer hastily completed the Myopic recordings, tweaking and nudging them into radio-ready singles to release the first week of January. Second's new album would release the week after, to be capped off by a live performance of their first single at the Grammy Awards in Los Angeles. Emmi was already brainstorming ideas for an over-the-top performance and it already weighed heavy on Deis' mind.

But tonight wasn't the time for outside worries. Tonight was for enjoyment and for seduction.

She released a calming breath as the elevator door slid open on the second floor. She approached slyly, silently on the toes of her stilettos and peeked through the cracked door of Charlie's room.

Inside, he stood with his right side facing her, pulling on a black suit jacket over a shirt the same dazzling blue as his eyes. Slim leather belt, soft raven hair brushing over collar, clean shaven face. But his heavy boots under the dress slacks made her giggle aloud before she could mute it.

He turned, eyes narrowed as she tried to hold back the laughter with her palm, leaning against the door frame. When his arms crossed, a judging scowl on his lips, she stepped inside with palms out for peace.

"No, you look amazing. It's just, did they forget your wingtips?"

He followed her glance down to his feet. "Did I wreck this already? I thought this was a fitting compromise."

"It is," she grinned, wrapping her arms around his waist. "It's perfect."

"Uh oh, the *P* word," he muttered, drawing her in close. "I thought we decided to avoid that word."

"You're right," she sobered dramatically with a pout. "Forgive me?"

"Let's negotiate the terms."

When their lips touched, she went as weak and silly as a teenager. Trapped in his arms, his hands cupped her cheek and slipped back into her hair. The eager moan freed from her throat had him nibbling the firm, painted lips he'd craved.

Pulling back, he watched her hazy eyes refocus with utter contentment. "Enough stalling. Let's see this dress. Ruby said it took hours to pick out."

"She is such a stool pigeon. All right, here."

She swung the coat from her shoulders, and he gaped at the clinging velvet. It was simple but she was magnificent in it, all soft curve, toned leg, wild hair and sex appeal. He fought not to pant like a mutt in summer.

"Christ Almighty," he breathed, resting his hands on his hips with a sharply blown exhale. "Um, I... So, yeah, that's... Wow." He cleared his throat with a raspy cough.

She giggled, tossed the overcoat onto the chair, sauntered over and laid her arms gently on his shoulders. "Oh, Charlie, I'd been hoping for a reaction like that. This is all for you."

The brazen flirting, the lilt when she uttered his name, skipped up his pulse in an instant. With a fast whirl and sudden strength, he forced her back against the wall. Pinioning her hands above her head made her gasp. His pulse raced, his vision red and his body aching for more after her assault days before.

"This kind of reaction is good, too," she admitted with a brow raise.

His gaze skirted every inch of her face, his eyes feral and his pointed incisor nipping his bottom lip. A long, liquid pull consumed her belly. One hand held hers high while the other traipsed down her silken cheek, chin and neck.

"Deis," he whispered intoxicatingly. "You have no idea what you do to me. You're here with me, and I will never," he nipped her neck as her eyes fluttered closed. "Never," he lapped at her exposed collarbone. "Never let you go. You're mine now."

She melted back against the wall as his hand swept up her side, over the curve of her breast, up her arm and back to where the other hand kept hers imprisoned. He brushed his lips up her neck, over her jaw and murmured. "Are you mine?"

Hearing the words, knowing it meant all she'd hoped for, her eyes looked to the heavens. Her heart squeezed, ached, longed. Bewitched, undone, she whispered. "I'm yours."

With a sly smile, his eyes narrowing, he pulled a tender kiss from her lips, bringing her arms down to his shoulders. It was deep, intoxicating and painfully sweet. She leaned against him, her heart humming in her chest as the world spun.

"Mm," she moaned, leaning back, lightheaded. "I…"

"Ssh," he hushed her, pulling her away from the wall and toward the door. "Come, I've got a surprise for you."

She giggled and clutched his hands, following a step behind as he led her to the stairwell. "Where are we going?"

"I said _ssh_," he reminded, sending a paternal look of raised brows over his shoulder that had her mouth swiftly closing with a smirk.

She tiptoed after him, praying not to sprain an ankle climbing up to the third floor. How Emmi did stage shows in these sky-high heels, she'd never understand. He kept a slowed pace, guiding her with a firm handhold.

They turned the corner, nearing the Diagnostics Department with each step forward. The doctor inside wanted to probe, to ask the questions filling her mind, but his firm scolding resonated in her ears as he led her inside the office she'd once occupied. The empty desk and settee she'd left behind waited, barren and unused, alongside the tall bookcases that once held her manuals.

He released her hand, turning to her as he backed toward the interior door leading from office to lounge. The curtains were drawn, but colorful lights winked from inside when he pushed the door open.

"For you," he murmured, holding out his arm as she approached.

Stepping into the lounge, her body froze as her mouth dropped open.

Inside, curtains were drawn over the outer and inner windows for privacy, and where the table had been, where she'd spent so many hours stewing and pondering, a few blankets overlapped to form a makeshift picnic space, complete with a huge wooden basket, clear wine bottle and glasses. To the side was an electric fireplace with a roaring yet heatless blaze nestled inside. A miniature version of Haven's nine-foot flawlessly decorated Christmas tree sat atop a table on the far wall and a few gifts of varying sizes waited underneath. And on every flat surface, miniature lanterns of wrought iron held flickering red and gold candles, lighting the space in a glow that warmed her soul.

"Oh, Charlie," she breathed, her palm over her heart. "It's lovely. I'm..."

He stepped up behind, laid his hands on her hips. "Perfect."

She narrowed her eyes over her shoulder as his brows lifted.

"Now we're even," he mused, leading her over to the cushions atop the blankets.

"You're... This is..." She stammered, words just outside her reach as she sat. "How did you manage all this?"

"Oh, I had plenty of help. Ruby insisted we have a real, romantic date. Anna hand-selected the menu and wine pairing, Henry did the tree. The hospital was all right with the decorating, and Devon brought my suit here."

"It's all so beautiful. And this fireplace?"

"It's from Bernie's place. Rai and Steve brought it by this morning. You said my gift will take a while, but I think you should open yours before I get sidetracked by your lips again."

He carried over the wrapped bundles, four in total, and laid them beside her as he sat alongside. She lifted the largest one, a light, broad box in plain red paper, shaking it like an impatient child. He laughed as she scowled at the silent package, glad to stretch out the anticipation a little longer.

"It was worth a shot," she shrugged, tearing away the paper anxiously and opening the box.

Inside was a scarf of gold and crimson fleece alongside a pair of matching socks. She cradled them in her fingers. Both were enchantingly plush and flawlessly made, though there were no labels or brands printed on them.

"There's no gift tag. Who is this from? They're so soft."

"Christine," he told her, handing her a wine glass half-filled with a fragrant white. She sipped and handed it back. "She's gifting Ruby a matching pair, too. I bought her a crochet set last Christmas. She's a natural, eh?"

"It's outstanding." She praised, tossing on the scarf. "She could sell these."

"I'll suggest that. Maybe she could do a little online shop while she's at university."

"She'll make a fortune. It's unique and stylish. I love it."

Setting aside the box, she grabbed the smaller rectangular gift next. It was solid, heavier. "No tag here, either."

"Open it. I bet you'll sort it out straightaway."

Under the silver paper, she found an onyx box with "Littmann" printed on the label. With a knowing chuckle, she flipped out the insert, revealing a top-of-the-line stethoscope in classy black and stainless steel.

"Wow, this is a nice one. Mine is so dinged up and ancient, I don't even carry it."

"The nurses and fellows took up a collection, got you one so you'd quit nicking theirs."

She admired it longingly, her mind traipsing back over her time treating patients alongside the dutiful staff. "It's too much. I was only here, what, two weeks?"

"You made quite an impression. And you did a lot of good, from what I hear."

"I made a few enemies, too," she admitted, repackaging the instrument and setting it aside.

"You took chances, did whatever it took to solve the mystery. And I think the naysayers reconsidered when they saw you do whatever it took to save me."

"I thought I punched you, broke your rib."

She shifted her gaze to him, watched his mouth curl into a smile as he held the dainty wineglass in his thick fingers. "That impresses us British lads. What can I say?"

With another laugh, she lifted the third box, wrapped in white and red, with a card on top. Slipping her finger in, she ripped open the card's envelope at the seam.

"Read that to me," he instructed after another sip. "I haven't got a clue what's inside this one."

She opened it to find youthful, loopy handwriting covering the left side, reading aloud as he'd asked.

> *Dear Doctor Deis, I just wanted to do a little something to thank you for all you did for me and my mum. She's coming around and we're better now than we've ever been. She quit her evening job so we can*

spend more time together and it's been really nice. In case Doctor Gordon didn't tell you, I got my new liver late Monday night. It took six hours. I'm doing well on the anti-rejection meds. I'll be here another week or so and on those meds for years, but I already feel better than I ever have. I guess I felt lousy for a long time but didn't realize it. Now I've got a future to look forward to. You made me better in more ways than one, and when no one else could sort it out, you did. I don't know how, but you did. I guess you really don't like losing. So have a lovely time here in England and I hope you find whatever it is that makes you feel better. You're the best doctor in the world and you deserve it. Sincerely, Miranda Victor

"Oh, Miranda," Deis breathed shakily, holding the writing against her chest with both hands as a tear slid down her cheek. "She's going to make it. What a miracle."

Charlie beamed, holding his tongue and waiting while she composed herself. He handed her Miranda's gift as she held out the card for a trade.

Inside, Deis found a framed picture of Miranda and her mother in the hospital's recovery room, smiling with their arms around each other. To the photo's side, tucked under the protective glass, rested one of her tiny notebook pages, one she'd torn, crumpled and discarded into Miranda's trash during the ten-hour inquisition. It was flattened out and showed a complex system of arrows, cross-outs and underlines Deis recognized as her own haphazard notetaking.

In the very corner, the word "hemochromatosis" was circled and crossed out.

"I'm so overwhelmed," she wept in trembles, handing him the frame. "This is too much."

"This is how you brainstorm?" He asked, eyeing the note stuck inside the frame. "It's bollocks."

"I know. And my pages of lyrics are, too, usually."

The last box, the square in pale blue paper, waited between them.

"And this one's from you?"

"Yes, but it's a two-part deal."

She dabbed her eyes with a cloth napkin then lifted it, shook it and noted a quiet rattle inside. "So generous of you. Okay, well, let's see what we've got."

She opened this one more carefully, slower than the others, and found a black velvet cube, the size of a tissue box, under the paper. The top third opened like a clamshell, revealing a beautiful platinum rope necklace with a three-stone pendant centered on it. Two heart-shaped and blood red rubies flanked a much larger round diamond that shimmered in the twinkling lights around her.

She gaped at Charlie, the box clasped in her fingers as she desperately held back more tears. "Oh, it's so beautiful. This is..."

"I know," he argued with an outstretched hand. "I know, it's not nearly enough, but it's symbolic. At least in my overly sentimental, hopelessly romantic mind, it is."

He sidled up beside her, used a fingertip to gesture to the stones. "See, Ruby's obviously one of them, but the other one's me."

She giggled weakly, her eyes damp. "I know, Charlie. Your birthday's July eighth. Ruby's your birthstone"

When he lifted a suspicious brow, she giggled again. "There's this thing called the internet. All sorts of info on it. You should check it out sometime."

He snorted and nudged her with his elbow.

"I get it and it's lovely. You and Ruby are around me, right?"

"That's it." He cradled the pendant in his fingers. "You're the bright spot in our lives and you're our center. We'll be right beside you even when you're on your own."

She slipped it from the box, handed it over, slipped off the scarf and turned her back to lift her hair. Without pause, he slid the necklace over her shoulders and fastened it. When she dropped her mane and turned to face him, the glow of the gemstones and her eyes enchanted him.

"Charlie, thank you so much. I…"

"Wait," he contended gently. "I told you this is a two-part thing."

"Oh, right. What's the second half?"

"It's right here."

He lifted his cell phone from his pocket, unlocking the screen before scrolling for a moment. And when his recorded voice emerged, her brows knitted.

"Hey, beautiful," his voice began.

"Hi, Daddy," Ruby's voice chimed in.

She covered her mouth with her hand, a conspirator's glint in her damp eyes as she continued to listen. He held the phone between them.

"How's Haven today?" He asked in the recording.

"Brilliant. Henry's taking me along for a tree, a massive one, so we can decorate it. He's leaving soon, on holiday for a week, and Anna's going, too, so we'll get it put up straightaway. I picked a big bow and Henry said we need a ladder. Anna's making cider and we'll play carols while we put the lights on."

"That does sound brilliant. Did you pick out ornaments like the ones we have at home?"

"No, these are like little candles and Henry bought ribbon to tie them with instead of those hooks. It's going to be lovely."

"Sounds like it. And where are Deis and Miss Rai?"

"She said, 'stop calling me miss, it makes me feel old' so it's just Rai now. They're both downstairs in the studio room with the music blaring. Deis has these big goofy headphones on and Rai just taps her foot a lot."

Charlie chortled. "And did Henry help you pick out a gift for Deis?"

"Actually, Daddy," her little voice was suddenly serious, intent. "We think you should get her something really fancy, like super posh, since she's so sweet to me and you made her cry so much. You know the necklace you got me? Like that, but bigger, with like hearts or something on it."

"Hearts?" Charlie's voice was suddenly shaky on the recording. "Why hearts?"

"Oh, Daddy, *come on*," she replied derisively, impatiently in that tiny tone. "Hearts are pretty. And she likes you. When she came home from seeing you Sunday, she was chuffed. No tears at all. And she had a bubble bath. Rai told me so. Bubble baths are only for when you're happy, Daddy."

Charlie cleared his throat, fell silent a moment.

"Daddy?"

"Yeah, I'm here, baby," he finally replied. "I just remembered our visit. It was very nice. I guess she thought so, too."

"So there. I know it would make her happy. If you can't leave the hospital, maybe Uncle Devon can go get it. Henry said he'd help out, and Anna said she would, too. Make her feel like a princess for a bit, like how you make me feel."

Noting that Deis went stiff as a board beside him, Charlie halted the recording playback. One gaze at her revealed how astonished, touched and emotional Ruby's words made her. He couldn't help reaching out for her palm. Her cheek rested on his shoulder as he touched the screen to restart the playback.

"Well, if you think it's a good idea," his recorded voice replied.

"I think it's a brilliant idea. And maybe she'll love us both."

"Oh, Ruby," he began in a no-nonsense tone. "That might be a bit hasty. I know she's crazy about you but it's different with Daddy and Deis. We've talked about love between adults before, remember?"

"She loves me for sure, even though she didn't say it exactly. She told me she really cares and stuff, and when she hugs me, it's like when Grandma does. I can tell she loves me, and I love her, too, Daddy. She's the best, and she tells me bedtime stories, and she picks me up when I'm too short. She brushes my hair. She makes sure I eat my veg even though I hate them."

"Don't say hate, Ruby. Especially not about silly things like veg."

"Sorry, Daddy. She loves you, too. She really does. When she came home that day they took you off the lung machine, she was knackered. She said she wouldn't leave you because she didn't trust anyone to take better care of you. And she acts like that with me, too."

"I know," he admitted in a quiet voice. "I know that, Ruby. And we talked about that, and how amazing it was that she agreed to take care of you for me, to take care of us both so well."

"If she's so wonderful, Daddy, and if you think she's so pretty, then you could love her back. Right?"

The recording went silent. Deis' eyes met Charlie's as she drew in a shaky breath. His eyes were warm, serene, as he glanced back down to the phone. The recording began again with Ruby.

"Daddy? I think your phone's..."

"No, Ruby, it's me. I... I'm not sure what to say. You know you are the most important thing to me, right? More than music, more than my job, more than anything."

"Uh huh."

"Right. I would do anything to make you happy, even more than I'd do for myself. You're asking me to love her back, and the reason I shouldn't is you, Ruby. How can I love anyone when my whole heart is yours? Neither of you should have to live with half my heart. That's not fair to either of you. It's us forever, remember?"

Deis trembled, pulling away from him. Her heart broke again, shattered into a million bits. But he grasped her hand fiercely, capturing her attention and shaking his head once quickly.

He gestured to the phone as the recording continued.

"Daddy?" Ruby's little voice asked.

"Yes, beautiful?"

"Half your heart's still a whole lot. Give her the other half. We'll share."

Deis let out a single desperate sob, her hands moving up to her eyes to hide the tears she could no longer hold back. Ruby's heart, her precious heart, was the most beautiful gift of all.

The recording continued as she quieted her bawling to listen.

"Ruby," Charlie sighed. "Do you love her?"

"Uh huh. If you love her, will she be my mum, then?"

"Is that what you want, a mum?"

"I think so. Mummy, she left us. And you were sad, but you were sad before that. I remember all the fighting. I was chuffed when that was over. She made you mean."

234

"Ruby," he began, but she continued before he could wedge in more.

"If you love me, and if Deis loves you, then she didn't. It's not the same."

Charlie's voice broke. "No, Ruby, I don't think it's the same, either."

"And she's been gone a while. And we've been good, right, Daddy? But Deis sings with me, she shares her coffee, and she's nice to me. She never yells."

"She'll never yell at you, Ruby. She might yell at me, but only because I'll deserve it."

"So, we can keep being around her? That'd be brilliant."

Charlie chuckled a little with an exhale. "I don't see why not, princess."

"I love you, Daddy."

"I love you too, beautiful."

He clicked his phone's side button, darkening the screen. Pink circled Deis' eyes, tears dripping down her cheeks like rain as he reached up to sweep them away.

"Don't cry, please. I don't want to make you cry anymore. I've done more than enough of that."

"I can't help it. Her little heart. She's so..." She exhaled a deep, shaky breath and calmed her nerves. "I can't believe her. She's an angel. A conspiring, underhanded, unbelievably darling angel."

"See why I had trouble sharing my heart?" He asked rhetorically as Deis nodded. "She's the best damn thing I've ever known. Well, she's tied for first now."

He took her hand gently, cradled it in his. "You've changed a lot about me. First, my life. You saved it, not just after the fire, but from the loneliness I'd simply learned to live with. I thought that was just a necessary evil. Emmi started a life for me by signing Light, but you've added so much to it. I've been doing nothing but writing lately, and when I think of you, the most incredible lyrics just come to me. You've restored my faith in life and in a music career just by being you."

She inhaled, pressed her lips together and tried desperately to stop her tears.

"Second," he continued, turning her left hand over to touch her palm. "You've changed my mind. I didn't think that was possible. I've been stubborn and opinionated so long. I knew my center was Ruby, and I knew I had to protect her. I built up a wall around us both, around my mind to keep us safe, but you tore it down. You showed me there was a better option, and thinking back on it now, I can't imagine it any other way."

He turned her hand back over, cupped it into a fist and surrounded it with warm fingers. "And lastly, you've changed my thoughts on love, and how it's supposed to be. I thought some people just don't get to love, that it just isn't meant for them. And when Ruby came along, I was so fixated and in love with her, I figured that was the best I'd ever get. And I thought I'd have been satisfied to just love her, but you changed my opinion again. You are the most lovable woman I've ever known, for more than just who you are or what you look like. It's not about what you can offer me or the life I want for Ruby. It's this," he paused as his free hand settled over her thumping heart. "Your heart grows, it expands, and it engulfs everything. I didn't think a heart could work so hard until I found yours. And it makes me want to be better, and it makes me want to love better. So, I will."

His hand fell away and lifted the box her necklace had been in. He moved her fingers, curling them around a small tab and urging her to lift the plush insert from the box.

When she did, a twinkle hidden deeper inside the black velvet interior exploded into glittering life.

A platinum band with an identical round diamond center stone and flanking ruby hearts was waiting below, matching the necklace perfectly. She took the box from his hand and held it while her chest squeezed, her heart pounding so hard that it deafened her ears.

"DeAnna Karine Sarafian," he breathed, drawing her welling eyes up. "Please stay with us. Be our center. Be my wife, be her mother, and be the heart we so desperately want to share."

When she froze, awestruck and speechless, he took her hand, lifted it to his lips.

"Be with us. I love you, and I swear it now, I always will. I want us to be a family. A real family. Please. Please say you'll marry me."

She drew him up in a fierce, sudden hug and squeezed the air from his recuperating lungs. Sobbing, she held him tight, fearing he'd take it all back, that he'd ruin the most beautiful moment of her life.

"Yes," she wept, warm drops falling from her chin to his shoulder. "You already know I will."

She pulled back, pressed her tear-soaked smile to his lips as his hands swept over her cheeks. He lowered her face to his shoulder again, hauling her up onto his lap to calm her weeping. When she finally lifted her head, he slipped the ring on her finger.

Warmth spread up her arm as he gripped her tight. This man, this gorgeous, loving and dedicated man, was hers.

She'd never finish a drink again, but she could live with that.

With a knowing giggle and eyes wiped dry, she glanced up at him. He met her gaze, petting her hair.

Suddenly, his head lifted and tipped to the ceiling as he shouted. "She said yes!"

The door from hallway to lounge swung open as a rush of bodies flooded into the space. Abruptly surrounded by her medical peers, friends and family, Deis exploded into hysterical laughter. Confetti was thrown, balloons were set aloft and exploding cheers echoed around them.

In awe, she jumped to her feet, just in time to accept a robust hug from her father and mother, both in tears.

"Dad! My God, what are you…?" She took his shoulders, touched her forehead to his. "Mom? When did you…?"

"We're here for you, baby," her mother blubbered, stealing her for a comforting embrace. "Thank your future husband. Oh, we're so excited for you both!"

Anna and Henry, with Rai and Steve right behind, stepped in with shouts of congratulations. Doctor O'Leary dabbed her eyes with a handkerchief while Doctor Murphy crossed his arms with a pleased smirk. Doctor Gordon set a bottle of high-priced champagne by Charlie's knee with a wink. A few nurses stepped up and covered them with more confetti, laughing like loons as Ruby edged in, dressed in a matching green-striped holiday top and leggings. Charlie opened his arms and accepted her embrace, a few of his tears dampening her party outfit's shoulder.

When all the guests were greeted and the ring glittered in everyone's view, Deis finally asked with scrutinizing eyes. "Tell me there's not a marble cake waiting for us somewhere."

Epilogue

Thursday, December 25

When her SUV pulled into Haven's front circle a little before noon, he wasn't surprised to see a half-dozen cars clustered nearby. He knew a houseful of guests waited for them.

His mid-morning hospital discharge had gone smoothly, and his first outpatient treatment was scheduled for the following week. He originally waved off the treatments despite Deis' ire, but to avoid the screaming matches Ruby had spoken out against, he deftly reconsidered. She added his appointment to her phone, the first of many checks she'd likely do in their years together.

But he could get used to that.

"Is the whole extended family here?" He asked, removing the seat belt.

"Most of it. It wouldn't be Christmas without a full house."

"You Americans make too much of it," he groused. "A roast dinner, maybe a gift, that's all you need."

"Miser," she retorted with a brow lifted. "You have a little girl, so you should at least be somewhat merry, damn it."

"*We* have a little girl," he reminded, taking her hand and kissing it. "You got both of us in the deal. And besides, you're merry enough for us all."

"For the moment, but you better keep it that way. Wanna try?"

She puckered and he accepted the bait.

His kiss was more than she bargained for, the kind that tied her belly in knots as his hands fisted in her hair and his tongue explored daringly. She embraced the heat, the demand, as she edged across the center console. She wanted desperately to climb into his lap as he nibbled her lip.

239

"Later," he breathed as their lips pulled apart. "I think we have an audience."

Her eyes fluttered open, looking over his shoulder to see Rai and Ruby standing outside the closed front door, both with arms crossed impatiently. Her hands were still tangled in his jacket, brushing over the skin of his neck as she replied in a velvet whisper. "She'll have to get used to it eventually."

She stole one more kiss before sliding back and opening her door. Ruby rushed forward as Charlie stepped out, holding her arms high for a lift. She squealed as he swung her over his shoulder like a flour sack. Her tightly spiraled onyx hair swung as she reached out to Deis for rescue. When her doctor and future stepmother only shrugged, she shrieked dramatically and beat her little fists on his broad back.

"Hey," Charlie greeted Rai with a cheek kiss, tossing his free arm around her. "Thanks for watching the cretin."

"My pleasure," Rai smirked, watching as Ruby kicked and thrashed. "She was far easier for me. Then again, I didn't carry her around like a wild hog."

"Eh, she's easier to keep track of this way."

Deis accepted Rai's hug and they showed each other their engagement rings once more. Charlie hauled Ruby to the door, swinging it open wide.

"Merry Christmas!" The flurry of voices called out from the marble atrium, the excited faces of their friends and her family all around.

He set the squirming girl down so he could accept a hug from Emmi, his mentor and musical savior. The radiant blonde held his cheeks a moment, centering his gaze on her face. He was stunned to silence by the intense violet of her gaze, the unspoken pride in her eyes. She released him with a soft, loyal smile.

"So, let's see it," Emmi asked Deis, less than a step behind him.

Deis offered her left hand and the blonde swooned.

"It's me and Daddy. We're the hearts!" Ruby announced, wedging between the ladies.

"I see," Emmi beamed. "And Deis' heart's pretty awesome, huh?"

Simon approached Charlie, offering his hand to the healing hero. Fully dedicated to his role as a superhero, Simon was easily twice his width and solid muscle. Afraid of more broken bones, Charlie was careful to return Simon's grasp lightly as Emmi's beau cupped his forearm with a pleased grin, nudging him farther inside.

Liam and Devon waited impatiently by the steps. When Simon stepped clear and signaled them, they rushed him like rugby hooligans, lifting him with hoots and hollers. Shaken and jostled, Charlie fought for balance in the four thick arms. They all ended up in a heap on the floor as Ruby ran over to watch. When he was finally dragged back to his feet, they group-hugged and squeezed the breath from his still weakened lungs.

"You bugger!" Charlie called to Simon. "You set me up."

Despite the judging look from Emmi, Simon simply lifted his pint of beer to his lips with a satisfied smirk.

Liam ruffled his mate's hair as Devon lifted Ruby to his hip. She fiddled with the small silver hoop in his ear.

"Where's Robbie?" Charlie asked, scanning the crowd.

"Eh, you know," Devon replied with a lowered voice. "He's a miserable bastard."

"Especially when the party's at Haven with these ladies," Charlie murmured with a sigh. "Is he still that sore?"

"Getting him in good with these birds might be a lost cause, mate," Liam replied dismally before taking a long drink of beer.

Deis, after returning to Charlie's side, saw the concerned looks on the men. When she didn't see Robbie among the guests, she surmised the reason and held her tongue.

"See? I knew you'd claim that beauty before any of us could," Devon remarked quickly, changing the subject and gesturing to her.

"Sorry ol' chum," Charlie replied with a snicker. "She's only got eyes for me."

"Good luck with her," Deis' father interjected, stepping up dressed in a dated brown suit and offering a hand to his future son-in-law. "Keep your rooms tidy and your laundry folded."

"She's hard to please." Her mother, the golden and beautifully aged version of her daughter, added with a smile as she approached. "Make sure you give her what she asks for or she'll just take it from you. But, from what I hear," she snuffled, peeked over at Rai with a lifted brow. "My girl's already done that."

"Ooh!" Liam hooted with a colossal laugh, trading high-fives with Devon while Deis blushed scarlet. Emmi covered her eyes with her hand and Simon's heavy brow lifted suggestively.

"Mother!" She chided, stepping to Charlie's side. "Can we not?"

"I don't think you're built any differently than me," she told Deis, stepping up to brush her chestnut hair with wrinkled fingers. "I used my wiles and took your father for myself all those years ago, too. And see all the good it has done for us all? This place, these friends, it's all so beautiful."

Deis sighed with a headshake and embraced her mother as Devon handed Ruby off to Charlie's waiting arms.

"Where are Bernie and Steve?" He asked, cupping Ruby's bottom with both arms.

"They should be here any minute," Rai replied, handing a full beer to Deis' father. "Last minute gifts to get, apparently."

"Oh, the gifts!" Emmi exclaimed. "Ruby, help Simon and me bring them downstairs, would you?"

She hopped down, eagerly following the blonde and her gent upstairs on her red, glittering ballet flats, the broad red velvet dress with white fur trim lifted by little fingers as she ran.

"You guys didn't get me anything, did you?" Charlie asked Rai. "I got all I could've asked for this year already."

Deis' Purpose

The satirical coos and the kissy faces from his band mates had him glowering. Their mockery only intensified when he reached for Deis, pulling her in for a sweeping kiss to keep up the theatrics.

Gifts were placed around the tree in stacks by the time the front door swung open once again. Bernie's arms held a few boxes while Steve quickly swept up Rai in his own. Jane followed behind with a pie plate wrapped in foil.

"Hi darling," Steve smiled up to his little prize. "Miss me?"

"Every moment," she replied, her arms draping over his shoulders. "Quit being gone so long, damn it."

Ruby danced around them until Steve lifted her high above his six-foot-seven frame, spinning her twice as her frantic giggles echoed through the manor.

Charlie helped Bernie arrange his gifts before accepting his handshake. His red hair and bright eyes, and the tacky holiday sweater he'd chosen to wear, helped ease Charlie's trepidation at meeting such a national celebrity so casually. His tone was jovial, uplifting. "Nice to meet the hero, finally, and good to hear you're up and about again. Now you've got yourself a sugar momma so you can stop catching yourself on fire, eh?"

Charlie chuckled. "That's the goal. Thanks for coming."

He nodded once as Jane handed the pie off to Emmi for a hug from the firefighter she'd seen on the news.

"What's this?" Emmi asked as Jane stepped back from Charlie.

"My family's traditional Christmas pie, banoffee. We've been making it religiously as far back as I can recall."

"Sweet Jesus," Emmi murmured excitedly, lifting the lid to see chocolate drizzles and toffee bits on the fluffy whipped cream below. "I'm off the treadmill this week, but with the guys all here, I might not get a piece. I'll hide it."

Liam, alerted to the pie like a dog to a bone, murmured to every male within range. "Let's tuck in, boys."

Emmi dodged Simon's long arms and Charlie's band mates' advances, bee-lining to the kitchen while they followed with clomping feet. The singer's high-pitched scream from the kitchen scared Jane, but she relaxed when Simon returned with Emmi thrown over his shoulder. The pie was nowhere to be seen.

"How long is the household help excused?" Jane asked Rai, rubbing her chilled hands together.

"I approved them off until the second of January. They've done enough this year."

"Generous," Jane replied while she and Bernie gladly accepted pint glasses of pale ale from Deis. Both guests insisted on seeing the ruby and diamond jewelry. The newly betrothed smiled grandly as she showed them off, beaming ear to ear.

With full glasses of beer or mugs of cocoa in all hands, they retired to the lounge area off the atrium. The tall windows revealed intermittent snowflakes drifting down and melting on the dormant bushes and plants of the garden. Rai had the piano carried up from the studio and Charlie listened with fascination while Ruby played basic Beethoven and simple carols to the gathered friends.

"When did you learn those?" He asked as his daughter climbed into his lap after her impromptu recital.

"Rai's been showing me. She's brilliant. And Henry taught me to ride a horse, and Anna taught me to make a cake. Oh, Emmi!" She remembered with glittering eyes, turning to the blonde. "Can he see it yet?"

Emmi rose dutifully at her call and strode off to the kitchen on golden heels with Ruby close behind, dancing in barely contained excitement. Charlie lifted a brow at Deis, waiting for explanations.

"This is her second home," his fiancée murmured with a sip of sauvignon blanc. "I told you she's been a joy. She's become a part of the family here."

"I wanted to know about this cake."

"Oh," Deis chuckled. "You'll see for yourself in a second."

Charlie's eyes shifted to the doorway as Emmi reappeared. A huge cake, covered with white chocolate curls, rested on a silver platter in her hands. She ferried it over to the guest of honor, taking a moment to kick Liam in the shin as he approached with outstretched fingers. He winced and sat back down as Devon eyed his friend's dented leg with a snicker.

"Your favorite, from what I hear," Emmi commented as Charlie inspected it closely.

"Looks like it," Charlie grinned. "I'm guessing it's full of coconut, then."

"Sous chef's demands," she replied, gesturing to Ruby before turning back to set the cake on the cabinet beside the hors d'oeuvres and wine bottles. "I'll cut it later, after we all have the roast dinner I slaved over this morning."

"You're spoiling him," Deis commented. "I don't cook, at least not well."

"I do," Charlie pecked her cheek. "And if Ruby's welcome here to enjoy Anna and Emmi's cooking, then I am, too, right?"

"Anytime," Emmi stroked his raven mane and winked at Deis.

"Gifts!" Bernie shouted suddenly, jumping up and scaring Deis' parents into shrieks.

"Sorry, he's a bit high-strung," Steve explained to the room. Rai and Jane nodded in corroboration at his side.

Bernie returned with boxes in his arms, handing one to each member of Second and a smaller one to Charlie. "It's just a little something to help you out, mate."

Charlie lifted a brow. Slipping a finger under the wrapper and tugging it aside, he revealed a household smoke detector.

Bernie sat back down alongside the scowling Jane. "See, it works like this. When there's a fire, it makes a hell of a racket, and so then you know not to run in the building."

Jane smacked his arm and Deis laid her forehead on Charlie's shoulder as the room laughed and toasted the comedian.

"Thanks, I think I've heard of these. Seems useful. And what did he give you?"

Deis shrugged and tore away the paper. Underneath was a new copy of a medical book she'd read many times over the years. Dry and uninteresting to most, it was a critical tome to possess. Ethics and proper practices in emergency medicine were listed in extreme detail inside.

When she lifted it with a questioning look, Bernie lifted a brow innocently. "I heard you're jumping on patients, punching them and whatnot. I figured you needed a refresher on the basics."

Deis threw the hardbound book and it smacked against Bernie's chest while he laughed boisterously.

"I saved his life," Deis retorted.

"You stabbed me, punched me and broke my rib," Charlie corrected from her left before pecking her cheek. "Love you."

Emmi eyed her gift with renewed suspicion. "Now, what generosity should I expect? Maybe a Kama Sutra guide?"

"We've no need of that," Simon murmured with a grin around the rim of his pint glass.

Liam reached over and high-fived him.

With an eye roll, Emmi ripped away the paper, revealing a plain shirt box. Inside, wrapped in gold tissue, a violet satin bustier with a designer name on the label greeted her.

With a deep moan, she lifted and nuzzled it. "Fan*tastic*."

Bernie waved a blasé hand. "Jane picked it. I guess I pick dim gifts for diagnostic geniuses."

"Jane, you can pick her outfits anytime," Simon grinned, taking it from his lady's hands and holding it to her chest. "Seems a bit snug. You think the girls'll fit in that?"

"Maybe. We'll see later." Emmi's brow lifted provocatively. Simon wrapped her up and burrowed in her neck as she squealed.

Deis shot her band mate a broiling look, suddenly reminded of her parents' presence, but her mother only gestured nonchalantly with her wine glass. "Oh, they're young and beautiful. Let them enjoy it while it lasts. You couldn't get me into that top with a shoehorn and a barrel of butter."

Rai received a set of charcoal crayons from Bernie and Jane to go with the easel and paints Steve had given her the week before. Though she'd always appreciated the arts as an observer, her fiancé encouraged her to give art creation another chance. She was already spending time each day doodling and dabbing in her suite.

"I'm still trying to figure out which medium I'm best at," Rai confessed. "Steve's just going to keep buying supplies until I figure it out."

"You buy yourself everything else. You ladies are hard to shop for."

"No, we're not," Deis argued, gesturing to the rings that gleamed from hers and Rai's fingers. "And Emmi's is strangely missing. What's holding you up, Simon?"

All eyes on him, his brown eyes slipped away. "Aw, damn it all..."

"I am," Emmi interjected, taking his hand. "He knows he has all the time he needs. Besides, no one's more patient or understanding than I am."

Jeers and scowls filled the room as Emmi gaped in feigned shock.

"What an amazing year it's been," Charlie breathed, dreamily and exhausted, upstairs on Deis' grand bed with the cold night beyond the fogged window. She fit perfectly against him, cradled at his side. Her bare, silken leg wrapped up and over his, her arm over his sweat-dampened chest as she sighed against his neck.

The glow, the warmth of him, and the exhaustion his lovemaking brought with it made words impossible to find.

His head bent down, his lips brushing her forehead. "You're sure you want me? You're signed on for years with a hapless gent and his kid, you know."

"Mm," she moaned against his neck, where the peppery scent of him teased her senses. "Please."

"Again?" He grinned as she jabbed his side with a weak fist. "Ow, okay, *okay*. I'll give you five minutes to recover. Blimey, you could've asked nicely."

He reached down, dragging the blanket up around them as she settled in. Having him near, feeling his heartbeat and seeing the scars would always be a bitter reminder of her path to Haven and her choices after. Without the stress of med school, the hell of all the years touring, the toil of Emmi's perfectionist expectations, she'd be somewhere else, likely apathetic and without this satisfying purpose for it all.

"You happy?" He asked softly, interrupting her thoughts.

"You have no idea," she admitted, lifting her wistful eyes to his. "This won't be easy, and you're probably going to hate me at times. I'm headstrong, determined, a pain in the ass. I'm sure we'll be on the road again before long, but for the first time ever, I feel like I have a reason. I've found a reason to want to come home. You and Ruby, you're more than I bargained for. And I couldn't be happier about it."

His pleased smile, and the kisses it so often delivered, was all hers.

"Challenge accepted, and I'm sure Emmi will have us on the road soon, too. Now I have even more beautiful souls around to care for my, err, *our* daughter."

When she smiled and exhaled contentedly, he pulled her into his arms. He relished the smell of her hair, the arch of her brow, the bow of her top lip. When his voice emerged, it was the gentlest Deis had ever heard it sound.

"It's not me sorting it out anymore, on my own and removed from the living, breathing world. You had me at word one, my love, and I've come too far to go back to that old life. And you're a lot smarter than I am. We'll sort it out."

She sighed, absorbing his warmth and his promise. "We'll get it done."

"Again?"

She lifted a brow as he rolled her over, grinning as he coveted his prize all over.

Coming Soon...

Second Saga, Book Four:
Destiny's Passion

Enjoy this sneak peek into Destiny's life…

As the sun set, Destiny sorted through her obsessively organized wardrobe, choosing bits and pieces to assemble into a night-out ensemble. Rai and Deis were too exhausted from working to tag along, and Emmi was far too prudish and careful to be seen out enjoying the club scene. She'd spent the day memorizing and practicing Robbie's drum lines, preparing as Emmi had instructed, and was ready for reprieve.

Not unlike nights in her recent past, she'd go out on her own. She'd flirt, play, enjoy some company and come back to share her exploits with her newly domesticated roommates.

With a red leather skirt, matching over-the-knee boots and a sheer, lacy black top chosen, she brushed and dabbed at her porcelain face. Accentuate the green eye, carefully line the full lip, highlight the sharp cheekbones, darken the soft brows. A few canisters' spray kept her crimson curls tame as she pinned a few back, showing off the emeralds dripping from her earlobes.

Henry knocked politely, two soft raps, before stepping inside with a bow.

She prayed her ensemble would elicit a response from the dapper professional. Her pride waned as he maintained his frustratingly solemn demeanor despite the leather and lace.

"Dante and the car await you. And for your ride home?"

"I wish he'd give me some peace," she griped, rising from the cushioned stool of her vanity. "I'll find my way home. No worries, okay?"

With a grin, she watched the remarkable servant depart as industriously as he'd entered.

Such a timid thing, she realized. Too bad Emmi had forbidden any seductive tactics. Entertaining as it would've been, squaring off with the blonde pit bull wasn't worth it.

Her slim phone slipped into one bra cup while some cash slipped into the other. A long pocket stitched into the inside of her boot was the perfect spot for her tube of gloss, disposable toothbrush and penknife. Made of ceramic and wood, it passed unnoticed through security and metal detection at even the most exclusive nightspots.

It was her duty to protect herself, and while she played fast and loose, she was far from careless. The privilege of going out and representing the organization without Emmi's supervision was a hard fought-for and glorious coup. Though she'd never had to use it, the silent weapon was an insurance policy she never went without.

A wool cape covered her neck to knee, tied with a red satin cord. She checked her makeup once more, flipped off the lights and strutted down the stairs. Dante waited in his intimidating suit and sunglasses.

"A little dark for those, isn't it, slugger?" She jibed, taking his massive arm in hers.

"Adds to the look," he replied, leading her out the door to the waiting car.

Two hours later, she was seated at a VIP high-top table alongside a packed dance floor. Flashing lights and lasers over the crowd revealed bouncing bodies, arms held high and chemically intoxicated faces. Music exploded from towering speakers in the corners, pounding in her chest like a jackhammer. Onlookers crowded around for selfies, autographs and to greet the gregarious redhead. A bouncer stood nearby, shrugging off anyone who got too close or reached out for a touch of her leather get-up.

Across the table, the club promoter shook a few hands, nudged Destiny's arm as other celebrities came into view and kept up her endless bottle service. Thrilled that she'd replied to his email and acquiesced to visit the nightspot, he accepted the accolades of the club owner and introduced him to Destiny. Not a single word escaping the mid-thirties, chestnut-haired owner was discernible amidst the thumping sound, but she smiled and posed for a picture with him good-naturedly.

The drinks and hours disappeared as the night stretched on. At times, she allowed the crowd to coax off her stool so she could sway among them and laugh as they sought to impress with their breakdancing or urban dance routines. Feeling warm, loose and relaxed, she spotted two guys at the bar's corner, beer bottles in hand and narrow-fitting tees over firm chests. In a well-practiced move, she bowed and backed away as the crowd filled in the chasm, undulating to the deafening bass.

She edged around a few patrons to position herself just inside the lads' peripheral vision. She tossed her garnet curls back, pressed a hip to the bar and watched them from the corner of her eye.

There was clearly a debate between the two gents. The one with a dark military buzz cut nodded toward the redhead while the other, with cropped golden locks, shrugged him off. A few more seconds passed before the darker haired male approached, stood beside her as she turned toward the bar, pretending to ignore him.

"Beg pardon, love," she heard over her shoulder in that posh London accent.

A wicked grin curled her lips while her back was turned but was slyly replaced with an off-guard smile as she whirled to face him. "Yes?"

"You... Blimey, you are Destiny. I tried convincing him." He gestured to the guy standing a few feet away, who lifted his beer in response. "Didn't believe me."

Her lips edged closer to his ear to both keep her voice from sounding shrill as she shouted, but also to feel his heart speed up at the pulse point of his neck. "The one and only."

"Wow," he said, his head tipped to the side, only inches from her cheek. "You're brilliant. Keith, he's a huge fan. Waited in line for hours for Wembley, paid over the odds for tickets right up front."

"I'll thank him. And where were you that night?"

"Girlfriend's," he replied casually. "Keith's not so lucky."

Slick.

She grinned at the wingman before peeking at his buddy. "Damn shame. No luck tonight, either?"

"Too shy."

Oh, I bet, her mind interjected sarcastically.

"Thank God for a chum like you," she replied, pressing her cheek to his for a split second. "Intro."

He nodded once then steered her through the crowd toward his mate.

The tawny friend inhaled sharply as she approached, surprise and awe clear in his eyes. She laid a palm on his thick forearm with a sweet smile and felt the muscle below turn to stone. The smell of musk and spice, woodsy and impressively masculine, leapt to her nose as she leaned in. His slate eyes narrowed on her face as she edged dangerously close.

Her lips neared his lobe as she cooed, "Hi Keith."

He pulled his head back, his eyes wide and fascinated. "It is you. Smashing, and so lovely."

"Thanks, handsome." She turned on the million-watt smile. "Having fun?"

He shook his head, feigned a pitiful look. "Lonely."

"Not anymore. Your friend?"

"Tom. A total bore."

She giggled and leaned back to toss her hair back off her shoulder while slyly watching his eyes skim south to the cleavage on display through the sheer bodice. With fiery eyes and her bottom lip in her teeth, she edged back in closer to his firm frame. "Wanna keep me company?"

He set his beer down on the rail to his left without pause, his palms moving to her leather-clad hips. The bodies around them shielded public view as she hooked her index fingers into his jeans pockets. She tipped her chin up provocatively and stepped in, his muscled chest pressed to hers. She felt the unspoken acceptance of her offer, and his excitement over it, press against her thigh.

Her lips edged back to his ear. "Come," she whispered, giving his middle one quick tug.

They passed the bar, disappearing through a dark, curtained hall beyond. The heavy beat still pulsed through the walls of the hidden corridor, but voices and laughter were muted as she traversed the narrow passage, headed to the club's VIP room. Up two narrow stairs, she opened a thin wooden door, stepping in with him on her heels.

A mini bar stocked with bottles and glasses waited in the corner of the otherwise empty lounge, lit only with dim bulbs in ceiling inserts. Along the far wall, a two-way mirror above the club's jam-packed bar displayed the churning crowd on the dance floor.

"Ah, much better," she murmured, closing the door and flipping the latch.

He stepped farther in, toward the cloudy glass between them and the club scene before turning back to her. He was still, silent as she sauntered over.

"Keith. Lovely name," she told him in a sultry voice, the alcohol warm on her breath. "And fantastic body. Looks like you work hard for it."

Her nails skimmed up his chest, drew circles on his cotton-covered pectorals as she eyed him curiously. He was unable to hide his excitement as he pressed against her, ready for action.

His palm caressed her cheek, their eyes locked. "I'm a diligent lad. I'll show you."

She took a step back, bit her lip. "Go ahead."

CPSIA information can be obtained
at www.ICGtesting.com
Printed in the USA
BVHW070841120520
579562BV00002B/152

9 781647 183516